REMASTERED
Time Travel Didn't Go As Planned...

Hallie Baur

Culicidae Press, LLC
918 5th Street
Ames, IA 50010
USA
culicidaepress.com
editor@culicidaepress.com

Ames | Berlin | Lemgo

ISBN-13: 978-1-68315-046-6

Library of Congress Control Number: 2023930415

Cover design and interior layout © 2023 by polytekton
Some images generated by DALL-E AI system at openai.com/dall-e-2/

For the menders of our time.

Contents

Glossary

Original Time (OT): Time Travelers' native era of existence.

Time Travel (Travel): Term coined by the Time Regulatory Network; the act of transporting to another era. Often written and referred to as 'Travel' to distinguish between Time Travel and common, same-era travel.

Time Regulatory Network (TRN): Agency of scientists, health care professionals, investors, system developers, lobbyists, and other affiliates who manage the logistics of Time Travel.

Psilopram: Pharmaceutical created by one of TRN's founding scientists; used to bring Time Travelers into their optimal mental state before and during their journey through time.

Aid: Emergency safety device sent to Time Travelers from TRN.

UpgrAid: Enhanced version of the Aid. Includes several additional communication features.

Acclimation: Recovery period for Time Travelers when they arrive to their destination.

Acclimators: TRN employees assigned to Time Travelers; facilitators of the Acclimation process.

Monitors: TRN employees whose purpose is to ensure safety of Time Travelers and respond to emergencies when signaled via the Aid or UpgrAid.

Menders: New network of Time Travelers comprised of previous TRN employees and current TRN employees whose mission is to rectify past societal faults.

Ideal Future (IF): Era, individual to each Time Traveler, where societal conditions allow for their best life.

Block: Underground device created by TRN system developers. Used to block TRN's audio access to the Aid and UpgrAid.

Chapter I

"We're almost there," Eva pointed at the sign. "Hang a right down Cherry Street!"

Rae followed Eva's lead and the pair of Time Regulatory Network stylists trudged through the city's warehouse district. The streets were so quiet they could hear grains of snow scratch across the empty sidewalks.

"Hallelujah!" Rae replied through chattering teeth. After snaking through the abandoned streets, Rae questioned whether the UpgrAid's GPS would ever take them to their New Year's Eve destination: a rave. A night of fun before buckling down on their mission. Rae wondered if TRN was onto her secret group's project, if the all-powerful organization had decided to misguide Eva and herself through the icy streets until they froze to death.

Rae reached into her oversized pants pocket for the "block." She intended to use the device once she was forced into the role of monitoring Time Travelers, a position neither herself nor any stylist had initially signed up for, but had been pushed into by TRN's supreme ringleader, Adrian Glass. Rae and Eva smuggled the UpgrAid's blocking device to their last nineties vacation, independent from TRN. The stylists could still receive messages from TRN, but their conversations were muted to the organization's listening ears.

Rae and Eva first accepted their jobs as TRN stylists with optimism. They were promised the freedom to Time Travel at no cost. Flexible hours were assured. Shortly after Rae and Eva started in their hub's salon, the nineties became a very popular destination, and they assisted countless Travelers in achieving the authentic look of the era. The money rolled in, and they were fulfilled in their careers.

Then, TRN got desperate. Employees were stretched beyond their limits. Those in charge of monitoring Time Travelers' safety were spread too thin. There were errors in distributing the Aid. Once the Aid was readily available and the UpgrAid was launched, Travelers became even more demanding and fluctuated throughout the eras at a rate TRN couldn't sustain.

Next came Adrian Glass' ultimatum.

"All TRN employees must monitor until demand is met. If you're not in, don't bother showing up tomorrow."

Rae and Eva chose to monitor, but on their own terms. Eva's boyfriend, Josh, a tech wizard, opened a door of opportunity with his sound-blocking device which clipped onto the UpgrAid. The block allowed Rae and Eva's growing unit, which they referred to as menders, the secrecy to do the work required to rectify past-society's mistakes without TRN's ever-listening ears. Overwhelming uncertainty still lied in the outcome of their mending endeavor, but they motivated each other to harness their advantageous position while more and more brilliant individuals such as Dr. Chandra and Francis Platt joined in the efforts to mend the past.

As Rae and Eva approached the building, the music inside became audible. They stood outside the rusty door and the music's volume sounded as if it would cause the old facility to explode. They snapped the block onto their UpgrAid devices. Eva and Rae exchanged a look of excitement, the distant streetlights gleaming off their metallic makeup and stick-on face jewels.

"You ready for this?"

Rae nodded.

"One last night, just for us. To remember why we're doing this. Peace, love, unity, and respect."

They opened the industrial doors and were immersed into the bizarre world inside.

Mia came to the swift realization that she was in over her head. The abandoned warehouse was packed with the most whacky get-ups she had ever seen. Though Rae, Mia's TRN stylist, stressed that nineties attire was far more maniacal than Original Time's imitation of the era, Mia didn't believe Rae until she saw rave culture for herself.

Before Time Traveling to 1997, Mia would have turned around and left as soon as she entered the building. Her heart would have raced in the confined space, but Psilopram, the drug which facilitated her journey both mentally and physically, worked its magic again that New Year's Eve.

Mia laughed as Macy leaned into the party's madness.

"Of course, she feels at home here," EJ chuckled with Mia.

Macy was enamored with the wildness of it all. She was glad the eccentric group they'd met in the hotel elevator dropped a flyer on the floor. Within minutes, Macy was lost in the methodical, trance music's build.

EJ kept tabs on Macy as she diffused into the crowd. He was overwhelmed and Mia noticed. She wished she could have shared TRN's miracle drug with her friend.

The rave was like nothing EJ ever experienced. Earlier in the year, he and his brother's Halloween bash has been a shameless night of fun, but their little party was nothing compared to the rager into which they'd stepped.

Tiffany, ready to let loose after a Christmas break which was filled with her stepsibling's naivety, rushed to the bowl of bodies to join Macy.

Mia cupped her hands around her mouth and yelled into EJ's ear.

"Macy wasn't messing around when she said she wanted to do something crazy for the new year!"

"What?!" EJ replied over the blaring volume.

"Never mind," Mia shook her head. The energy got the best of Mia, and she started to let down her barriers. "Let's go!" She took EJ's hand and led him to the floor where Macy and Tiffany danced.

They melded with the other dancers and were engulfed by the assortment of homemade costumes. All around them, people smiled with paint-streaked faces. Bright, sunny costumes were contrasted by dark creatures of the night, clad in leather and spikes. The gathering was unbridled.

Finally, Mia and EJ reached their friends. They approached just in time to witness Macy downing the contents of a red cup. Mia was tempted to ask for whatever substance Macy may have swallowed, but heeded Dr. Lowell's advice. She knew better than to dystrophy the fortification her mind had undergone.

EJ looked around with panic in his eyes.

"You good?" he asked Mia.

Mia nodded.

"Me too," EJ said, attempting to sound cooler than he felt in the edgy scene. "I'll be back. I'm going to get some water."

With that, EJ stepped away to a nearby water cooler. He filled four cups and attempted to carry them without spilling.

Mia scanned the makeshift club. She was fascinated by the underground culture which she'd never known to exist. Then, her eyes landed on a familiar face. At first, Mia couldn't place how she knew the young woman, then she realized it was Rae, her stylist. Mia was delighted to see a friendly, Original Time native, especially after Vaughn's departure over the holidays. Mia gestured to EJ who was carrying their cups back to the place where Macy and Tiffany danced.

"Can one of you help him? I'll be right back!" she said and pointed to Rae. "I have to say hi to someone. I'll hurry!"

EJ sighed and rerouted himself to a seating area which was set up beside the dance floor.

Mia ran up to Rae.

"Rae!" Mia shouted.

Rae turned to search for the voice shouting her name. She was struck with a tinge of alarm, wondering if TRN had come to retrieve her and Eva. Instead, the lights illuminated one of her favorite TRN client's face.

"Girl, you look great!" Rae said with pride.

"Couldn't have done it without you!" Mia stated. "This whole thing is off the hook! I remember you saying to get crazier with *everything* I wore," Mia continued. "This is what you meant, isn't it?"

Rae laughed, "It is!" She paused and took in her surroundings. "Shit, this is even next level for me and Eva!"

Eva heard her name and turned to see with whom Rae was talking.

"Eva, this is Mia," Rae made the introduction. "She's one of my all-time favorite clients."

"I see why!" Eva yelled, giving Mia an impressed once-over.

Rae's eyes traveled to EJ. He was keeping tabs on Mia from the couch. Mia followed her gaze.

"A friend," she explained, "his name is EJ. He's basically our bodyguard tonight," Mia joked.

"That's so sweet!" Rae exclaimed. "Well, we're heading to the dance floor! Care to join us?"

Mia glanced at EJ. He looked bewildered.

"I should probably get back to my friends," Mia replied. "Nice to meet you Eva! See you around, Rae!"

Eva held up a peace sign, paired with a brilliant smile and Rae blew Mia a kiss.

As the stylists headed to the floor, Mia returned to her and EJ's reprieve. EJ handed her a cup of much needed hydration. Unable to help herself, Mia glugged down the entire cup. From where they were seated, EJ and Mia watched their wired friends move tirelessly. They exchanged an amused look. Rather than resuming small talk, EJ held Mia's gaze longer than usual. She couldn't pull away from his deep-set eyes and allowed a delicious tension to enter their ethos.

Since the eradication of Lars from their lives, a weight had been lifted from their band, the Tuesdaze. Though the band had been apart for winter break, they picked right back up where they left off. Their ride to the city that night brought warmth to Mia's heart following Vaughn's departure. Mia still hoped she made the right decision to stay.

EJ was becoming more and more of a safe harbor. During their drive, he only played Mia's favorite tunes from the passenger side. He was constantly attentive to her well-being, and Mia welcomed his consideration.

Just as Mia let herself sink into EJ's stare; she felt the UpgrAid buzz in her pocket. The device, gifted from Vaughn after Mia lost the original Aid, had yet to make a sound since it came into Mia's ownership. A burst of adrenaline caused her skin to prickle. Mia pushed herself up from the couch to look at the device in private. She saw a look of disappointment on EJ's face, their intimate moment severed.

"I, um," Mia started, unable to think of a reason to break away.

The music pulsed, mimicking her heart's thump. Mia took a deep breath to steady herself. She hoped the UpgrAid would never be necessary, and her mind reeled at what emergency was at hand.

"I have to g-go outside for some fresh air," Mia stammered.

Before EJ could follow, Mia raced through the crowd to the heavy front door. She burst out into the frigid air and pulled the shiny, rectangular device from her pocket.

A dull, yellow light glowed in the corner of the device. The UpgrAid sprung open along its seam. Inside was a tiny screen. Digital text moved across the screen, reminding Mia of a Wall Street ticker.

'Remain calm,' the ticker read. *'Family emergency, your parents have been in an accident. TRN Employee will meet you inside.'*

———

Just as Rae and Eva felt the infinite well of energy bubbling up within them, Rae's UpgrAid began to vibrate.

"Ugh!" she shouted to Eva. "I thought we'd get away with no situation notifications tonight!"

Eva looked to Rae for an explanation and Rae patted her pocket where the device was stored.

"Emergency strikes," Rae stated.

She fought her way to the warehouse's grungy bathroom for privacy. Her stomach turned as she remembered that TRN emergencies were significantly more frequent and severe during the holiday season. She remembered Mia was inside and her heart sank. She didn't want to break any type of emergency for her beloved client.

Rae stood in an empty stall and plugged her nose at the putrid smell. She opened the UpgrAid and the situation flashed across her screen.

'Mia Hayes,' TRN's dispatch messaged, *'at your location. Traveler is aware to be on the lookout for TRN employee. She knows you, yes?'*

Rae clicked the 'Yes' button.

'Her parents are on life support. Find an excuse for her to get to the TRN hub.'

The nearest hub's address remained frozen on the screen with no further explanation for Rae. She shed a tear for Mia's loss, wondering if monitoring to mend would be worth the heartbreak or if she missed her chance to get out of TRN unscathed. Rae got her wits in order and made her way to deliver the news.

———

The screen went black. Mia verged on hyperventilation. She wasn't sure if she could go back to the center of ecstasy with so much dread. EJ opened the front door and came outside, intensifying the situation.

"Mia, are you okay?" he asked in a panic.

Mia was in shock. She nodded, scraping herself together as much as possible.

"Sorry," she stated. "I just needed to step out."

"Are you feeling okay? You're pale."

"Y-yeah, I've got to go back in. There's someone I need to meet." Mia struggled to grasp any viable story. "EJ, my parents have been in an accident."

EJ's eyes widened, "*What?* How do you know? When did this happen?" He placed his hands on Mia's shoulders.

"I can't explain, but I have *got* to go inside. Someone is meeting me. Let me go," Mia shoved his arms from her body, "alone."

Disheartened and confused, EJ hung back as Mia launched inside to the rave. Her eyes darted around the strange gathering. Then, standing at the edge of the floor was Rae with an expression Mia would never forget.

———————

Tiffany gazed at a clock on the wall. The clock was crusted with a layer of debris and had a crack in its glass face. Twenty minutes had passed since they downed the house punch. Tiffany and Macy had heard the warnings, the adult version of, "Don't take candy from a stranger."

They took it anyway.

In November, when they first planned their trip to the city, the Tuesdaze shared a mutual understanding that all rules were to be set aside. It was their post-finals/pre-spring semester vacation, and before going out that night, the four of them made a pact to look out for one another, but to live it up without apprehension.

"I'm not judging a *thing* any of you want to do," Macy had said. "Let's get wild."

Though Tiffany was particular and organized when it came to certain things, when she let loose, she released all inhibitions. Macy was an instant flame to any gasoline the group had to offer, and that night, Tiffany brought the propane.

The high set in. Each flash of light was more vivid than the last, every song was a calling to something higher than their humanity, and everyone at the rave was there to be loved. Tiffany looked at Macy with wide eyes. They nodded at one another.

'*It kicked in.*'

A new rhythm surged through the enlivened warehouse. The DJ's white gloves curated another galactic track, and his dance floor throbbed. Macy looked over to spot Mia and EJ taking a break in a secluded area close to the wall. Three, beat up couches offered reprieve for the overheated and overstimulated.

"They're so precious," Tiffany stated.

Macy pursed her lips, "I guess."

EJ and Mia's growing care for each other hadn't gone unnoticed. Though Macy felt a tinge of jealousy, she knew the mistakes she'd made with Mia. Macy's protective mechanism of cool casualness backfired last fall, but she was happy to see Mia across the room with someone they all adored and trusted.

Half of the Tuesdaze watched from the dance floor as Mia and EJ inched toward one another then Mia's expression changed. She stood to her feet and bolted for the front door. Just as Macy and Tiffany looked at one another, mutually obligated to rush after their friend, the DJ went heavy. Simultaneous with the shift was the potent onset of Macy and Tiffany's punch.

The big room crowded, and Macy and Tiffany were locked into the surge. Trails of lights streaked across their eyes, like fireflies from another dimension. An urgent sense of visceral affection filled their bellies and emanated into their surroundings.

A group of colorful beings accumulated, unable to satisfy the closeness they so fervently desired. Eventually, fatigue set in, and Macy and Tiffany were desperate for water. They spotted the cooler and went to fill their glasses. EJ and Mia were nowhere to be found, but Tiffany and Macy were at peace with their absence.

"Pace yourself," a towering man in a bright yellow vest stated. "Too much ain't good."

Macy nodded. She slid her teeth across one another like tectonic plates.

"Here love," another raver offered Macy and Tiffany pacifiers from her tiny backpack.

Replenished by the culture of kindness and sips of water, Tiffany searched the room for EJ and Mia. She was unsuccessful in her efforts and her short thought sequence moved on as Macy took her hand and led her back to the dance floor.

––––––––––

Rae hustled Mia from the warehouse.

She was annoyed at EJ's persistence to accompany them. Despite the inconvenience of his trailing back to their hotel, his unwillingness to leave Mia's side after Rae spewed any reason she could think of for him to remain at the party, Rae was touched by his genuine concern.

"An accident, what happened Mia? Are they okay?"

"They're in critical condition," Rae stated.

"Your name is Rae, right?" EJ clarified.

Rae nodded.

"How do you know all this? Did you come to the club to tell Mia?"

"Not exactly, it happened while we were there. EJ, don't you want to keep an eye on the other girls you're with?"

"Mia, we can go straight to the airport," EJ offered, ignoring Rae's attempt to brush him off. "It's not far. I can drop you off and pick up Macy and Tiffany before dawn. I know you said Maine is expensive to get to this time of year, but I can help a little."

EJ melted Rae's heart with his kindness, but she had to get Mia alone, and EJ proved hard to shake.

They needed to get to the TRN hub as soon as possible, before it was too late for Mia's parents. Rae sighed and clung to her responsibility over the situation.

"I have my car a block away," Rae bluffed. "We're staying nearby. EJ, you saw that party, do you think those other girls are safe in there?" She played on his big heart. "What do you say we divide and conquer? I'll take Mia, you check on your friends."

"Yeah, EJ," Mia piped up, "go. Make sure they're okay. I'll call as soon as I can."

"Okay," he said, suspicious of the long-lost friend taking the reins.

Before departing, EJ cupped Mia's face with both hands and kissed her forehead.

"Everything will be okay," he said, "no matter what happens. We'll be in Birchmont when you get back."

Hot tears streaked down Mia's cheeks. She took EJ's hand and squeezed. Mia uttered no words and feared she would crack. EJ shuffled down the street, back toward the abandoned warehouse on Cherry Street.

———

Mia and Rae rushed to the TRN hub. The building's façade was made to look like a dry-cleaning business. Inside, behind the front desk, was a small TV. Mia watched the screen as the party in Times Square erupted.

1998.

"This won't take long," Rae said. "Let me see if Psilopram is available."

Rae snaked through rows of faux-dry cleaning bags while Mia paced and breathed heavily. She knew what an emergency Travel situation potentially entailed: no Psilopram. Before she could overthink what Travel would be like without the drug, Rae returned and extended her hand toward Mia. In her palm was a dose of the life-altering medication. Mia swallowed the pills. Rae attempted to comfort Mia by rubbing her back, but it took minutes for Mia's breath to regulate.

"Ready?"

Mia replied. "Ready as I can be."

———

EJ didn't return to the rave. He wasn't in the mood for boisterous countdowns or blaring music. 1997 had been the best year of his life, and he wasn't in a hurry to let it go. He didn't want to sing 'Auld Lang Syne,' and decided to return to the rave once the new year was celebrated.

Instead, he walked the streets in solitude. At midnight, he heard cheers drift from city balconies and stoops. He hoped that night was as bad as the year would get.

———

A bright winter sun beamed down on Macy's leg.

She cracked open her eyelids. She could barely move. Macy evaluated the gargantuan bed on which she lay.

To her left was a man wearing only a yellow vest. Next to him lay the pacifier supplier from the previous night. On Macy's right, Tiffany was curled up next to a lean, clean-cut man. Macy chuckled, unsure of what they'd gotten into.

Macy nudged Tiffany awake. Tiffany groaned and opened her eyes. Macy held back laughter at Tiffany's confused expression.

"Where are we?" Tiffany mouthed.

Macy held a finger to her lips to shush Tiffany.

"Let's go," she mouthed.

The two of them fished enough clothing from the floor to shield them from the winter air. Before exiting the random raver's apartment, Macy took one last look at their three partners from the night before. She sent them a silent 'thanks' for the night of feeling alive.

Once they got outside, Tiffany and Macy burst into laughter at their state. The sun glistened on remaining patches of glitter, and their bizarre assortment of clothing was nothing compared to the wildness of the previous night's events. They were on their way down but enjoyed the ride before the plummet.

––––––––––

Mia sat in her father's recliner. The fabric still smelled like him, and the aroma settled her post-Acclimation stomachache. Though she was shaken and nauseous, Mia knew how much she lucked out on her emergency journey back to Original Time; there was enough Psilopram.

Rae ensured that Mia had a high enough dose to both eliminate her claustrophobia and assist in her impending grief cycle. Mia also learned how fortunate she was that she and Rae were in the same place at the time when Mia got the news. There was a shortage of monitors and Mia may have been left in the dark for weeks had Rae not been there. She would have missed her parents being laid to rest.

The days following her arrival were a blur. Family gathered at the Hayes' home. Jon and Ellie's legal representatives called to set up meetings. The funeral commenced.

But Derek wasn't there.

Mia called their local TRN hub but was put on an endless hold. She fumbled with her UpgrAid to try and signal TRN, but it seemed the device was deactivated. She wondered if the UpgrAid had been turned off while she was Acclimating to prevent her signaling yellow or red.

As Mia's aunts, uncles, and cousins puttered around the Hayes household, Mia couldn't muster the energy to move from Jon's leather office chair. Hours into her family's obligatory, drawn-out presence, Aunt Donna, Ellie's closest sister, approached Mia.

"Mia, sweetheart," Donna said and stroked Mia's hair, "someone's here to see you. She's in the living room." Mia's aunt offered a weak smile. "I think you'll be happy to see her."

"Can she tell me where Derek is?"

Donna hung her head, "No, honey. We're trying our best to find out, though."

Donna helped Mia to her feet and guided her to the living room.

On the couch sat Francis Platt, Mia's TRN legal representative. The grooves of Francis' face appeared deeper than Mia remembered. Francis took Mia's hands.

"Mia, I'm so sorry…" Francis started.

"I don't know what to do," Mia said. "I don't know where to be. I should feel a certain way right now. Everyone's crying. My parents died. And I feel numb."

"Don't worry about that right now," Francis stated as she patted Mia's back. "Your place is wherever you are. I just worry about when the drugs wear off."

"I worry too," Mia said.

"You know, I lost my parents at your age, and I wish I could have fast-forwarded through the five years that followed. I was a mess. Maybe Psilopram will be a blessing to you."

"Time will tell."

"I know I can't do anything to influence this process for you, but I want you to know I'm here to sort through all the papers that are thrown at you the next few weeks," Francis said. "You're probably not thinking of this right now, nor should you," she continued, "but your life without this tragedy is still there in the past, waiting for you.

With your permission, I can be your stand-in here. I've got some free time. You're gonna want to go back to ninety-seven soon."

"Ninety-eight," Mia replied. She considered Francis' offer, but with Francis' status as a lawyer recruited by Time Regulatory Network Mia couldn't imagine her rates. "I appreciate your willingness to help, but I don't know what our finances look like yet," Mia said. "I don't think I could afford to have you sift through the documents of my parent's life."

Donna overheard the conversation and approached Mia and Francis from around the corner where she'd been eavesdropping.

"Mia," Donna began, "your uncle and I are your godparents. I know you're technically an adult now, but we're here to help with anything you don't know how to handle. Your parents," Donna's voice cracked, "they left very few stones unturned. The only thing you and Derek have to decide is what to do with the shop and venue."

"If that's all there is to sort out, don't worry about hourly rates," Francis said. "I know the whirlwind that comes with this kind of loss. I'm here to help, kid."

Mia's first smile in days emerged.

"Thank you," she replied.

A knock on the front door stalled their conversation.

"I'll get it," Donna stood and went to open the door.

In stepped Vaughn.

Mia's anger surrounding Vaughn's lack of follow-through in obtaining an Aid for Derek was immediately dissolved by his comforting familiarity. She rose to her feet and ended up in his arms.

"Come in," she said.

Vaughn stomped the snow off his boots and with full hands, attempted to remove his parka. Mia noticed that he held a plastic container filled with food. Mia took the container and let Vaughn de-winterize. She set the food with the other dry holiday sweets dropped off for the Hayes' mourning.

Mia came back into the living room to see Francis and Vaughn catching up.

"I'd better be off," Francis said to Mia. She gestured to Vaughn, "This guy knows what's been going on lately. There's a lot I need to fill you in on, Mia, but now isn't the time. I'll send the paperwork for your aunt to sign. We'll take care of things."

Francis gave Mia one more tight hug, then piled on her extra layers and left.

"Sit with me," Mia said to Vaughn.

A spark of Mia's emotions returned as she felt upset with Vaughn.

"What happened to getting an Aid for my brother?"

Obtaining the emergency device for Derek had been suspiciously challenging.

"Can't he just walk into a TRN hub there and get one?"

Vaughn sighed, heavy with guilt.

"I wish it was that easy," Vaughn said with a low voice.

Donna took the hint to leave the room.

"We are nearly *out* of the device. The sixties are completely out. TRN might seem like they have it together, but they weren't even close to being prepared for this influx. Not only that, but TRN employees are leaving without trained replacements. Some monitors are going off-grid once they arrive at their destinations. Many just can't handle this job."

Mia remembered Rae's expression at the rave. For the first time, the intense spectrum of TRN's employees' job dawned on Mia. Her perception of Vaughn evolved.

"There's a lot to it, isn't there? I guess I had too much faith in TRN."

"You and me both," Vaughn said. "It sounds crazy, but things were better *before* the Aid. Time Travelers were prepared to be vagabonds. Travelers knew they had an out, but they didn't have the expectation of staying so *connected* to Original Time. Now that TRN's monitors are at Travelers' beckon call, there is way more back and forth Traveling than we anticipated. People are being reckless now that the support is there 24/7. The safety measure backfired."

Mia shook her head and processed Vaughn's words.

"While I'm being honest, I have to tell you," Vaughn continued, "back in ninety-seven, I was trying to recruit you to be a monitor. You'd be good at it. Plus, I wanted you to join me," he admitted. "We are desperate for more people like you who are beautiful, adaptable, lovable…" Vaughn trailed off.

They sat in quiet while Mia debated the authenticity of her and Vaughn's short, sweet time together in the nineties.

"Aid or not, we have to let Derek know *this* happened," Mia gestured to the room where her mourning family lingered, "even if I have to Travel to the sixties myself."

"It's more complicated than that. The waitlist to Travel is weeks, maybe even months out. We have a shortage of flex-Shells. Mia, there's only one way you can go back to the sixties right now."

"What is it?"

"Like I said, TRN *needs* employees. And they're willing to negotiate, to pull strings if they can bulk their staff with monitoring recruits. But there's a hefty price. For example, I had to agree to be on-call for weeks just to earn a trip here. I've been working way more now than I ever had to in the nineties with you or with Derek in the sixties. I'm facilitating Acclimation locations, I'm breaking news to Travelers like Rae did for you, I'm coordinating Shell-repairs, answering emergency calls from the Aid," Vaughn rambled. "It's *exhausting*. We need help."

The dots began to connect for Mia. The only way she could Travel back to see her brother was to help TRN with their predicament. She had to play their game, and to get Derek out of the dark, she would.

DEATH.

Chapter II

Renee flipped the second card. Her heart sank when she saw the image.

"Ten of Swords," she sighed. "I really am no good at this. Don't take me for a proper fortune teller. Honestly, I don't know why we couldn't just stick with Rummy or Crazy Eights."

"Renee," Lorraine said, "these cards are *so* far out. We couldn't just leave them in that old hat box of Sylvia's. What a wonderful keepsake these cards are."

"The anticipation is killing me, what does the card mean? This is the card signifying my present, right?" Derek asked.

Renee hesitated, hoping the words to reframe the notorious card would reveal themselves. She wished to be back on holiday. Back where her calendar was clear, and no one expected anything of her.

———

Every year, for the winter holidays, Renee, Germain, and Marcel, Germain's father, had a standing invitation to visit the quaint French village where their family first settled. They were welcomed by Corrine, the daughter of their grandfathers' Spanish

Influenza nurse. Corrine exuded warmth, but Germain saw the confusion in her eyes upon their arrival.

"We're missing some faces," Corrine remarked on Grant and Angelene's absence.

"Grant's dealing with some… health issues," Germain offered. "But we brought our friend, Carole. She accepted one of the extra train tickets. Thank goodness we had a second spare ticket. Renee and Carole filled the open seat with shopping bags after our maintenance stop in Paris."

Renee laughed, "Don't blame us. You bought a few items yourself," she nudged Germain.

"Yeah! Many of the pieces were for *En Blum*," Carole chimed in, "they weren't *all* for us."

"Well, I can't wait to see what you've bought. Welcome dear," Corrine opened her arms to Carole for an embrace. "I've never disliked any friends of this lot."

In the house of their ancestors, the next-of-kin spent many late, festive nights at a card table, surrounded by empty bottles. Jovial laughter reverberated from the gingerbread-like house. They visited Corrine's friends, shopped at the local boutiques, and went through Corrine's attic which was full of the family's historic treasures. Renee and Germain came back with boxes of heirlooms from their grandparent's first home in France.

On the last day of their visit, a winter storm pummeled the village. Marcel inched his son and friends to the train station in Corrine's Citroen. He parked and let out a sigh of relief. "I'm going south this winter," Marcel stated.

"Okay, *Papa*," Germain chuckled. "You've said that for years."

"I mean it this time. Corrine has some connections. Maybe a place for me to stay. I'm done with this bitter cold."

"If you're serious, you must write me when you arrive. Keep me current on your state and whereabouts," Germain instructed.

"My state," Marcel chuckled. "I must not look as young as I feel. I should say the same to you. I don't hear from you enough. We didn't have adequate time to get caught up on life," Marcel stated.

"We'll both do better. See you in the new year, Pa."

With that, Germain kissed his father on the cheek. Marcel popped the trunk and the friends rushed outside. They shuffled around the car, suitcases in hand. Renee and Carole blew kisses to Marcel, and he winked back at them.

After a long train ride, Renee, Germain, and Carole were welcomed back to England with a New Year's party at Tom's pad. Despite sixty-seven's rollercoaster of events, the whole crew reunited for the year's end; Renee, Germain, Carole, Derek, Lorraine, Grant, Angelene, and Tom were all in attendance.

Lorraine insisted that Renee bring her interesting family relics to the party to share, including a hat box full of Sylvia's treasures.

"I wish I could have seen the village, it sounds like an absolute dream," Lorraine swooned, "but I've felt… under the weather. The train would have been a nightmare. Anyway, show me these pieces of history you've returned with!"

Though Renee would have preferred to look through the heirlooms on her own, she knew that her inner circle held the same reverence for Sylvia as she did. Together, they sifted through old, rigidly posed family photos, discolored train tickets to England, badges of honor from the First World War, and finally, two sets of cards.

One set was a deck of playing cards, the other, Tarot cards. Lorraine, who had recently become fascinated with ritualistic, pagan culture, plucked the cards from the hat box. Edges of the cards were worn, and the deck was tied together with a piece of yellow ribbon. Lorraine untethered the cards and shuffled them. The card's musk diffused into her nostrils.

"Can you read Tarot, Renee?" Lorraine asked, delighted.

Renee hesitated then nodded.

When Renee was a little girl, her grandmother warned her that not everyone was open to the art of fortune telling. "They think it's the devil's hand."

Despite Sylvia's apprehension, Renee insisted that Sylvia agreed to show her the spreads and explain the meaning of each card.

"Only if you promise to keep them private."

One time, Renee kept one of the cards in her pocket and 'the moon' card fell out on the middle of *En Blum*'s show floor. An aristocratic customer saw, and stormed out of the boutique, muttering words about witchcraft as she exited. Following the incident, Renee thought her grandmother had disposed of the cards, but they'd been waiting for her in Corrine's attic all along.

Lorraine persisted, "Give us a New Year's reading!"

"Yes! Tell us what we need to prepare for in sixty-eight!" Carole demanded.

Renee caved.

"Oh, alright," she agreed, unable to resist the cards' allure. "Just three cards each. I'm not doing an entire spread for everyone. I'll pull past, present, and future."

"You can skip me," Grant said. "I'm not sure I want to know," he muttered.

Though Grant was on a steady incline toward stability after his bloody, forgotten night, he didn't want to see what the cards had to say about his past and couldn't handle a potentially ominous card for the future.

"Skip me too," Angelene stated, always the skeptic. "I don't believe anything is predestined."

"It's not that things are predestined, the cards are based on the trajectory of *this* moment, that's it." Renee said.

Angelene rolled her eyes.

'Not worth my time,' Renee told herself.

She went on to pull auspicious cards for Carole, cautionary cards for Tom, and finally, landed on her old flame Derek.

"First card: past. Interesting," Renee stated, "five of cups. Abandonment. I've never known you to leave anything uncared for," she said, hoping to exude appreciation for his essential help at the boutique.

Based on his reaction, the card hit home a little too hard. Renee realized she must have struck some mysterious nerve, buried deep within her dear Derek. For their first time together in months, away from the spotlight, she became aware of his shadows.

"You've experienced real loss, haven't you?" Renee registered aloud.

"Yeah," Derek answered. "Let's move onto the present."

Renee pulled the second card in Derek's spread and paused.

The Ten of Swords depicted Derek's present. An armored man held ten swords on his back, not yet cutting him, but inches away from piercing the weak spot in his armor. Renee didn't want to alarm Derek, but Sylvia had informed her of the warning card.

"This card—" Renee started but was interrupted by a knock at the door.

Tom turned to face his entryway. He moved the tiny curtain from the window and saw an unfamiliar face; outside stood a young woman with wavy hair and a big mouth. Though her identity was unknown, she was unthreatening and quite pretty, so Tom opened the door.

From the sunken living room, Tom's guests turned their heads from Derek's round table Tarot reading to the new face in the entryway.

Derek's mouth dropped open when he saw his sister. He rushed to the front door and shoulder-checked Renee on the way. She dropped her deck of cards. They splayed onto the carpet, all face down but one.

Death.

───────────

Before Mia's departure to 1967, TRN reminded her that the further she went back, the earlier in the year it would be. She was reminded of the change as she walked down the street to Tom's flat and she heard New Year's parties commence. For the second time, she found herself irritated by the celebration of the new year; a year beginning with tragedy.

Mia double-checked the address TRN provided. Derek was to be found inside. Mia knocked on the door and a man with red hair answered. He let Mia in. She scanned the room and found Derek. Mia watched his face blanch.

———

'Mia. Here. In Tom's doorway. This can't be good.'
Derek's mind reeled as he approached his sister.
"Who are you?" Tom asked Mia.
"I'm Derek's little sister, Mia," she told the eclectic group.
She wished she could have introduced herself under different circumstances. Mia took a deep breath. Before her journey, Vaughn crafted a backstory for Mia which she repeated to Derek's friends.
"I just got in from the states," Mia explained to those emerging from the host's conversation pit. "Our parents were in an accident."
"*What?*" Derek panicked. "Are they okay?"
"No. Derek, we have to go. I'll explain more at your apartment."
With minimal questions from the shocked group, Mia directed Derek outside. She made him guide her to his apartment. They paused to manage his emotions as needed. Mia became aware of the full effect of the fresh dose of Psilopram administered during her journey to sixty-seven. Derek was inconsolable. She couldn't imagine the chaos of the moment if neither of them had an emotional buffer.

Mia had yet to shed a tear for her parents since she left the nineties. Her absence of grief was advantageous in acting rationally after such a heartbreaking loss, but upon seeing her brother's unbridled sadness, she felt eerily unhuman and wished she could extract the numbing Psilopram from her system to share Derek's pain.

———

The day after Mia broke the news, Derek slept until dusk. When he finally emerged to the living room, a harsh wind whistled by his balcony door. Sleet pelted the glass as he took a seat on his sofa, still dazed.

"When do we need to go back?" Derek asked. "I assume you have an Aid since you're here."

"I do, and I have one for you as well," Mia replied. "I've only caught a glimpse of the madness, but TRN is in way over their heads. Travel around the holidays was *insane*."

Derek nodded, "You're telling me. I've tried to go into the nearest TRN Hub multiple times, but there's only one person working there. After the holidays," Derek explained, "I decided to check on the hub's Aid stock to see if I could get a device. I wanted to wish Mom and Dad a lovely holiday," Derek choked on his words.

Mia joined her brother on the couch. She put her hand on his shoulder.

"I wish I could have told them too," she said.

The siblings spent the next three harsh, icy days holed up in Derek's apartment. Mia was still fatigued by her expedited Acclimation process, and they spent most of their time asleep. Derek smoked every bit of weed he could find and almost drank his flat dry. When their stomachs began to eat at themselves, they picked at a crusty loaf of bread in Derek's kitchen.

On their third day of self-confinement, the sleet dissipated. Mia listened to the icicles drip and waited for her brother to wake up. She was getting antsy to Travel back to OT solely for the sake of Psilopram's ability to move Derek through the grieving process at the same rapid pace she experienced.

Derek stumbled into the living room. His eyes were red, and defeat was written all over his face.

"What do we do, Mia?"

Mia answered, "I wish I knew. Though logistically, things are sound for now. You'd be surprised at how much Aunt Donna has done. I hope you're okay with this, but I put her and Francis Platt from TRN in charge of the legalities," she paused, "all we have to decide is what to do with King's and the Court."

Derek trusted their aunt and TRN's caring legal specialist, but he couldn't imagine anyone running their family's record store besides Jon, Ellie, or their grandparents.

"Aunt Donna is keeping daily operations running for now," Mia stated. "She assured me they have it under control until we make a decision."

"Make a decision?"

"Whether to sell or keep the business," Mia said.

Derek shook his head, "It won't be the same without Mom and Dad. Nothing will.

"It won't," Mia agreed, "but we have time to figure it all out. And we have the right connections. I am working for TRN, Derek. We can come and go to other eras as we please for a bit, at least until I'm on call."

"On call?" Derek repeated, "And working for TRN? Since when?"

Mia hesitated. She wanted to avoid dropping more bombs on Derek than necessary. She collected the right words while Derek went to pour himself a glass of amber liquid. He took a long swig and emptied the small glass.

"Working for them was the only way I could come back here to tell you what happened. There is a huge demand for TRN employees right now. They're giving me two weeks to stay here, then I'm going back to monitor for a while. Hopefully, after that, I can return to the nineties to see how my sequence there plays out. I was told about," Mia paused, "Mom and Dad at a rave in the nineties. Luckily, my stylist, Rae, was there or I may have gotten the notification about the accident but not been able to leave for days, weeks even. I found out that you didn't know what happened and Vaughn pulled some strings for me to get here, but for a price."

"So, you're working with Vaughn?"

"I am, yes," Mia started, "but my position is a bit different than his. I wouldn't know how to handle the things he controls. Considering how desperate TRN is for help, they were really understanding of our situation."

Mia's circumstances began to sink in for Derek. To keep him informed, his sister was working for TRN, an organization he didn't trust. And his parents had *died.* Deep sadness flooded in and began to suffocate him. Derek looked around at the full ashtrays, empty bottles, and dirty dishes. Clothes littered his floor. The only clear space in his apartment was the cushion on which Mia sat.

He had to get out.

Derek rushed to his entryway, sat on a bench, and laced his shoes. He threw on his coat.

"Derek, where are you going?"

He couldn't answer his sister because he didn't know himself.

"Don't go off by yourself," Mia pleaded. "Here, let me bundle up and come with you."

Before Mia could gather her TRN-provided outerwear, Derek was out the door. He flew down his stairs to the door of his building. Derek burst through the double doors. The crisp air stunned his lungs.

Derek ran with no destination. Heavy trees dumped wet snow on his head. Derek's feet moved beneath his body. Tears began to streak down his cheeks.

Little time passed before Derek grew short of breath. He hadn't run or worked out since his arrival to the sixties after replacing his Original Time fitness regimen with long walks and daily calisthenics.

Derek stopped to regulate his breath, but just for a moment. Before hysteria could catch up with him, he resumed his erratic run. The scarce passers-by followed Derek with their gaze, concerned by his bewildered state.

Eventually, after drawing in the harsh winter air, he panted but continued down his unknown path. His chest ached for the balm of summer. Suddenly, he hit a patch of residual ice from the pool of a nearby gutter. Derek slipped and fell onto the hard cement.

The immense pain and bottled-up emotions caused him to wail in a way he hadn't since his childhood. He half expected Ellie to help him to his feet with sympathy and reassurance but realized that would never happen again. Derek pulled himself off the slick sidewalk and into a bank of snow.

Alone, propped against a packed drift, Derek sobbed.

Through his blurry gaze, he saw a figure approaching.

Mia embraced her brother; her long waves warmed his frigid cheeks. She held him as he cried. Guilt bubbled up as Mia felt it had been years since their parents passing. She wondered how long the Psilopram would keep her emotions at bay.

A knock on the door pulled Derek from his light slumber. He walked to the entryway and opened the door to see who was there. Grant and Angelene stood on his doormat.

"Derek," Grant started, "I don't know what to say man..." he trailed off and wrapped his arms around Derek.

After Grant released Derek, Angelene took her turn in attempting to comfort their grieving friend.

"There are no words I can say to make it better," Angelene stated, "but we're here for you. All of us. Tom and Germain send their condolences too."

Mia's stomach growled loudly, and Derek chuckled. The melancholy mood eased. Derek pushed the door open to include Mia in the conversation.

Angelene half-grinned at Derek's little sister.

"Shall we get some food?"

"There's a place nearby," Grant stated.

Angelene gave Mia and Derek a once over. Her penetrating gaze darted to the siblings' disheveled hair and mismatched clothing. Derek looked down at himself, suddenly aware that he hadn't showered in days. As he leaned down to brush dirt from his pants, he suppressed the shooting pain from his recent tumble.

"Why don't you two clean up and meet us at the pub around the corner," Angelene suggested.

"That sounds great. We'll clean up and be there as soon as we can," Mia replied.

"Alright. See you in a bit."

Derek closed his entryway door and meandered to the kitchen to pour himself a glass of water. After that, he stepped into the shower. Something about the stream of water dredged up a new round of emotion. Derek wept; his tears mixed with the water drops. From the living room, Mia heard and even her Psilopram-fortified heart was shattered.

"When will you go back to the States?" Grant asked.

Derek paused, uncertain how to answer. Mia chimed in.

"Most of the pressing arrangements have already been made," Mia explained. "Our aunt has everything under control. Our parents didn't want a funeral," Mia bluffed, remembering the blur of faces as she watched her parent's coffins perched at the altar.

"So, you're not going back?" Angelene asked, surprised.

Mia replied, "No."

Later, Mia would explain to Derek that there was little to go back for, only the skeleton of their previous life. King's and the Court, their childhood home, their grandparents house, now up for sale; all that was left was a shell.

Mia was distracted when a welcome diversion from the conversation arrived. She remembered them from the party where she found her brother. Germain and Tom approached their booth.

"My deepest sympathies mate," Germain said as he squeezed Derek. "And to you too, love," he uttered as he smoothed Mia's hair.

Tom followed suit and muttered condolences before they took their seats.

"Renee sends her sympathies," Germain explained. "She phoned this morning. She's off to Paris and couldn't be here to tell you herself. She wanted you to know the Uni girls have the store under control for the remainder of their holiday break. She's quite impressed with them."

Derek nodded and images of Renee cluttered his mind.

He longed for the previous summer's rush fed by Renee's endless stream of star-studded events. Derek craved something to soften the harshness, to lend a new lust for life.

A waitress arrived and they put in their orders. They drank their pints in silence. Finally, she returned with their food. At first, Mia and Derek had little appetite, but that changed after sipping a few spoonfuls of stew.

Germain looked upon the siblings with sad eyes.

"Eat up," he stated, "this is on me."

Derek recalled that, aside from Tom, everyone at the table was without at least one parent. As the sustenance rejuvenated Derek's mind, he remembered that Tom and Germain had just returned from a trip to see Germain's father. He felt selfish for neglecting to ask about their travels.

"How's your father doing?" Derek asked. "Where was he staying for the winter? Somewhere in France? South of where you visited, right?"

"Marseille," Germain answered. "I hope to receive a letter or call from him soon." Germain got a far-off look in his eyes. As Derek and Mia devoured the contents of their dishes, Germain's wheels turned. "Let's go visit *Papa*," Germain stated, "all of us."

Derek and Mia processed the notion.

"You just got back. Leave? Again?" Angelene asked.

"I think that's a wonderful idea," Tom replied. "Print's dead this time of year. Let's get away before it picks up in the spring."

Grant remained stoic, contemplating the idea.

"C'mon," Germain proposed, "if you're not going back to the states, what's the harm in taking a trip to get away from this... darkness? Do you have to get back soon, Mia?"

Mia wasn't sure how to answer. TRN had granted her two weeks to do what she wanted before monitoring. Marseille seemed a far better option than going back to OT's excessive sympathizers or jumping back into the nineties.

"What's it like in Marseille this time of year?" she asked.

"Well," Germain began, "it's not tropical, but it's better than this," Germain gestured outside the pub where a light snow began to fall. "It's the sunniest place in France."

Mia and Derek exchanged a look. For the first time in days, a smile lit their faces and answered Germain's invitation.

———

When the four travelers emerged from the train, they were welcomed with bright rays and the aroma of sea-brine.

Derek scanned the crowd for his envisioned Marcel.

"*Papa!*" Germain shouted.

Marcel emerged from the crowd and hugged his son.

"I did not think you would visit so soon!" Marcel stated. "Tell me, is this an excuse to dote on your aging father? You know I can take care of myself."

Germain hesitated, "I know *Pa*. We've come to visit as a bit of a getaway," he said and gestured to Mia, Derek, and Tom.

"Our parents," Mia started, "well, they were in an accident. They didn't make it."

Marcel's expression dropped. He approached Mia, rested his hands on her shoulders, and squeezed.

His hands were warm.

"My most sincere condolences," he offered. "The sting of loss cannot be cured by sunshine, only softened by time," Marcel stated. "We will do our best though, yeah?"

Mia and Derek nodded.

Marcel's loving nature was undeniable. His parental quality was an instant source of comfort to the siblings. The group of travelers followed Marcel down from the train platform.

"I hear you like cards," Mia said to Marcel.

Marcel grinned, "Am I in good company?"

"You are indeed," Mia smiled, reminded of her and Derek's euchre-filled family Christmases.

Marcel beamed. He lifted Mia and Derek's shared suitcase and led them to the street to signal a cab.

Marcel opened the door to his humble flat. The space was welcoming, but very cramped. Mia's eyes were drawn to the plethora of instruments perched throughout the common space.

Marcel followed her gaze. He scratched his head.

"I'm still figuring out what stays and what goes."

A trumpet case was squeezed into the space between a sofa and the wall. On top of the horn, other various, smaller cases were stacked. A monstrous standup bass took up a third of the wall space upon which it leaned.

"I am sorry," he said with concern. "I did not anticipate so much company this soon. I have very little storage."

"No need to apologize," Mia said.

She was grateful to be somewhere new, somewhere with no ties or heaviness, however she hoped that most of their time would be spent wandering the city rather than being stuffed into the tiny apartment.

"*Pa*, is there storage in this building? Perhaps you can put some of your instruments away for a bit, you know. Just keep out your horn," Germain suggested. He scanned the room and attempted to figure out the logistics of where they were to sleep that night.

"It's not so crowded when I'm here by myself. And I spend much of my time… elsewhere."

Before Germain could ask where his father was spending his days, or nights, Marcel continued.

"I've branched out from traditional jazz. There's something new," the excitement in his voice was audible, "something soulful that makes you want to groove. Something," he paused, "there's no name for it yet, but you must come to listen during your visit."

"I'd love to hear it," Mia stated.

A smile lit Marcel's face.

"*Papa*," Germain said, "I'm so excited to hear more about your new music and I'm glad you've settled in here, but it's growing late. Do you know of nearby lodging?"

A knock tapped at the entrance and Marcel answered the door.

"Guests I see?" a voice said from the open-air hallway outside Marcel's flat.

"My son and his friends," Marcel said. "You remember, right?"

Mia stood on her tiptoes to view the woman whose lovely, accented voice floated from the hallway.

"Auntie Corrine!" Germain exclaimed.

Tom, Derek, and Mia couldn't help but give in to the excitement as Germain cut past his father at the door and hugged the petite, silver-haired woman. He picked her up and spun her in a circle.

"I didn't expect you'd visit your father for another year! Or at least not until summer. You missed me, was that it?"

Germain beamed, "You caught me!" He turned to face his friends. "This is my Auntie Corrine," Germain paused, "well, not aunt by blood, but by choice."

"My mother housed Marcel's father after the first Great War," Corrine explained. "Now, we can't stop housing the family. As of last fall, I came to own this building. My uncle left it to me upon his death."

Germain's mouth dropped open.

"You *own* this building? Why didn't you give *Papa* a bigger flat?" Germain teased.

Marcel nudged his son.

"This residence is a trial run to see if I wish to retire here," Marcel stated. "Those English winters have felt colder and colder. My flat is fine. I don't need much, and I didn't realize you'd visit so soon. Corrine, love, this is…" Marcel trailed off and presented Germain's friends with an open hand.

Derek extended his introduction first, "Derek Hayes."

Derek reached out to shake Corrine's hand, but his gesture was disregarded and replaced with a delicate kiss on both of his cheeks.

"And I'm Mia."

Corrine went on to welcome Mia.

"Americans I hear," Corrine stated. "Derek, why do I know Derek? Oh yes!" Corrine clapped her hands together. "You are Renee's 'saving grace' were her words. She carried on about you over the holidays, how you helped her at the boutique, your summer rendezvous," she raised her eyebrows and Derek blushed. "Then, she grew too busy in her stardom."

Silence fell upon their conversation and Tom took the opportunity to introduce himself.

"Tom," he said and kissed Corrine's cheeks, "a friend of Germain."

"What brings you all to visit? Though I'm quite fond of Marcel in Marseille myself," Corrine made eyes at Germain's father and giggled, "there *must* have been some sense of urgency. You just visited the village over Christmas."

Their speaking halted once again.

"Our parents," Mia spilled, "they have passed."

Corrine shuffled over to Mia and took her hands.

"We wanted to get away, but could not go back home," Derek stated. He finally understood what awaited them in Original Time and vowed to himself not to return until necessary.

"I am sincerely sorry to learn of your loss," Corrine stated.

"Corrine, dear, now that you've welcomed Germain and his friends, I must ask, do you have a vacant room?"

Corrine nodded, "Children, you may rest in my *pied-a-terre*," she smiled and smoothed Mia's hair.

"Marcel, I trust you have extra space for me at your place."

Corrine's dwelling felt like home. The living room led outside to a quaint, wrought iron balcony. There were four small bedrooms and they each claimed one. Mia opened her bedroom window and drew in the sea's aroma fused with spices and cuisine she couldn't identify. She unpacked a black shift dress, the only clothing she brought besides the white blouse and blue skirt she wore.

She sat on her bed and took in her surroundings. Based on the opulent décor, she knew the room she chose was Corrine's. Mia kicked off her shoes and snuggled the soft blanket. She fell asleep as soon as her head hit Corrine's pillow and she dreamed of floating on the salt water.

Mia woke up to a buzz. She looked around the unfamiliar room, then remembered the events of the previous week and how they ended up in Marseille. She wished that she could have stayed in her dream, that the reality of her reason for being there vanished at once.

The buzz's source finally became clear to her. The UpgrAid.

She was about to answer her first test TRN alert. Test alerts were a part of her conditioning to monitor. Mia read the device's text.

'Two blocks to the north. Young woman, 23 years old. Name: Emma. Language: English and Spanish. 5'4", brown eyes, straight brown hair. Has taken heroin. CAUTION: Danger may include gang activity.

Mia groaned. She dreaded the commencement of her penance to TRN. She felt unequipped for the huge responsibility, but TRN assured Mia that any help she could offer would suffice.

Before departing for the sixties, Mia was informed that before she was officially on call as a monitor, she would receive several of these mock alerts. She was encouraged to imagine what she would do in the situation. Once her allotted two weeks were up, the alerts were set to go live, and she would train on the job.

'In a real situation, I'd call the authorities,' she thought to herself.

With that thought, Mia picked up Corrine's bedroom telephone to ensure its functionality. TRN recommended that she get in the habit of securing open communication wherever she was on call. Just as she set the handset back on its hook, a gentle knock rapped on her door.

"Come in."

Derek opened the door and stepped inside. His eyes were red.

"I'm sorry," he stated, causing Mia's heart to sink. Derek lowered his voice. "I wish I had just Traveled, like you. You're so even keeled about this, but I'm not," Derek said as his voice cracked. "I know I'd be better with Psilopram. I see the way you're handling this. It's like you skipped over grief. I'm your big brother. I'm supposed to be strong for you, but it's the opposite way around."

"It's so strange, Derek. I wonder how much of a trainwreck I was in the Shell. I must have gone through so many emotions, but now, I can't recall any of them. The last time I felt the weight of what happened was after the rave when Rae was leading me to the hub. It's like I cheated and skipped the sorrow. I'm so sorry that I can't *feel* what you're going through right now," Mia said and squeezed her brother's arm.

Derek sat next to Mia and sobbed on her shoulder.

Finally, he sat up straight and looked his sister in the eyes.

"I don't know how to go on *here*," he said, "but I can't go *back*."

Mia nodded, "I know."

The siblings heard a rustle in the living room and turned their heads in that direction. Germain shuffled to the doorway and his expression saddened when he saw Derek. Germain offered him a handkerchief and sat down on the corner of the bed.

"I never knew my mum. Sometimes I feel lucky for that. It would have been harder to let her go," Germain stated. "Whatever you need to do here, do it. I know nothing will bring them back, but they would want you to *live*. That's what *Papa* always said about Mum. 'Give her a life worth watching.'"

Derek drew in a deep breath to compose himself.

"Shall we wake up Tom and go see this city?"

———————

Corrine opened Marcel's balcony doors and listened to the evening sounds. Cars splashed through puddles left from the late afternoon rain. The breeze ruffled Marcel's frumpy, moth-eaten curtains.

'I have got to help him decorate.'

A knock sounded at the door, and Corrine hurried to answer, giddy to see their guests.

"Did you rest well?" she asked as she invited them inside.

All their eyes were refreshed and their skin more aglow. All but Derek's. His eyes were bloodshot, and his cheeks were rosy and damp.

After seeing Corrine's expression, Derek looked down at his color-blocked polo from *En Blum* and saw wet splotches. He smeared the moisture into his shirt, hoping to make the tear-soaked spots less visible. His shirt reminded him of the boutique, and he hoped the Uni girls hadn't left the door unlocked or mischarged any transactions.

"Though I'd love to keep you here, if you want to go see Marcel play, I can give you directions to the club where he is," Corrine offered.

"You're not coming with?" Mia asked.

Corrine laughed and answered, "I know how Marcel gets at his shows. I think it's best if I'm waiting for him right here," she paused and winked at Germain. "I'll have the cards ready."

The directions Corrine gave made no sense to Derek, Mia, or Tom, but Germain seemed to understand where they were headed. As they cut through the city, Mia grew aware that she was the only female when they passed several darkened allies. She turned her cheek from the aggressive shouts, expelled from the narrow walkways. Mia was still uneasy from her TRN mock-alert. She saw how a young woman could be held against her will in one of the secluded paths.

Mia thought about the bits of advice given by TRN over the last few days. Through the Aid, they began to offer tips and tricks to heighten her skills as a TRN employee before throwing her into the job.

"Two Travelers in trouble are worse than one," one of the training tips read. *"Keep your entanglements to a minimum. Let the authorities and medical professionals handle most emergencies, then get the Traveler to the nearest hub."*

With every bit of advice she received, Mia further respected Vaughn's expertise. The Psilopram softened her feelings of complication surrounding Vaughn, and she saw him only as a helpful ally.

Finally, the four of them reached a well-lit area and Mia began to ease.

Germain led them to the exact site of Marcel's performance. They could hear the bump of the music inside.

"Ready to go in?" Germain asked.

"Ready," Derek nodded.

They went inside and Mia was shocked at the difference between the club's shabby exterior and the lively happening beyond the creaky front door. The energy was fresh and upbeat, a stark contrast to the last week of her life. She felt the light come back into her eyes. Germain noticed.

"It's wonderful, isn't it?" he said into her ear.

Tom's face held the same awe. He hadn't heard anything like the music being played and fell into the smooth groove. They mellowed with the drum's steady, relaxed beat. Marcel lent his trumpet's flair to the guitar's offbeat chords.

Germain shook his head, "My father," he said and gestured to Marcel.

Marcel's somewhat reserved façade unraveled onstage. He leaned into his bright, brass bars as if in another realm. The front row was studded with enamored fans.

"Shall we go up there?" Germain asked.

"Yes!" Mia answered.

Once they established a place to stand, Germain went to get a round of beers. They took turns refilling the libations and all sense of rigidity evaded them.

Germain looked at the clock. '1:30AM.'

The few remaining audience members stumbled, laughed, and shouted to one another. Germain's heart warmed when he saw Derek's unbridled laughter at Tom, who was on a roll with his stories. Mia was equally delighted by Tom.

They hit a second wind.

The band wrapped up fifteen minutes before, unable to be torn from the stage at midnight, as had been expected. Finally, Marcel emerged from backstage with the handle to his trumpet case in one hand and guitar case in the other.

"You can play any instrument, can't you?" Mia asked.

Marcel grinned. Now that he was offstage, Mia noticed Marcel's aging frame and the sweat that accumulated on his back.

"Let me take your trumpet case," she said, no stranger to the post-show tear down.

Marcel looked at her and raised his eyebrows, then gestured to the trio of men.

"You mean to tell me," he raised his voice, "there are three, able-bodied men and this little *bebe* is the one offering to help?"

They all laughed, and Derek took the trumpet case.

"She always was the favorite," he joked and elbowed Mia.

On the way home, though Mia was sure danger lurked, she felt invincible. They danced back to Corrine's building and stumbled upstairs. Corrine's kitchen was lit by a glittering chandelier and light sparkled across the entire space. Smoke drifted up from the table as Marcel flicked his ashes into an ashtray. He picked up a deck of cards.

"Miss Mia, you will be my *belote* partner, yes?" Marcel proposed.

"Of course," she agreed. "One of us needs to know what we're doing."

He laughed, "How you never play *belote?*"

"Americans…" Corrine teased. "Derek, I will show you. And Germain, Tom, you know how to play. Or Germain, did you forget after your time away?"

"You better watch what you say, or I'll be less easy on you than usual," Germain answered with a mischievous grin.

Marcel handed his slim, piquet deck to Mia. Mia began to shuffle the deck and Marcel promptly stopped her by placing his hands on the cards.

"No shuffling, just cut them like this, see?"

He explained the rules and the game kicked off in their favor with an excellent hand. As they played, Mia and Derek exchanged several looks of contentment.

They leaned into the familiarity of a family card game. Mia witnessed her brother's fluctuation between a sense of belonging and utter heartbreak. Despite Mia's recognition of his state, she was impressed that Derek held it together for the remainder of the game. When Germain and Tom concluded the first game with a victory, Mia tipped her head toward Corrine's balcony, ushering Derek to meet her outside for some fresh air.

"We're going to step out for a few minutes, is that okay?" Mia asked, hoping she wasn't being rude.

Corrine waved them on, "Of course, take the time you need."

"Take these," Marcel offered the siblings a pair of cigarettes.

Mia took them graciously, "Thank you."

Marcel tossed her a lighter.

"Throw on my coat, love," Corrine gestured to a burgundy trench by the balcony door.

The coastal breeze was sharp, but the solitude unified Derek and Mia. After a struggle to light their cigarettes, they finally succeeded. The Hayes stood in silence and took in the scene.

Lights reflected off the rippling water and vessels swayed in the marina. The moon was veiled by a passing cloud. Derek took a long drag and spoke to his sister.

"What a year it's been."

Mia nodded, "We haven't had the chance to catch up on what *we've* been doing yet, have we?"

She closed the balcony doors for privacy but was reassured of their discretion after she heard bursts of laughter coming from the kitchen table.

Mia went on to tell her brother about the Tuesdaze, Macy, and Vaughn. She explained how when their parents had visited the nineties, they seemed more at peace with Derek and Mia's decision to Travel.

"They were really focusing on their own lives, finding out who they were before us," Mia stated. "The night," she paused, "*it* happened, they were on a date in the city. Dad took Mom to the Nutcracker."

Derek drew an inhale deep into his lungs. It burned.

"These last few days have given me whiplash," he said. "Hour to hour, minute to minute, I've gone between wanting to be alone and process this to the need to feel nothing and completely forget about it. I don't know what to *do*."

Mia placed a hand on her brother's shoulder. He continued.

"Even more bizarre than what has happened is your reaction to it. You're healed," he let out a sigh. "I'm jealous. I feel like a wreck."

"Within the last week, I've had *two* doses of Psilopram," Mia stated. "You're not a wreck. If anything, I am. Who reacts so numbly to losing their parents?"

Derek sighed at the strangeness of that moment in time and pulled his sister in for a half-embrace. Their cigarettes shortened, and they went back inside to join the game.

The next morning, Derek awoke to the radiance of sunshine. He had a stinging headache from the wine the night before, but the sunlight was irresistible, and he pulled open the curtains. A blue mass of water sparkled beyond his window. He pulled on his trousers and walked into the living room.

The rest of the bedroom doors were still closed. On the table sat four empty wine bottles and a stacked deck of cards. In need of separation from the oppressive weight of indoor cigarette smoke, Derek pried open the balcony doors as quietly as possible. A bite in the air reminded him it was still January, and he went back inside to put on a sweater.

The patio doors' suction caused one of the bedroom doors to open. Derek tiptoed across the creaky floor and wrapped his fingers around the open bedroom's door knob. He began to close the door but paused to process the sight before him.

On the bed lay Germain with Tom cozied onto his shoulder.

A smile lit Derek's face, and he pulled the door closed. Derek found his coat by the door. He wrapped one of Corrine's knitted scarves around his neck to walk along the harbor.

The streets were quiet, aside from a church bell's hourly mark. *'Only seven chimes.'* He reveled in the alone time which had been so scarce over the previous days.

Derek knew almost nothing about the city, so he veered away from empty alleyways and stayed in the public eye. The cool air vaporized his breath. His mouth tasted like cigarettes, and he regretted not gargling with water before his walk. Just as he began to contemplate the nature of Germain and Tom's relationship, he was distracted by shrieks sounding from near the water. He slowed his pace and turned to see what the excitement was about.

He saw a curly-haired woman with a knitted blanket draped across her shoulders. She ran across the beach and splashed in the water's edge. Her squeals were the product of the early January water. After further evaluation of the scene, he saw that three other young ladies stood up-shore and cheered her on. Derek's mouth dropped when he saw that she wore nothing under the blanket.

The nude woman gestured to the group and another member of the blanketed calamity joined her frigid frolic. Derek could see the water rendering her breathless but the sheer look of glee on their faces made him envious of their mad endeavor. The woman lured the rest of the group to join her.

Derek's conscience kicked in, and he felt guilty for ogling the women's bare breasts and shocked gasps. Despite his best attempts at decency, he couldn't tear himself away from the spectacle. He was reminded of Carole's time-halting window display at *En Blum.*

After a few more minutes, the women gathered at the corner of the beach. A blonde woman pulled a worn backpack from the ground and doled out clothing.

Derek feigned disinterest as the sirens trudged up from the beach to the walkway where he stood, frozen. They spoke amongst themselves in Spanish. As they neared him, he met eyes with the curly-haired woman. He was breathless, as though he'd been the one splashing naked through the icy water; her rich, umber eyes and brunette swirls stunned Derek.

"*Buenos dias,*" he offered as they crossed paths.

She responded, "*Buenas noches!*"

Derek's eyes remained glued to the beauties as they laughed and made their way into Corrine's apartment building.

—————

Derek went straight to Marcel's flat to probe Corrine about the women from the beach. He knocked on the door. After a few minutes with no answer, Derek put his ear to the door and heard the clanking of dishes. He knocked louder.

"It's Derek!" He shouted, seeing that she had no peep hole.

"Hold on!" Corrine shouted from the other side. "Marcel, let him in."

Derek heard Marcel's footsteps and he was greeted with a smile.

"You are up so early," Marcel stated.

He saw the scarf wrapped around Derek's neck and the rosiness of his cheeks.

"Come in from the cold. Did you take a walk?"

"Yes," Derek answered. "It really is a beautiful city. Corrine," Derek started, "who are the Spanish girls in this building? Are they tenants?"

Corrine rolled her eyes.

"Yes, they are staying here temporarily. Vagabonds," she shook her head, "loud and messy. But they paid for their lodging up front," Corrine shrugged.

Derek could still hear the voice that wished him a good night and imagined how the previous evening would have gone if they'd met. To suppress the image of the siren's magnificent body, he busied himself and went to the kitchen to assist Corrine.

"Can I help with anything?"

Corrine moved with grace around Marcel's modest galley kitchen. Derek watched as she chopped vegetables and placed them into a large pot. He noticed a small bowl which held spiky, red-orange herbs.

"Lovely, isn't it?" Corrine plucked the luxurious spice from its dish. "Only the best for our guests."

Derek's stomach growled. He realized the only food he had since arriving was a dried-up pastry from Corrine's counter the night before. Marcel hovered in the kitchen, also uncertain how to help. Corrine chuckled.

"Go," she said, "let me take care of the cooking. Get some bread and this will be ready by the time you return."

———

On the way to the market, Derek and Marcel passed the same beach where hours before, Derek stumbled upon Corrine's unruly tenants. Derek scanned the beach.

"Too cold this time of year," Marcel stated. "Summertime is a different story. Nude beach," he raised his eyebrows.

Derek chuckled. Walking with Marcel felt natural, comfortable, just as it did with Germain.

Marcel continued.

"Corrine does not go down to that beach anymore. She thinks she's too old. Then, I point out the wrinkled, fat men," Marcel and Derek laughed. "Maybe this year she will be tempted."

"Are you leaning toward a permanent stay?" Derek asked.

Marcel paused and Derek regretted prying.

"For now, I'm living day to day. I spent many years busy with late nights, keeping the kids out of trouble. You know, Germain, Angelene, Grant, Renee. Luckily, they didn't complain about tagging along to the clubs and," Marcel chuckled, "the clubs didn't mind the kids. They put them to work. Now, I want to live for me, you know? I'm figuring out how to spend the rest of my days."

"Mia told me our parents lived their final days like they were young again," Derek barely uttered.

"I'm so sorry, man. I understand loss. Losing Germain's ma, well…" Marcel's face grew pained, and he trailed off. "I didn't know I could love again, *really* love, not just love for the night. The timing was always off with Corrine. I was married when I met her, then she was married shortly after my wife died. Though we're old now," Marcel nodded, "the timing is finally right."

"That's great," Derek stated and offered a smile. "It helps that Germain loves Corrine too. It seems like she's already family to him."

"She is. Marseille is full of sunshine, both from the sky and from Corrine. Germain worried that I was too old to uproot, but if I've learned anything, all that we've got," Marcel gestured to the marina, to the open sea, and finally rested his hand between Derek's shoulders, "is this."

Chapter III

Derek studied her face.

Lucia, the curly haired woman from the beach, sat across from him. She was unbothered by his presence. She had her eyes closed. Her shoulders were relaxed, and her lips were slightly parted. Lucia was lost in her morning meditation; a ritual she, and all of her 'sisters' practiced daily.

The day before, Lucia and Derek ran into each other outside the building. They made their introductions, then took a short walk through the city. She helped him pick out a new camera after he shared that he left his Leica in London.

"A tool to imprint every moment here," she said as she convinced him to make the purchase.

After a day of capturing Marseille together, Lucia invited Derek downstairs the next morning. Derek was thrilled to spend a second day with Lucia, but he had a hard time zoning out with such beauty seated before him. The rest of the sirens sat in the common room for their ritual, but Lucia had pulled him aside to a corner room.

"Meditation will relieve your mind of the heaviness," she said.

Derek furrowed his brow. He had mentioned nothing of this parent's death.

"What heaviness?"

"Shh," Lucia quieted him. "You don't have to explain."

Derek closed his eyes. He tried meditation back in Original Time but was not as disciplined about the practice as Lucia. But he was motivated to give it a shot. Lucia had a light within her, and he could tell she benefited from the daily practice. She understood something Derek had been missing.

He finally settled into the present.

"Nothing exists but your breath," Lucia told him.

After days of a restless mind, Derek's thoughts dropped off and he thought of nothing.

Minutes passed and Derek opened his eyes when Abra, the maternal figure of the group, signaled the end of meditation with a bell chime from the next room. Lucia and Derek remained in their secluded corner of the unit. He heard the others prepare breakfast while they planned their day. Lucia shared that her 'family' hailed from various areas of Spain. They exiled themselves from their home country's fascist turn of power.

"We attempted to make things better there before leaving. We spoke out and did our best to strengthen the opposition, then we departed from Spain," Lucia explained, "the danger was too high. Now, we've landed in Marseille, though I don't know how long we will stay. It depends on how long we are needed here."

Derek was surprised at how on-purpose the vagabonds seemed to live. To "stay until they were no longer needed." He thought of his own ventures and realized how purposeless they turned out to be.

Darting off to the sixties. His fling with Renee. Working at the boutique.

Though, early on in his trip, he convinced himself he was entitled to the lack of commitment. Especially after working so hard for Artificial Intelligence, something, he was told, would make a *positive* change in the world. After his drama with Anna, he reasoned that perhaps his lighthearted relationship with Renee was alright. He was still uncertain about Angelene. Rather than pick apart his emotions, he engaged with Lucia.

"How did you get so… involved with the opposition then leave?" Derek asked. "How do you know when it's your time to go?"

Lucia shrugged, "Abra makes the call. And her decisions have not failed us."

Abra, who was eight years older than Lucia, took in the young ladies after finding them in a troubled state. The family went on to create an existence filled with both spiritual and visual beauty.

Lucia shared that, over the last month, they had lent their efforts to countless social movements, spent time with several well-known artists, and, according to Lucia, they meant to press forward on their unnamed mission to change the world for the better.

Derek wondered why she chose to spend time with him when she could be on her way, illuminating others in the crossroads of Marseille, but her light was contagious, and he let her rays soak in for as long as she was around.

That afternoon, Derek led Mia downstairs to meet the sisters. Derek's attitude underwent a dramatic shift after his morning with Lucia, and Mia's heart fluttered with excitement as Derek knocked on the vagabonds' door.

"It is open," Abra called from inside.

A smile crept onto Mia's face as she turned the doorknob.

As they stepped inside, Mia noticed that there was no furniture, just pads and cushions scattered about. A breeze came in from the patio and ruffled beautifully dyed dresses, which hung from a line on the balcony. Abra approached Mia first and was soon joined by three other women. Mia automatically knew which one Lucia was based on Derek's description.

"So nice to meet you," Abra said and smoothed Mia's hair. Something about the way Abra's eyes glinted made her seem just as young if not younger than those she oversaw.

"Wonderful to meet you as well," Mia responded.

The rest of the non-biological family introduced themselves; Chiara with copper hair, sprite-like Phoebe, and finally, the fabled Lucia.

Nothing about Lucia was inhibited. Her crown of dark curls bounced as she walked across the room. Her eyes gleamed from beneath unkempt eyebrows. Even Lucia's long, wide-knit, sweater couldn't confine her luscious curves; the garment's loose stitch left nothing unseen.

Mia adored the bohemian sisterhood. She and Derek spent the day absorbing their philosophies. By the time the sun dimmed, and the hour came to go upstairs for Corrine's cooking, Mia was more inspired than she anticipated to make a difference through her role as a nomadic protector of Time Travelers.

The Hayes siblings spent Mia's final week before her commitment to TRN kicked in, bouncing between Germain's family upstairs and the oasis below. An increasing amount of Mia's days were spent downstairs, but Derek struggled to find his place in the new, interwoven dynamic of old and new acquaintances.

Derek joined the vagabonds' ritualistic morning practices but felt obligated to give adequate attention to Germain and his family, so he often went upstairs by noon. The Londoners gathered around Corrine's table for lunch, but Mia often remained downstairs and came upstairs only for evening meals.

By the time Mia and Derek finished supper and made their plans for the evening, the sisters' space was always vacant, and the Hayes grew curious where they went for the night.

Corrine noticed the Hayes' intrigue with the vagabonds. Initially, she was skeptical of the four unkempt tenants below, but she noticed the spark they ignited within the siblings. One night, before she began to cook, Corrine encouraged the Hayes to join her renters in a night out.

"I've seen you watch them from the balcony. Perhaps they are not what I expected. They've paid their rent. They never disappear for days on end. They don't seem strung out. Why not join them for a night?"

Mia turned to Derek and beamed.

"Let's go with them. Tonight! Before I have to go. I've got only two days left," Mia stated, "before I must go back to the states for school."

Corrine nodded toward the balcony.

"Looks like you'd better hurry!"

Below, the vagabonds were gathered outside. They pointed to their uphill destination. Abra's cigarette shortened as did the Hayes' time to join the family.

Just then, Germain, Marcel, and Tom stepped inside Corrine's flat from their day out in the city. Germain saw Mia shove cash into her jacket.

"Where are you headed?" he asked.

"We're going out with the downstairs tenants tonight. If they'll have us, that is," Mia explained.

Germain and Tom looked to Corrine for a reaction as she washed tomatoes. Corrine laughed.

"Go with! You don't have to dote on me and Marcel. We could use a night alone," she smirked.

Germain shook his head, "Well then, let us be on our way."

The four of them hurried downstairs.

"Care to go out with us tonight?" Mia asked Abra. She caught the family right before they began their uphill trek. "I leave Marseille in two days. It seems you know the city well as you are always out for the evening. Where shall we go?"

"Let us discuss," Abra said and gathered the vagabonds close.

They whispered to each other. Mia kicked herself for intruding in on their plans. She heard Chiara whisper, "Will they be alright without us?"

"Break away… then meet…" was audible.

They loosened their huddle and Abra turned to face the four friends.

"Shall we head uphill?"

Within minutes, the group was carried away, into the night.

———————

The first hints of dawn began to emerge. Uphill from the city, from where they spent the night, a soft, steady illumination bled into the sky's darkness. Birds chirped and Derek caught a third wind as he sat next to Lucia on the balcony. Lucia's curls blew and tickled his face. Her brown swirls were infused with the aroma of incense.

After the whirlwind of a night at a local musician's hashish den, Lucia and Derek sat outside and talked on her balcony. She went on about her life as an exile and explained that she'd lost her parents when she was young.

"Abra found me in my most dire state. She showed me this life and I haven't looked back. The way we live, our stability is always challenged, but we are free. And we can make a difference."

"What do you do to afford," Derek paused, uncertain how personal to get with the woman he hardly knew, "moving around? Food? Clothing?"

"We have a lot of friends who help us out. But we have helped them as well. And the artists," Lucia chuckled, "they always take us in. They understand what it's like to be in a constant state of transit. We give them what we can and open our doors when we have doors to open. In our travels, we've taken in several musicians, photographers, painters…" Lucia trailed off. "They bring life to the dark areas we've been. They must be nourished. Housed. Given a place to find their voice when the world has tried to homogenize them."

"You're a refuge," Derek stated.

Lucia smirked, "*We* hope to offer a refuge. Perhaps it is a moving refuge, but, one day, maybe we can all have access to a place of true safety."

Lucia looked across the sky with her dreamy gaze.

Derek couldn't help but pick up his camera.

"Do you mind?" he asked.

Lucia answered with a smile, then went back to admiring the ethereal beginnings of a new day.

"Stay just like that."

The more outrageous, the better.

Mia was both lost and found during their night with the vagabonds. They fed on each other's free and easy attitudes, and it led them all around the city with no moments of melancholy or friction. Spontaneous actions, romantic pursuits, and complete openness were not only accepted, but encouraged in the nonjudgmental environment of their group.

In Original Time, feminine support had become blasé and ingenuine, something many people just said to *sound* supportive. The vagabonds' fierce authenticity was a phenomenon Mia had not yet witnessed in her life. The closer Mia's betrothed time to TRN grew, the more she leaned into their one-day-at-a-time philosophy.

At the end of the night, Mia, Germain, and Tom floated upstairs to their flat and Derek remained at the vagabond's apartment. Mia opened her bedroom window and heard Derek talking with Lucia. She smiled to herself.

"What was I supposed to do? Leave you in the dark?"

Derek sighed, "Mia, Vaughn should have taken care of things like he said he would. He should have gotten me an Aid months ago. Hell, considering his 'elite' position, he should have been the one to deliver the news to me. This is unfair to you, and it makes me so angry. Things are amazing here. Knowing you have to leave tomorrow…" Derek hung his head.

"The anger you have toward Vaughn isn't going to help anything," Mia stated, uncertain of where her instinct to defend Vaughn came from. "He's basically running the U.S. Northeast's TRN region. He *got* us here. It's just how it played out, Derek."

The siblings snapped their heads toward Mia's door as they heard Germain and Tom rouse in the living room.

"Let's not talk about this now," she said. "Let's just *be* here for as long as we *are* here. Lean into this time with Lucia and the vagabonds. Just because I have to go doesn't mean you must return home too. Stay with her. She's good for you."

"I know. But I can't put my baggage on her. Plus, they won't stay long; I can feel it. Perhaps I should monitor with you," Derek considered. "Things won't be the same when I go back to London. So much has changed since last summer. It all started so bright and sunny," he paused, "you know, Psilopram."

Mia nodded.

"You're still on that high. I'm not. And I'm dealing with this loss *alone*."

"I'm sorry, Derek," Mia grasped at any shred of emotion she possessed. "I haven't intended to make you feel alone. Honestly, I fear there will be a day when it all hits me at once."

Mia paused and contemplated her brother's consideration of monitoring.

"Take some time today and *really* think about monitoring. Make sure you *want* to commit to ensuring the safety of Travelers; that you're not just trying to escape this transitional season of your life," Mia nudged her brother, "or keep track of me. I can take care of myself."

"I'm sorry," Derek uttered, "it's just you and me, now. I can't help but want to look out for you. Plus, the dose of Psilopram would be welcome. Lucia is helping but, again, I can't rely on her to fix me. I've been there before."

Just as Derek was scared for Mia, she was concerned about him. The free-wheeling Derek, whom Vaughn previously described to Mia, had expired.

"I don't know what the right answer is for you," Mia said. "All we can do is live. That's what Mom and Dad would have wanted for us."

A knock came at the door and served as a welcome break in the siblings' intense conversation. Derek went to open the door. Germain and Tom stood on the other side.

"Everything okay?" Germain asked. "Mia, we can't have you cooped up on your last day here."

"I agree. Derek is just worried about me and the girls downstairs getting into trouble," Mia bluffed.

Germain and Tom laughed.

"I would be too if I had a little sister," Germain stated. "I remember I used to worry about Angelene, that's probably why she's so reserved now. Once she grew out of her ugly duckling phase and became the beauty we now know, it took both me and Grant to keep the bad boys away from her."

"Especially the cats in her beloved beat scene," Tom added. "Even worse than their terrible hygiene is their pretentiousness."

Derek rolled his eyes, "That's an understatement."

"Shall we have some tea before going out for the day?" Tom suggested.

The siblings agreed and sat with Tom and Germain at the kitchen table. They sipped their tea in silence. Germain fumbled with the tablecloth and exchanged a look with Tom. Tom nodded.

"We're going back tomorrow," Germain revealed. "Tom received a call from the ad agency. They signed a big account and are in dire need of his artwork."

"That's wonderful," Mia said.

Tom scoffed, "Wonderfully mind-numbing. 'That's not *quite* the angle we had in mind. Can you draw her profile rather than straight on? And make her look younger, like one of the mods.' It's never done the first time." Tom took a long drag of his cigarette.

"He's got work piling up. There's no timeline on your stay though, Derek. I'm sure Corrine and Papa would be fine with you prolonging your visit."

"Thank you, Germain. I'll consider what I want to do. Mia and I were just discussing what's next for me," Derek stated. He turned to face Tom. "Congrats man, I didn't even know you got the ad job."

"It's not all that exciting," Tom said. "The job didn't seem so urgent to share after learning what happened with you two. But I suppose more dough will be welcome," Tom nudged Germain, "Germain's just glad I'm on the straight and narrow."

Germain raised his eyebrows, "You can say that again. Things were getting a little dicey. This time away was just as essential for us as it was for you two. Cut some... ties, you know? But enough about our entanglements in London. Let's plan the night. Papa has a show. Should we invite the girls from downstairs and live it up for our last night here?"

The Hayes nodded. The four of them finished their tea and went to notify Corrine and Marcel of their plans. They knocked on Marcel's door. Minutes passed before Corrine opened the entrance. Her hair was disheveled, and Marcel fumbled to button his shirt.

Germain shook his head.

"Sorry to interrupt, we just came to notify you that we're leaving in the morning."

"All of you?" Corrine asked.

"Well," Germain turned to face Derek, "do you want to extend your stay?"

"You are welcome to stay in my apartment for as long as you'd like," Corrine stated. "Or I'm sure you have an open invitation downstairs," she winked.

Derek shrugged, "I-I'll probably go back too. I don't know yet, I'm sorry."

"He's taking today to consider his options," Mia said. "But more importantly, we must know the location of your show tonight, Marcel."

"Ah yes. Tonight, we will give you a proper send-off."

"Seriously, how many instruments does your dad know how to play?" Mia asked Germain.

He grinned and shook his head, "I'm not sure. I wish he would have passed on his talent to me."

The vagabonds swayed along to the band's signature drumbeat. The entire club was fixated on their beauty. Chiara danced with Mia, Lucia with Derek. Tom and Germain exchanged glances, uncertain of how close to each other they could dance without provoking attention. Abra and Phoebe flitted around the club and lent their energy to the crowd. At one point, the group gathered and passed around a small blunt. The high kicked in and they surrendered to the rhythm.

Finally, Marcel's band wrapped up their set. Time passed and they came around from backstage. Abra's face lit up when the lead singer stepped out from behind the curtain.

"Daniel!" she exclaimed and ran to wrap her arms around his neck. "I couldn't believe my eyes when I saw you onstage. I've waited the entire show to talk to you!"

"I thought my eyes were playing tricks on me when I saw your face in the crowd. My dear, Abra. You've come so far. All the way to Marseille," he said.

Derek chuckled. He was tempted to stay with the vagabonds, to extend his trip just to hear the tales of their involvement with the era's music scene. After Abra and Daniel moved past their initial excitement to reunite, they turned to the rest of the group.

"Would you like to come to my flat?" Daniel asked.

Marcel sighed, "I've got to be heading home," he stated. "But the rest of you, go. Daniel, what a small world that you and Abra know one another. Go ahead, catch up. Corrine and I will send you kids off with breakfast in the morning."

As Marcel made his exit, Germain watched his father go with a surprised expression.

"Just a year ago, *Pa* would have stayed out all night with us. He would have wasted the entire next day and gotten himself into trouble. Love looks good on him."

Upon stepping outside the venue, a sea-tinged breeze sharpened their senses. Mia breathed the briny air into her nostrils. She could feel that her time in the city was drawing to an end.

"This way," Daniel said and led them up the street.

———

Outside Daniel's flat stood a few seedy characters. They doled out some unidentifiable currency between themselves. Their faces were shadowed, the dark added further mystery to their intentions. Daniel's group took a unanimous sigh of relief when the suspicious men dispersed as if nothing suspicious took place.

"Sorry," Daniel stated, "you never know what you're going to find around the corner here."

The group filed into his place.

"Welcome to my pad," he said. "Make yourselves comfortable."

Rather than flip a light switch, Daniel struck match after match and brightened the living room with candles. Germain, Tom, and Mia took their seats on a large sofa. Chiara sat at Mia's feet. Abra and Phoebe shared a chaise lounge and Lucia nestled onto Derek's lap. Their host was just about to sit on the floor near Abra when a knock came at the door.

"My flat-mate," Daniel stated. "Probably pissed by now."

Derek couldn't tell where Daniel was from. He had dark hair and eyes, like Lucia, but his accent didn't sound Spanish. He also struggled to guess the vocalist's age. He looked as though he could be older or younger than Abra.

Daniel opened the door. In stumbled a drunken British man.

"You been toking without me, Dan?" he asked.

Daniel grinned.

"If you would have come to the show, you could be on our cloud," Daniel stated.

"Well lucky for all of you," the Brit said, "I scored a dime-bag of the good shit from the group down the way. Turns out the gangsters in this town are good for something." He pulled the stash from his pocket. "I'm Reg by the way."

The rest of the group introduced themselves and Daniel went to his room to retrieve rolling paper. On the way back into the living room, he stopped in front of his album shelves and pulled a record from its sleeve. He set the record in its place and put the vinyl in motion. A bossa nova tune played, and the music's samba set the mood.

Daniel and Reg pulled kitchen chairs up to the circle and rolled two big joints. They lit the joints with a silver lighter. Reg passed one joint to Mia, and Daniel passed the other to Abra.

They took their turns inhaling until the embers met their fingers. Daniel went to open the window for some fresh air. Light from the streetlights coupled with the waxing gibbous moon poured in as he pushed back the curtains.

Mia studied Reg.

From the moment he walked in, his form and attitude demanded her attention. A black denim jacket hung on his shoulders. Reg walked to the couch where Mia sat and placed his keys in front of her on the coffee table. His reach exposed a bit of magnetic, waistline flesh. Then, he returned to his chair. The distance between Mia and Reg proved an obstacle as her body grew heavier and heavier.

The record stopped and left the room in a dazed silence. Mia's ears buzzed. She mustered her energy and stood to flip the record. She brushed her leg against Reg's hand on the way to the turntable.

As she placed the album's B side face-up, she heard footsteps draw near. Reg joined her at the record player. They stood together while the record spun and gazed at the moon and the downhill city lights.

Mia got a better look at his face. He looked somewhat familiar. She found it not so far fetched that his face may have adorned one of King's Records shelves.

He turned to face her with a wider grin than her own.

"Come sit with me, love."

Reg took her hand. Rather than return to his chair, he led her to his bedroom. They sat on the edge of his bed with the door ajar. Mia took stock of his simple room; a wire framed bed, an amplifier as a nightstand, littered with various daily pocket-findings, and a guitar case propped in the corner. Mia wanted to open the carrier, to place her fingers on the strings.

Observant of her gaze, Reg asked, "Do you play?"

"I do," Mia answered. "I might be a little rusty though."

For the first time on their vacation from reality, Mia felt homesick for the nineties, for her band, the Tuesdaze.

"You play? I think that's so sexy," he stated.

Mia leaned into his sensuality. She felt her chest grow hot and a jolt of adrenaline shot through her body. The sensation was prolonged by her high.

The volume in the living room increased and Mia peeked outside Reg's room. Abra and Daniel shared old stories. Derek seemed in a great mood as he made the entire room laugh. He had his arm around Lucia. Tom and Germain held hands as the group's attention was focused elsewhere.

"Do you want a blanket?" Reg offered.

Mia didn't realize she'd begun to shiver. The late January air flowed in from the window.

"Sure," she answered.

Reg reached for a scant quilt on his floor. His shirt, which was slightly too short, flashed the skin of his low back to Mia. Unable to suppress the urge, she reached around his side and fit her fingers in the waistline of his pants.

He turned to face Mia with a half-smile. His dimples became more apparent and his lips more luscious in the moonlight. He wrapped the blanket around his shoulders, then outstretched his arms and veiled himself and Mia out of the living room congregation's line of sight. Reg pressed his lips against Mia's.

Starting with her waist, he touched her in a way that pulsed electricity throughout her body. Mia didn't care that his moves were from experience, he was sure to be a highly skilled lover. Before they drew too much attention to themselves, Reg extended his foot and nudged the bedroom door closed.

"Corrine really must be something special," Daniel stated. "I haven't seen him like that with anyone since I joined the band in September."

Germain nodded, "She *is* something special. For years, I dreamt of her being my mother, but then, you know how Dad's life has been. Busy with us, busy with music, or busy with the ladies from the show. I don't blame Corrine for saying yes to such a serious suiter as her husband was, someone with less strings attached."

Lucia chimed in, "We watch them walk together in the morning sometimes, you can see it is real love."

The group continued doting on the sweet, elderly couple, but Derek's attention went to Reg's bedroom when he heard the door close. Lucia saw his distraction.

"Let her go," Lucia stated. "She has much to explore in this world and she's only got so much time."

"True," Derek stated, amazed at how accurate the statement was with Mia's commitment to TRN looming nearer.

Suddenly, he was very thirsty.

"How's the tap water?" Derek asked Daniel.

"Help yourself to the kettle. Glasses are in the cabinet to the left of the sink," he answered.

Derek went to retrieve a glass and was trailed by Lucia. On the way to the tiny kitchen, he passed a large, hallway mirror and gave himself a quick glance. Since his incident at Tom's, he had avoided mirrors, but this time he stopped to look at himself. As Derek studied his reflection, Lucia came up behind him and rested her chin on his shoulder.

"Look at him," Lucia said and wrapped her arms around Derek.

Derek looked into his own eyes. He noticed the ways in which his face changed over the previous year. He had more lines; his cheekbones were more pronounced. Then, he noticed his eyes were different from just days before. The light had returned.

After taking a long drink of water, Derek excused himself to the restroom. As he washed his hands, he saw a familiar face looking at him from a stack of magazines.

Renee.

———————

Hours later, Mia awoke to a bright, midday sun. She looked around the room and remembered where she was. No one lay beside her. The bedroom door was open, and she heard voices in the main area. She fished her clothing from the floor and was taken back to the prior autumn's Halloween night with Macy. After Mia pulled on her dress, she shuffled into the living room.

Reg stood shirtless in the kitchen.

"Good morning, lovely," he smirked with a cigarette between his lips.

Mia grinned. She wished for the bravery of the previous night's high.

"Good morning," she answered.

"Fuck," Reg said, "you are something."

He was even more beautiful in the light of day.

"I should say the same," Mia said and attempted to match his swagger.

Reg put out his cigarette in a nearby ashtray. He walked toward Mia and smoothed her hair from her face. He held her face and intoxicated her with his kiss.

"Shall we get you home?" he asked.

Mia nodded reluctantly. The time to leave had come.

Mia's heart raced as she knocked on Corrine's door.

Her brother answered and shook his head. She hadn't examined herself before leaving Reg's love nest, but she could imagine how she looked.

"Oh, give her a break," Mia heard Tom say from inside.

Mia pushed the door open, and Derek stepped aside to let her in. Mia avoided his gaze and walked past him to go to her room and pack. Tom and Germain's bedroom door was open and, as she watched them fuss with their suitcases, she realized she couldn't take anything to OT but the clothes on her back. Derek trailed Mia to her room.

"I guess packing won't take long," Mia stated to avoid the subject of the previous night. "Maybe I'll give my clothes to the vagabonds."

Derek was quiet. Mia was too exhausted, too daunted by the impending trip back to the TRN hub in OT to try to determine her brother's life's course for him or answer questions about herself and Reg. Instead, Derek broached another topic.

"I saw Renee in an article. I don't know what's wrong with me," Derek admitted. "I'm still hung up on her."

Mia patted her brother's back.

"What about Lucia? Angelene? Monitoring?"

"I don't know," he stated. Derek lowered his voice and closed the door. "Who am I to think I can keep Travelers safe when I'm so... unstable myself? I'm going back to London with Tom and Germain. I've started something there, now I've got to see it through."

They packed their belongings and went to Marcel's flat where Corrine had breakfast ready. They ate, then started in on their goodbyes. The departure felt premature.

"What a wonderful surprise this visit was. We hope to see you all again before the holidays," Marcel said.

"You can come back to visit England, you know," Germain stated. "Corrine, you are always welcome too."

Tom chimed in, "Yes, my flat is very spacious. I have extra bedrooms if you wish to visit at any time. I know Germain's place is rather small," he elbowed Germain.

"Thank you," Corrine said with a smile.

"That is most generous of you, Tom. Maybe once it gets warmer, we will return," Marcel stated.

"Mia, Derek, lovely to meet you. Mia, don't forget the rules of *belote*. I can't be stuck with a bad partner," Marcel winked.

A twinge of sadness struck Mia.

"I will have to practice in the United States," she said. "Maybe I'll share the game back at college."

Marcel nodded, "Well, should you be on this side of the pond again, come see us."

Marcel and Corrine embraced Mia.

"Thank you both for everything," Mia's words came out muffled by Corrine's soft sweater.

After another round of well-wishes, the four travelers made their departure. As they stepped inside the train's cabin, Mia gasped and felt her bare wrist.

"My bracelet!"

But it was too late to go back. The train was set in motion, and she was on track to move further and further from life as she knew it.

Germain, Tom, and the Hayes siblings stepped back onto English soil.

"Thank you for bringing us here and for all the accommodations," Mia said. "I'm off to catch my flight home."

"Of course, little sister," Germain said and winked as his father had done.

Germain and Tom took their turns hugging Mia goodbye.

"Catch up later this week?" Derek asked his friends.

"Right on. We'll stop by *En Blum*," Tom said and caught a cab for himself and Germain.

Derek was left alone with his sister. He faced Mia and placed his hands on her shoulders.

"You really got the word that there's an UpgrAid for me at this TRN hub?"

Mia nodded, "I did. Just down Carnaby Street, there's a laundromat. 'Suds and Duds.' Go to the back office and knock on the door. Give them this piece of glass," Mia pulled a round, iridescent piece of glass from her pocket. The decryption glass had lost its luster after months of owning the decoding trinket without use.

"What is this?" Derek asked as he took the piece of glass and put it in his pocket.

Mia whispered into his ear, "TRN used to send out newsletters. Travelers used this glass to read the letters, but I've learned they will no longer be communicating via mail. Everything is going to the UpgrAid now. I'm glad they have the device ready for you."

Derek pulled Mia in close. Once he released her from the embrace, he messed up her hair.

"I'll write to Marcel about your bracelet. I'm sure Daniel will find it at his and Reg's place."

Mia's cheeks grew red.

"I hope so."

"Six months minimum, huh?" Derek said. "Hopefully, it will go by in a flash. Have they said where they need you?"

Mia shook her head.

Derek knew the agreement had been made but couldn't help his concern.

"Just be…"

"I know," Mia interjected. "I'll be careful. And same to you. Don't get so caught up in finding someone that you miss out on everything else you came here for."

Derek nodded, "I won't."

"I'll keep in touch once I know what we need to do with King's. Francis can manage things for a few months, but let's meet in Original Time in late summer or early fall," Mia said. "As long as they don't extend my contract."

"Love you," Derek said.

"Love you too," Mia replied.

With that, they each signaled a cab and returned to reality.

Chapter IV

*B*zzt.

Rae woke up and looked at the clock.

'5:30AM.'

Her UpgrAid continued to vibrate. A new message. She moaned and reached for the device on the nightstand.

The past month challenged her motivation to follow through on her plans to mend the past. It was the dead of winter and every beckon from TRN proved to be more demanding than the last. Rae was limited in the amount of time she had to connect with other monitors and gauge their interest in making a difference in history.

Rae read the screen.

'Mia: Back from the sixties. In Acclimation. Vaughn told me to reach out to you for training.'

Despite the early hour, Rae's heart went out to the newly orphaned Traveler.

'Rae: I'll pick you up and we can go to the hub.'

'Mia: Thank you.'

Rae smoothed things over after Mia left the nineties and, in doing so, she found Mia even more endearing. She informed Mia's concerned bandmates of her necessary semester off from college. When they asked for Mia's home phone number and address to send their condolences, Rae struggled for an excuse, but finally landed on, "She's staying with various family and will be hard to contact."

After two weeks of relentless interrogation, especially from EJ, Mia's loyal group of friends left Rae alone. Rae went on to prepare Mia's TRN monitor training documents. Though Rae knew TRN somewhat alleviated Mia's predicament, her heart was heavy with the fact that Mia was forced to monitor as a penance. Rae wished there was another way for the young, beautiful musician to go about life with the same lightheartedness she carried for the duration of her time in Birchmont.

Rae had empathy for the long nights, early mornings, and emotional responsibility that Mia was about to take on. Rae leaned on the hope that, if her side-project took off, if they could mend the past, she and all overextended TRN employees could take back both their own lives and those taken by unfortunate events of the past.

––––––––––

Mia heard Vaughn giggle with her Acclimator.

She was annoyed that they were having fun while she was so exhausted. Mia wanted Vaughn at her bedside. Alone. For him to stroke the hair from her face like he did in her apartment in 1997.

Mia drifted in and out of consciousness for what felt like hours, then, she awoke to a sound on her nightstand. Vaughn was standing next to her. Mia grinned and reached out to take his hand. Rather than taking her hand, he handed her the UpgrAid. The device buzzed without stopping.

"You have a message," Vaughn stated.

Mia mustered the strength to keep her eyes open and read the UpgrAid's message.

'Rae: I'll pick you up. We can go to the hub together.'

'Thank y—,' Mia began to type, then Vaugh stopped her.

"You can speak into the device now and it will type for you," he said.

Mia spoke, "Thank you."

She looked at her previous message to Rae about being in Acclimation and didn't remember sending the notification.

"How long have I been here?" Mia asked.

"Since yesterday morning," Vaughn answered. "We didn't have time to prepare a custom Shell, so your Acclimation is taking longer than usual. Those Flex-Shells are brutal. You've been lucky to have Psilopram everywhere you've gone, or you'd be hurting even more than you are now."

Mia struggled to sit up, but once she did, she looked around the room. "Where's my Acclimator?"

"I let her go for the day. Look at you," Vaughn said, "you're almost fully recovered. She's been putting in crazy hours, so I figured now that you're past the intense part of Acclimation, you can handle yourself from here. Independent recovery is good practice for when you're monitoring on your own. Now, let's get you ready. Rae's coming to pick you up, right?"

Mia nodded.

"Great. She'll take you under her wing."

Mia fought to hide her disappointment that she wouldn't be training with Vaughn. He noticed and offered a weak smile. His eyes looked tired.

"I'm sorry I can't be your monitoring trainer. I've got too much going on. Too many people to look after. Perhaps there will be a time, down the road..." he trailed off. Vaughn sighed and kissed Mia's cheek. "Need help up?"

Mia shook her head and pressed herself into a seated position. She noticed a folded outfit at the foot of her bed. She swung her feet off the edge of the bed and got lightheaded.

"Easy," Vaughn said.

Mia spotted a glass of water by the UpgrAid on her nightstand. Beside the glass was a syringe.

"What's this?" Mia asked.

Vaughn answered, "They've found ways to fortify monitors and speed up Acclimation so they can get out in the field faster," he reached for the syringe and removed the cap. "I can do the first one if you'd like. The needles are so small, you'll barely feel it. You'll be injecting yourself in no time."

Mia's eyes welled with tears. She was frustrated by her surfacing emotion but couldn't suppress the urge to cry. Vaughn rested his hand on her shoulder.

"This is normal," he reassured. "You've been through a lot. This shot will take you past what you're feeling."

"So, they're just pumping people full of this injection and Psilopram to get through this? Travel is no different than OT. Just numbing anything that bubbles up."

"Baby, you're just tired. And I get it, you've been through a lot. I'll give you the shot, just let me do it before everything catches up with you."

"Okay," Mia's voice cracked.

A hot tear streaked down her face as Vaughn inserted the needle into Mia's glute. Mia was hit with the reality of her commitment to TRN and wondered if it would have been better for Derek not to know about their parents; to keep him in the dark and let him live in blissful ignorance rather than sacrifice her own human emotions just to deliver tragedy to his doorstep.

"It takes a few minutes to kick in," Vaughn stated. His UpgrAid buzzed in his pocket. "Excuse me," he said and meandered to the corner of Mia's room. He looked at his device.

Mia took a few sips of her water, and, as Vaughn promised, just minutes passed before the injection kicked in. Her overwhelming emotions subsided. Her vision became clearer, and she was motivated to get out of bed and meet her responsibility as a monitor.

Mia passed the final test.

After two months under Rae's guidance, Mia was officially an independent member of the Time Regulatory Network's team of monitors. She was trusted to orchestrate an escape route for Travelers signaling a 'yellow' through the UpgrAid. Though Mia was assigned to a very entry level position in TRN's hierarchy, she was done with a third of her penance for the emergency trip to the sixties.

Though the training wasn't as intense as it was for those monitoring severe yellow signals and, even more extreme, red signals, many of the situations still caused Mia's adrenaline to spike. She saw Travelers mistake dangerous contacts for friends. Travelers with a zest for life stumbled into violent settings and had no way out besides TRN. Worst of all, many Travelers unknowingly got into situations like Mia's close call with Lars. Without the need for Rae's prompting, Mia adhered to the commitment of bettering every situation she encountered.

———

Rae was thrilled with Mia's progression through TRN's training program. She taught Mia to navigate the Time Travel landscape with care. Mia was unmatched in her genuine consideration for the Travelers and, upon cutting Mia loose, Rae did her best to implant the idea of *fixing* the scenarios they stumbled into rather than cutting ties with the imperfections of the past.

"It's not *their* problem. Every wrong from the past has led to where we are in Original Time. Whether we like it or not, their problems are also ours."

One night, to ensure Mia's continued sufficient performance in monitoring, Rae tapped into Mia's UpgrAid audio. The privilege to tap in was granted to Rae by Vaughn after Rae agreed to train Mia. She felt like a hypocrite as the block was strapped to her own device. Rae silently vowed to offer the accessory to Mia should she prove to be a good mending candidate. Rae listened to Mia calm a Traveler down.

"Breath with me," Mia said, "we're safe. You're safe."

"I can't believe he did that," the Traveler whimpered. "I'm so stupid. Why did I go there by myself?"

Mia took a deep breath.

"*You* didn't do anything wrong," Mia assured.

Rae continued to tap into Mia's rescues every few days when she wasn't taking calls of her own. Though she often lost Mia's voice in the chaos of the rescues, Rae knew she had found a new member of her mending team, she just had to wait for the right time to make it official; to extend the invite without TRN knowing.

———————

Mia was three months into monitoring. She spent countless hours calling past authorities, rescuing Time Travelers, and ensuring their well-being. Mia and Rae finally crossed paths again in the early nineties. They had just enough time to meet for coffee.

"Mia, your ability to monitor exceeds what can be taught," Rae said.

"Thanks, Rae. I often wonder if I'm doing enough. Doing this has given me purpose, but I can't help but wonder how Travelers are doing after I leave them. No justice is served to those who have put them in danger. It's…," Mia sighed, "painful to know that Travelers at rallies who are fighting with the era's natives to have basic rights, Travelers who are plagued by the dark side of their destination, Travelers who are," Mia searched for the right word, "assaulted, have no way to retaliate. No way to make sure what happened to them doesn't happen to more people throughout history."

Rae sipped her coffee and evaluated the seclusion of their surroundings. The patio they sat on had cleared; just the two of them were left. Their coffees were full, and no one was in sight. Rae reached into her pocket to hand Mia a block device, but paused when she felt her UpgrAid buzz.

She pulled the device from her pocket and Mia stood to block any potential bystander's view of Rae's UpgrAid.

Rae's stomach dropped.

"Dr. Lowell," she said. "He needs to talk to us. We're going to the nearest hub immediately."

Mia and Rae were silent as they walked to the hub.

Mia wondered where she would be sent next. And why Dr. Lowell was involved. She hadn't seen him since her consultation. So far, Mia had been called to the early seventies and the early nineties. Times that Travelers visited to party, to be a 'part' of a moment in history. But Travelers couldn't resist being sucked in by the currents of the eras and were often in need of rescuing from drowning in the circumstances.

Mia knew how they felt; she got caught up in other eras too. She often wondered how the Tuesdaze were doing without her. She had little time to learn the details of how Rae had "taken care of things" with her bandmates.

Next to Mia, Rae's mind reeled. She felt sick to her stomach and wondered what repercussions she would face for having the block. She wondered how Dr. Lowell had found her out. Or was it Vaughn who turned on her?

After Rae's ugly breakup with Vaughn, if their late winter hook-up even qualified as a relationship fit to require a breakup, Rae wondered if Vaughn had spilled her mending scheme to further advance his own position with TRN.

Finally, Rae and Mia reached the double doors of the nearest TRN hub. They handed their UpgrAids to the TRN employees who were disguised as hotel bellhops. They were validated with a nod and the bellhop returned the devices to them.

"Room 310," the bellhop stated and handed Rae a key.

Rae and Mia rode the elevator and walked down the hall to the room. They unlocked the hotel door and stepped into a vacant suite. Rae pulled out her UpgrAid. She slid the device open and called Dr. Lowell.

"Rae, Mia," he started, his soothing voice put Mia at ease, "I'm glad to see you found one another in this time. Always sweet to see trainers connecting with trainees. Unfortunately," Rae's heart pounded, "the time has come to separate the two of you. Mia, dear, good news for you. Vaughn has secured several monitors over the past couple of months. Just two more weeks here and you can return to wherever your heart desires."

"That's amazing!" Mia shrieked.

Rae suppressed a chuckle; grateful she hadn't completely fallen for Vaughn's charm. She knew his way of recruiting and she was glad her sexual health had prevailed beyond their hookup. Dr. Lowell continued and Rae's moment of relief passed.

"Rae, that means we need you to train more of Vaughn's recruits, but we are granting you two weeks of leave at the end of the month. Since it seems you and Mia have become friends, perhaps you can usher her into her chosen destination once her final two weeks are up. That's all I have for now. Discuss where you'd like to go, and they can coordinate the trip downstairs."

Rae had two weeks to make the decision; toggle between times and mend or go back to and see how things played out as a citizen of Original Time.

———

"How do I pick back up with the Tuesdaze? Can I see them again?" Mia asked.

Rae sighed.

"I've got to be honest with you Mia," she began, "I don't know how smooth that's going to go. I haven't told you this because you've been so busy, but they've moved on in ways you… might not like."

Mia's heart sank.

"Of course, they moved on," Mia stated. "I don't know what else I could have done."

Rae rested her hand on Mia's shoulder.

"I'm just saying it will take some time to get back to where you were with them before you left. I'm sure they'll accept you back into their lives, they're just confused. They don't *really* know where you've gone for so long. They don't know why you wouldn't accept their sympathy for your parents' accident," Rae said, downplaying the group's surprising persistence to contact Mia.

"Start small," Rae continued, "a hangout at the Loop or an MTV night with Macy. Reunite somewhere you can talk, but keep your story straight. Remember," Rae's voice shifted to that of a storyteller, "you've been staying with family, dispersing your parents' things. Making business calls for the record store. We'll get you a new place. I'll come back with you for a while and we can say that you're staying with me, your old friend, for emotional support. That will give you space to decide if you really *want* to stay before getting caught back up in things.

"I'm always here to back you up. Also, I would like to be there the night you meet with the Tuesdaze again," Rae requested. "I want to ensure the encounter goes okay, just in case your connection with them has changed."

———

Mia and Rae watched the Tuesdaze enter the Loop from a corner table. Mia's body buzzed, uncertain what the Tuesdaze reaction to her return would be. Earlier, her phone call to let Macy know she was back felt oddly natural. Mia was reminded of her first night in the nineties when Macy welcomed her into their group.

Mia tempered her excitement as she watched her friends' faces light up. In her worst imagined scenario of the night, she expected them to yell at her, to demand an explanation for her inexplicable absence. Instead, she was met with three embraces and her heart swelled in her chest.

"You're back!" Macy exclaimed as she squeezed Mia. "I called these two right after we hung up earlier," Macy gestured to EJ and Tiffany. "I can't believe everything that's happened."

Tiffany interjected, "Macy and I were crushed that we weren't there to help that night. EJ filled us in on everything the next morning and we were all sick. Well, some of that was our own fault," Tiffany cringed, "the rave got wild."

"We wish we could have done more," EJ said and shot Rae a look of distrust.

"Her family was taking care of her," Rae prompted Mia to recite their rehearsed story.

Mia thought of Derek's friends from the sixties and the vagabonds. "My brother and I had a lot to sort out. Luckily, our family is taking care of the details. I'm sorry I couldn't talk more these last few months. It was nearly impossible to make a long-distance call as we bounced around between relatives," Mia explained.

"I'm sure everything is under control, but let us know if we can help. I don't know what your bills look like, and we don't make much on our shows, but we're getting booked like crazy, and we can give you a bigger cut," Macy offered halfheartedly. "That is, if you still want to play."

Mia looked to Rae for guidance.

"I can't wait to see you onstage, Mia," Rae stated. "And Macy, you got the payment for her rent, right?"

"Right," Macy said. "Thank you. I can't quite cover the full rent, especially with my parents cutting back on helping me out. I pissed them off right after we got back from the city. 'Why can't you get a real job, honey? Think about your future,'" Macy impersonated her parents.

"Oh no. What happened?" Mia asked.

"Another time. Let's just celebrate your return tonight," Macy stated. Outside, icy droplets pelted the windows.

Rae stood and gestured to the window.

"I'm sorry, but I need to head out before the weather gets bad. I don't live as close as you all do."

"Wait, you live here now?" EJ asked. "In Birchmont?"

"My job transferred me here for the new semester. Guess the university is short on I.T. staff. That's why I was in the city on New Year's Eve. I went up there to celebrate after my Birchmont interview. I had just moved here from Maine, the same town where Mia is from. That night, my mom beeped me that there was an emergency, so I called her on a payphone at the warehouse and she told me about the accident," Rae hung her head. "Anyway, I've got a place on the other side of town. I don't know how long I'll be here, but maybe I'll see you guys around. I've gotta split while I can still drive," Rae said and downed the rest of her beer.

"See you around," Macy said.

"Mia," Rae turned her head before walking to the door, "you know how to reach me if you need *anything*."

With that, Mia was left to return to her life as though nothing in her world had changed.

———

Rather than approach the source of Mia's absence, the Tuesdaze danced around Mia's tragic few months by divulging spitfire facts about the year up to that point.

Tiffany had finally gotten into good study habits and was acing her classes.

"Some of Claire's nerdiness must have rubbed off on me," she giggled at her type A roommate's expense.

EJ was quiet and avoided eye contact. Mia opened her mouth to connect with him, but Macy interrupted.

"Tiff, you might like the preppy stuff my parents sent me for Easter, you academic," she teased. "They sent this atrocious, pink gingham button-up shirt. I think I'll cut it off and wear it onstage with leather slacks."

"Things must not be so bad with them," Mia reasoned. "They're sending gifts."

"Don't let the gift fool you. They only do things like that so they have something to hold over my head. If I wore the shirt and ate all the candy, they'd go bragging to their friends how they take such good care of me. But they only like me when I'm *their* version of me."

"I wonder if they've worn the Tuesdaze shirts you gave them for Christmas," Tiffany pondered.

"Well, they're about to sport it proudly wherever they go, especially now that *you're* back!" Macy winked at Mia.

"We've got some…updates for you," Tiffany said with a shaky voice.

"What's going on?" Mia asked.

Macy sighed, "It's a long story. I need you to have an open mind, okay?"

"Okay."

Mia looked to EJ. He rolled his eyes. Heavy drops fell harder onto the roof. Then the Loop's entrance opened, and Lars stepped inside, soaked from head to toe.

He spotted the Tuesdaze and hurried to their table.

"Did I miss it?" Lars asked with big eyes.

Mia's face twisted into a look of disgust.

"Why are you here?" she asked Lars, then looked to the rest of the group for an explanation.

"I told you guys this was a bad idea! We should have waited," EJ turned to face Mia. "I'm so sorry, I told them you needed time, you needed just *us* for a while until we could explain the whole story."

"EJ, don't be sorry, I'm the one who pushed it," Macy said. "I should have known better with all you've been through, we're just so excited and so much has changed. We didn't want to keep you in the dark any longer than we already have. You were just gone so *long*," Macy gazed at the floor, "we had to make some decisions."

Lars rubbed Macy's back and Mia understood what was going on.

He was forgiven. He was back in.

"How could you," Mia glared at Lars, "how could any of you? After everything you saw. Everything *he* did."

EJ rested his elbows on the table and cradled his head in his hands.

"I know how this looks. Trust me, Mia, I was so skeptical at first," Tiffany stated.

"You really were," Lars agreed, "and rightfully so. I was a piece of shit. I was so miserable and out of my head. I don't expect you to be okay with me, Mia, not tonight, maybe not ever. I just hope you'll step onto the Tuesdaze growing platform with us."

"We're playing in the city now, Mia. We're doing fine, we're getting by, but we need you. We're better with you," Tiffany explained.

Mia was at a loss for words.

"Lars has really turned it around," Macy messed up Lars' wet hair.

Lars fussed with his spikes. "I've gotten kicked out of this town's music scene. Justifiably. But I stopped drinking. I started scouting the good bands in the city. Then, one night, I met the right person: an agent from Chicago. I figured, what better way to try and make things right than hook the Tuesdaze up?"

Mia studied Lars. The face that once made her blood run cold had softened. His eyes were clear, and the dark circles had faded. But, despite multiple rounds of Psilopram and an existential shift, Mia struggled to accept that they allowed him back into the group's orbit.

"Whatever," Mia stated, "I'm calling Rae to come back."

She pulled on her raincoat and started toward the door.

"Mia," she heard Macy shout from the table.

As Mia reached for the front door, a hand wrapped around her upper arm. She turned, ready to fight Lars.

Instead, EJ stood there with his dark, pained eyes.

"Don't go. You just got back. I told them it was a bad idea," he began, "but I'm just the drummer."

Mia scoffed, "The drummer's the heartbeat," she eased her tone, "at this point you're the whole heart."

"If you're going to go, at least let me drive you," EJ pointed out the entryway window.

Outside, the world began to darken. Birchmont's grey scenery was blurred by the thick precipitation. Mia released the UpgrAid back into her pocket and followed EJ out the door.

———

Mia shuffled her feet across the Jaquez's entryway rug. Her teeth chattered from the cold rain. Though her enthusiasm to return was squashed, she took a bit of comfort from the brothers' household. Jaq, still the same, big brother, rushed downstairs to give Mia a big squeeze.

"Welcome back," he said.

"Thank you," Mia replied.

While EJ hung up Mia's rain-saturated jacket, Jaq retrieved three beers from the bottom drawer of his refrigerator. Mia kicked off her shoes.

"Take a seat," EJ gestured to the couch, "get comfortable."

Mia looked down at her wet jeans, "I'm not sure that's possible."

"True," he held the fabric of his own jeans and laughed. "It's a mess out there. You can borrow something of mine," EJ offered. "Come up with me."

Mia followed EJ upstairs to his bedroom which previously belonged to Vaughn. Mia chuckled as she remembered the black and white blankets that once concealed her and Macy on Halloween. The initial elation of the memory dampened when Mia thought back to the unexpected turn of events revealed at the Loop.

EJ passed a soft, grey crew-neck sweatshirt to Mia.

"This is my favorite one."

Mia hugged the sweatshirt to her chest. It was soft. EJ continued rummaging through his drawer and pulled out a pair of dark green flannel sweatpants.

"Thank you," Mia accepted them.

EJ stepped out into the hallway, but before closing the door, a half grin lit his face.

"It's good to have you back."

He closed the door just in time to miss Mia's reddening cheeks.

Mia struggled to remove her soggy jeans and t-shirt. She located a vent and stood over the warm air naked to dry off. Her mind conjured an image of what it would be like if EJ came back into the room.

———————

As the precipitation cycled between merciless sleet and a light patter, Jaq and EJ filled Mia in on what she missed over the last few months.

"Right after you left, we were all so worried," EJ began. "We wanted to be there for you, to come to the services. Why couldn't we be there?" he asked. "Why did Rae keep out those who care about you?"

Jaq sat in his recliner, rocking silently but asking a million questions with his gaze.

Mia took a deep breath to sort out her thoughts.

"My brother and I, we had so many things to settle, countless decisions to make. We couldn't have done it on our own. We had to travel around to family and, rather than give you several phone numbers, Rae offered to be my point of contact for that time," Mia explained. "I would have *loved* to have you all there, but it was impossible. Things moved so fast, and I'm not even sure you could have gotten there in time for the," Mia paused, "services."

"The important thing is that you're here now and that you know how much we care for you," EJ shook his head, "though it may not look that way with Lars back in the picture."

"How did he do it?" Mia asked. "I mean, Macy's never held him accountable; you two go… way back. But Tiffany loathes him. I never saw her being okay with his return."

"It happened slowly, but for you, it must feel so sudden. After the party in the city, the New Year's Eve rave, Macy and Tiffany went up to the city a couple more times. They heard a great band and found out that Lars had promoted the group.

I guess after the Holiday Bash, Lars went to the city during the weekends and stumbled upon a few bands. You know how he is, good at connections. Good at first impressions. Bands started relying on him to get the word out and fill venues. He got to know several musicians; then, one night, he ran into the girls. Tiffany nearly broke his nose!" EJ laughed. "Lucky for him, no one saw, and he maintained his credibility within his new scene. Then, he found his in," EJ sobered, "Macy. Like you said, she's never held him accountable. He gets her on the stage and, for her, that excuses everything else he's done."

———

Back at the Loop, Tiffany watched Macy and Lars from across the table. They spoke into each other's ears with hushed voices. She wished she left with EJ and Mia. Tiffany looked at the clock.

'9:00PM.'

The rain had slowed for the moment and Tiffany was tempted to drive over to EJ's, but she refused to leave Macy alone to spiral down with Lars. Though he was no longer drinking, he still had his vices and he shared them with Macy.

The first night they ran into him on the rave scene, Tiffany thought she sent a clear message, but the spell he cast over Macy increased in its potency every day. Lars drove a wedge between the

Tuesdaze. Tiffany knew that if she left Macy alone, she wouldn't hear from Macy for days.

Macy was all but failing her spring semester. She was living as though she had no responsibilities. Rather than taking walks, studying, and watching MTV, Macy's free time was spent in the city, at parties, or altering her state of mind with whatever tonic Lars fed her. Macy's focus was wavering, and they had to simplify their music.

Over Valentine's Day, Tiffany insisted that she and Macy have a girls night in. She hoped the night away from Lars and the hazy scene consuming Macy's life would lead to a breakthrough and ignite the memories of the wrong he did. Instead, Macy talked on the phone with Lars as Tiffany laid out three rented, romantic comedies for Macy to choose from. Tiffany caught sight of a box of chocolates on the coffee table.

'To my love beneath the lights,' was written on the box in Lars' scrawl.

"Lighten up!" Macy smacked her hand down on the table in front of Tiffany and pulled her from her thoughts. "I know tonight didn't go as well as we hoped, but we had to rip off the bandage sometime," Macy said. "And remember, *she's* the one who left us."

"Her parents *died,* Macy. What was she supposed to do? Check in to make sure *you* were okay? EJ was right, we should have waited to tell her *everything,*" Tiffany shook her head.

Lars chimed in, "Her reaction was fair. I was fucked up back then," he admitted. "It's gonna take time."

"We need to practice," Macy said, "you know, earn her trust back. I didn't get a chance to ask if she's staying back at our place or not. I'll give her 'til Monday to cool off, then we'll nail down a practice."

"Let's do Tuesday, like we used to," Tiffany suggested.

Macy shrugged, "I'm down."

Tiffany continued, "And Lars, don't show up. If you want us to perform, you need to stay behind the scenes, and I don't mean lurking backstage. Give her the time she needs."

Tiffany had fought a mental battle since Mia's departure. She didn't know how long to hold onto Macy. Often, she was tempted to let her slip away, but without Macy as the front woman, there was no Tuesdaze.

The shadows of tree branches danced across the living room floor. Limbs snapped in the wind and cracked their shells of ice. Mia pulled her blanket up to her chin.

Mia, Jaq, and EJ listened from the Jaquez' living room. After EJ's explanation of the last few months' events, Mia sat in silence and processed the information. A loud whoosh outside drew Mia's attention away from her thoughts.

"If we're going to get you home, we need to go now," EJ stated. "Sorry to keep you so long, I just wanted you to know everything."

"Thank you," Mia said with an exhausted smile.

Ice tapped on the kitchen window and Mia pulled the blanket tighter around her shoulders. An unexpected boom of thunder put inches between herself and the couch. Even Jaq was rattled and hopped to his feet.

The three of them hurried to the kitchen entrance to look out onto the patio. The wooden deck was glazed with a layer of ice. A flash of lightning illuminated the heavy trees. They exchanged a look.

"Yes Mia, you can stay."

"Nice digs," Rae joked and gestured to Mia's outfit when she picked her up from EJ's the next morning.

"EJ could use a styling session with you," Mia chuckled. "Did you see that storm last night? I got stuck here. I couldn't leave."

"I'm sure you couldn't," Rae said with a wink.

Mia blushed, "It's not like that with me and EJ," she paused, "or maybe it is. I'm still deciding."

Rae stopped at a red light; her tires slid an additional ten feet on the film of ice left on the pavement. Mia shrieked. Once Rae regained control of her TRN-supplied vehicle, Mia went on to fill Rae in on the changes that had occurred since her departure.

"I'm coming back to a whole different world, Rae. Lars, he was kind of our manager in my early days with the band, he tried to force himself on me over the holidays and was booted out of our group. Now, he's back and in control of the band. They all think he's changed. Even *he* thinks he's changed. Lars holds all the cards. He's got the hookups for gigs. I can't stand him, and now he's a fixed part of the Tuesdaze."

"I hesitate to say this," Rae paused, "but maybe it's a sign for you to put some distance between yourself and the Tuesdaze. When we met for coffee that day, you said you wanted to make a difference in the grand scheme of things. That you didn't want to leave Travelers you serve with no justice. Maybe this is your chance to make a difference, maybe not in the world yet, but within the Tuesdaze. Rather than Lars vanishing, getting away with hurting you, he's here. He must face his wrongdoings and correct them. Or else," Rae shrugged, "the Tuesdaze can't have you."

"I guess I haven't thought of it that way," Mia stated and understood the power she held in the situation.

Rae turned into an apartment complex. She followed a narrow drive all the way to the furthest building from the main road. Rae pulled into a parking space and shut off the engine. She gestured to the brick building's top floor, corner unit.

"Home sweet home," she stated.

They walked upstairs and Rae gave Mia the grand tour of her furnished apartment which, like her car, was provided by TRN until Rae was summoned to train Vaughn's new recruits. Rae led Mia to a walk-in closet which contained a full wardrobe.

"TRN supplied clothes, but not groceries," Rae laughed. "Want to join me at the store? I'll buy anything we need for the place. TRN gives me a food stipend. It's the least they can do."

"Sure," Mia replied. "You're sure it's okay if I crash here for a while? I'm not ready to move back in with Macy, especially with Lars around."

"Of course. You can stay until I'm called back to TRN. Maybe even longer if no one is using this space. Make yourself at home."

The weekend passed and Mia settled into the era.

Rae had meetings at the TRN hub on Monday and Tuesday, and Mia was left alone in the apartment. She dialed Macy's number on the landline.

"Hello?" Macy answered.

"Hey, it's Mia. I'm ready for practice, but under one condition; you get me, or you get Lars."

———————

Tuesday finally came. For the day's entirety, while the Tuesdaze were in class, Mia picked at her guitar. She attempted to recreate the same feeling Reg's melody gave to her in Marseille. She remembered that, as the sun rose, he had hummed a tune which Mia had never heard. Despite her best efforts, the tune was flat when not reverberated from his chest on which she'd lain. Her thoughts shifted to EJ.

Months had passed since Mia had any sort of romantic connection, and EJ brought her out of the dissociative state TRN's 'supplements' forced her into. Practice time came and Rae provided Mia a ride to Jaq's house. Mia trudged across the muddy driveway to the shed and the band took their respective places.

"Where have you been staying?" Macy asked. "With Rae?"

Mia nodded.

Macy chuckled, "I get that you're all pissed off about Lars, but why don't you talk to me about it rather than acting like a fuckin' baby?"

"Enough, Macy!" EJ snapped. "Let's just play."

EJ cracked his drumsticks together and started in on a beat. The tension led practice to start out differently than Mia expected. Not only was Mia rusty on the guitar, but she was lost in her thoughts.

The band muddled through a song which was, previously, one of their best tunes. They struggled to sync. The frustration built and Macy came to her wits end.

"Mia, why don't you just listen to what we've been doing. You can practice on your own this week 'til you get it," Macy blurted.

"Yeah," Tiffany said and rested her hand on Mia's shoulder. "This is a lot."

Mia held back tears of defeat.

She hit the right chords. She played the right rhythm, but the rest of their sounds had shifted. Mia did as she was told and sat on a wobbly chair in the corner of the shed to listen. Macy cued EJ's drum entrance.

The band was tighter, too tight. Macy's voice sounded like just another voice on the radio. Tiffany trucked along with a lackluster baseline, and EJ sustained a mechanical beat.

The Tuesdaze had gone pop.

"Why are you singing like that?" Mia asked Macy.

Macy furrowed her brow, "Like *what*?"

Mia backtracked, "Sorry, that came out wrong. You just sound…different than before."

Tiffany shot Mia a warning look.

Macy pursed her lips and pulled a cigarette from her pack. She lit the cigarette and paced.

"What have you been playing since I left?" Mia asked.

EJ reached for a stack of loose-leaf papers piled atop a workbench and handed them to Mia. Mia reviewed the list. The Tuesdaze were a different band altogether.

"I'm guessing Lars had a hand in this," Mia stated.

She saw everything she held onto so dearly about the nineties, slipping from her grasp. EJ looked at her with sad eyes and Tiffany stared at the floor. Macy turned to face Mia. Their eyes met and Macy had a stone-cold expression.

"Before you left, you were gung-ho about *making it* as musicians," Macy stated. "Remember? In the Cav the night of the holiday bash? Now, we have that chance. We gotta compromise for a broader audience, but we can get *paid*. We can be proud of this. I can keep it light. I don't have to thrash my voice every night for the show to be good." She shrugged and her arms fell to her sides. "I can tell my parents that the band's *not* a waste of time. You left, and we went for it," Macy continued. "Now, we have gigs almost every weekend. We've gotten tighter, we've gotten better. It's up to you whether you're in or out."

EJ sat on a folding chair with his head in his hands. He lifted his head and slicked back his hair. He looked exhausted.

Macy grabbed a notebook and scribbled on a sheet of paper. She ripped out the page and handed it to Mia.

"Practice these songs. If it doesn't go well," she paused, "I guess I don't know what we'll do."

"Let's call it a night," EJ said. "This is one of the few weekends we don't have a gig. We'll practice."

"Really think about this," Macy pointed her cigarette at Mia. "This is our shot."

Before Mia could respond, she felt a light vibration in her pocket.

The UpgrAid.

"You're right. Let's regroup this Friday. After you're done with class. I'll practice and get myself right with the setlist," Mia said to expedite her exit.

"Do you want a ride to Rae's?" EJ offered.

A honk came from the driveway. Mia opened the shed's creaky side door to a balmy Spring afternoon. Rae's car was parked in the lane. Rae rolled down her window.

"Figured I'd see if you were done with practice," she said.

Mia turned to EJ who had followed her out of the shed.

"You'll get the songs in no time," EJ said. He leaned close and spoke into Mia's ear, "Hopefully, we won't be playing stuff like this for much longer, now that you're back."

EJ's breath on Mia's neck caused her to blush.

"I'll do my best," she said and went to get in Rae's car.

"How'd it go?" Rae asked as they pulled away.

"Not great," Mia replied.

"I'm sorry," Rae said. "Listen, I didn't know what time you'd get home," Rae raised her eyebrows, "or *if* you'd get home tonight," Rae teased. "I saw how EJ looked at you," she winked. "I picked you up because I have something to tell you that cannot wait. I got my next assignment today and I leave on Sunday. I know, it's short notice. TRN said the apartment is available for another month. In the meantime, you can look for places if you want to stay here, or," Rae lowered her voice, "you can join me in my endeavors."

Rae pulled a device from her pocket and gestured for Mia to clip it onto her UpgrAid. Mia did as she was instructed. Rae grinned.

"Now, we can really talk."

––––––––––

Macy's phone rang.

It was Saturday. She let three phone calls go to her answering machine within the last hour. Macy was torn. Until Mia's harsh criticism the previous Tuesday, she had validated too many of her own actions.

That Saturday night, rather than finding the party, she stayed in. But she was lonely. She didn't know if it was worse to be alone in a crowd or in her apartment.

Macy lit a candle and contemplated whether to search for a subletter. She wanted Mia to come back, for things to be the way they were before. Macy hoped their opportunities would be a beacon of light to Mia as she returned to Birchmont. Instead, Lars, the orchestrator of their climb to success, overshadowed their potential. In her apartment, with a clear headspace, Macy felt foolish for taking the plunge and subjecting Mia's musical calling to Lars' continued presence.

She popped a couple of pills. An hour passed and, in her head Macy began to justify the changes Lars had made.

He no longer drank, heavily anyway. From what Macy saw, he treated girls with respect. Best of all, he got her on stage, in the spotlight.

Despite Lars' malice, for the last few months he stood as a placeholder for the partner she could flaunt in front of her family. He was eloquent and handsome and helped to keep Macy's parent's interrogations at bay.

He was bad, and she knew it, but he was convenient. And he had the substances to neutralize Macy. She'd been too much of something her whole life and found refuge in not being too much of anything at all.

———

Mia awoke Sunday morning to the vibration of her UpgrAid.

'Made it to the hub. Do what you can here,' Rae messaged.

Mia got out of bed with a sense of purpose. It was her second day as a committed mender, and she was determined to make a difference in the time; starting with the Tuesdaze. Mia went to the phone to dial Macy but was distracted when her UpgrAid vibrated again.

TRN: 'Traveler signaled yellow. Lost on the north side of your building.'

Mia furrowed her brow.

She was done monitoring. Why was TRN messaging her for a rescue? She was struck with fear. Did they know about Rae's menders' objective to fix what was wrong with the past? To explore the effects positive change had on alternate tracks of time?

Mia set her worries aside and walked out the door to assist the Traveler in turmoil. She burst through the exit, then rounded the building's corner. She spotted the Traveler, but he didn't appear to be in trouble.

He was tall and broad. When Mia got closer, she noticed his shoulder-length brown hair and spotted a signature dimple, highlighted by the morning sun.

Chapter V

Derek returned to his empty apartment.

'What now?'

He unloaded his suitcase. The task took less time than expected. Derek made himself a hot toddy and put a record into rotation. Eventually, the music stopped, and he was in desperate need of a distraction from the mundane winter evening. Even more so, he craved a break from his thoughts about Mia's monitor training. He went to *En Blum* a half hour before the boutique closed.

Derek expected messy racks, a short drawer, and expired New Year's '*Great '68*' décor. However, it appeared that *En Blum* was fine without him. He teetered between relief and disappointment. The Uni girls caught onto his melancholy.

"We did so well running this place because we had a great teacher," Bea, the sweet one, complimented Derek.

Ettie responded with her usual spiciness, "Glad *you* finally trust us. We'll see if we get any thank you from Renee."

Derek, feigned an aloof attitude and asked, "How is she anyway? Has she been in?"

The girls exchanged a look.

Ettie answered, "The only place we've seen her is in the dirty magazines."

"Well," Bea came to Renee's defense, "the money has got to be good. And she does look *great*."

They took Derek's bait and he fished for more information. Derek wanted to know about the state she was in, if she was safe, and if she was happy. He remembered seeing her face in the British musician's bathroom in Marseille. Derek agreed, Renee did look great, but when he thought back to the centerfold, he couldn't read Renee's expression.

"So, no word from her agent, William? I'd like to know when to expect her return to the country," Derek said.

"No. And I wouldn't anticipate seeing her anytime soon. Renee was just interviewed in Hollywood."

Derek chose to make his exit before he looked like even more of a sucker. "I'll start back full-time next week." He reached for the exit door handle then turned back toward the Uni girls. "Will you let me know if she calls?"

"Absolutely," Bea promised. "Same number to your flat's landline as before?"

"Yes," Derek nodded, "And Renee's working through the same agent, right? William?"

"Still William, yeah," Bea said.

"Perhaps I'll reach out, so she knows I'm back."

On his way out, he heard Ettie snicker. Something about being wrapped around Renee's finger.

"There he is!" Angelene said as Derek approached their booth in the pub.

Grant smirked, "Missing holiday yet? I'm sure you could have stayed longer rather than return to this dreary old town."

Derek sighed. He fixed his hair which he had anxiously tousled throughout the day.

"Perhaps I should have asked Corrine about her lodging fee," he responded.

After Derek's first full week back at the boutique, he doubted his decision to return at all.

Renee was away. Stars wanted the Uni girls, not Derek, to assist with their ensembles. He tried calling Renee's agent three times over the past week with no connection.

What kept him going was getting stars in front of his lens. With the right shot, Derek could transform a commoner into an up and comer. *En Blum's* A-list shoppers may not have asked him to put together their look, but Derek captured their essence with ease.

"I hope to go to Marseille next year, I think I'll be ready by then," Grant stated. "Well, I guess I was ready when you all went, but maybe I'm not as sure of things as I'd like to think I am. Or so you say, Angelene."

Angelene faced her brother.

"I'm just making sure you don't do anything you regret," Angelene stated.

Derek saw Grant's posture slump and felt a spark of anger toward Angelene.

"You can't keep making me feel like I'm the same person I was that night," Grant said. "It makes me worry I might be that person forever. I can't move on with you doting on me."

"Don't get mad. I was there the next morning. I saw," she paused, "everything. So did Derek." Derek shot Angelene a look. He didn't want to be involved in this beat-down of Grant.

"What? You needed my help then, and now you are angry with me?" Angelene asked Grant.

Grant didn't respond.

Derek attempted to change the conversation, but every topic fizzled out. Angelene finally put an end to the dull evening by covering the boys' drinks.

"Thank you," Derek wished they had more riveting conversation to make the evening worth her money.

"Welcome back," she said.

The trio stepped outside to an unseasonably warm winter evening. Derek was grateful for the air's gentleness and let his mind slip back to the previous Spring when he arrived in the sixties. He wondered how he managed to complicate things so much.

They walked together for a few intersections, then Derek's route split from Grant and Angelene's path. He wished them a good night and turned toward his flat. He looked back at Angelene and he caught her peeking back at him.

Her liquid eyes still shocked Derek every time. Derek thought of how, during Vaughn's visit to the sixties, he was encouraged in Angelene's direction. How she came back to his apartment after the night at the jazz club and they shared a long, warm kiss.

But the time away made Derek crave something else. Something visceral which he didn't feel with Angelene. The constant discernment he felt in her presence put him off. Angelene served as a persistent reminder of what he *wasn't* contributing to the sixties, what he *couldn't* contribute without breaking TRN's rules of detachment.

Derek's mind went back to Lucia, then to Renee. They were immersed in their existence rather than bobbing on the surface and looking below to see what was floating around to examine.

Derek returned to his flat. He clicked on the television, lay on his sofa, and fell asleep.

Lucia's dark brown spirals defied gravity and flowed with the water's currents. She smiled at him and spoke in the accent Derek had grown to miss.

"You can go anywhere," she said as bubbles drifted from her lips.

Derek let the rest of the air out of his lungs and descended to the bottom of the pool. He watched the light fracture across her face and looked up at the sun which was softened by the water.

"I don't want to be anywhere else," he said. "Just here."

A nagging buzz on the coffee table roused Derek from his dreams of paradise. Derek grabbed his device and looked at the text.

'Mia.'

Though he knew Mia could handle whatever was thrown at her, Derek's heart rate still went up when he imagined what situations Mia had to monitor

'Vaughn's here," flashed across his screen. 'And I'm free.'

Derek was relieved. The more he learned about his friend's status with TRN, the less worried he felt about his little sister's sacrificed freedom to keep him informed of their parents' death.

'Vaughn recruited enough employees to get me off the hook. I'm in the nineties for now.'

Derek furrowed his brow, unsure of how to respond.

'For now,' reverberated in Derek's mind. He was confused. In Marseille, it seemed Mia was excited to get back to the life she made in the nineties. Like Derek's experience, it was hard to remain a visitor for so long. At some point, they had gotten pulled in.

'For now?' Derek typed. 'Everything OK?'

He paused, then deleted the sentence, drawing inspiration from his realistic dream starring Lucia. Derek did his best not to project his months-long, lackluster mood onto Mia.

'You can go anywhere.' he said instead.

The night before, Derek fell asleep around seven-thirty. Now, it was four o'clock in the morning and he was wide awake. He flipped through the channels for a bit, then turned off the TV. Derek pulled a blanket across his body and laid back, hoping sleep would find him and he would return to the pool with Lucia.

Instead, a dripping icicle pestered him from outside. Derek opened the window and knocked the piece of ice from his balcony. The chilly air invigorated him, and Derek viewed the sleepiness of the city. He pulled on his jacket and his hat from Renee to go for a stroll. In his delirious, early-morning state, his eyes played tricks on him as the streetlight cast shadows in the alleyways.

Derek returned to the distinct restlessness he'd experienced before Traveling. He wasn't quite awake but was certain he'd toss and turn if he returned to his flat. Derek walked toward the boutique. He felt in his pocket for the backdoor key and decided that, if he couldn't sleep, he'd catch up on work.

As Derek approached *En Blum,* he noticed the backroom light's amber glow. Derek knew it wasn't the Uni girls. What he waited for had finally come; Renee was home.

———————

Derek turned the backdoor key and stepped into a golden kaleidoscope, created by Renee's shrouded lamp. Derek scanned the room and there she was, rifling through a stack of scarves. She looked irritated.

Upon seeing Derek, her annoyed expression completely dissolved. He was thrilled at her reaction. His mouth dropped open as he noticed Renee's short, modern bob.

"Welcome back!"

Renee smiled and went to embrace him. Derek stroked her dark, coarse hair and ran his fingers across the blunt, tucked-under ends. She pulled away and Derek looked into her green eyes.

"You cut your hair," he started, "I love it! How long have you been here? Did you just fly in from… somewhere?"

Though Renee's eyes were bright, her eye makeup was smeared, and her hair was unkempt. Derek took stock of the disheveled storage room. Renee always had a loveable sense of madness, but it seemed she was really tearing apart her inventory.

"I haven't been up *all* night. I slept on the flight back. Then, after we landed, I went out with some friends," Renee responded.

"Well, I'm glad I ran into you," he said. "That's hard to do these days."

Her expression dropped and Derek felt bad for his comment about her absence.

"Can I help you with anything?" Derek offered. "What happened here?"

Renee looked around at the mess she created. "I knocked over a few boxes." Renee stepped away from her desk and picked up one of the many scarves on the floor. Derek followed suit and helped her collect the squares of fabric from the dingy concrete.

"Be right back," Renee said and ran to start the backroom record player. She moved with the music and flailed the scarf around with her hypnotic motions. Renee signaled Derek to join her. His previous, half-conscious mood began to lift with her high energy. Derek was upset it was so late, or early. He wished he would have met up with Renee rather than fall asleep after another disappointing dinner with Angelene and Grant.

Derek let himself go and waved a scarf in the air along with Renee. Renee went on to wrap her checked scarf around his neck and looked at him in the way only she could gaze upon her subjects.

"Ready to go?" Renee asked.

"Where would we go at this hour?" Derek replied.

"The circus."

Renee guided Derek across several blocks. Rays of dawn illuminated the rowhouse, their destination, which was large but looked quite plain and run down with rotting sideboards and overgrown shrubs. A hum of voices inside hushed when Renee rang the doorbell.

"What are we doing here?" Derek asked. "Do I know anyone? Germain? Tom?"

Before Renee could reply, a tall man answered the door. He wore grey trousers which were secured by suspenders. A thin layer of perspiration lay across his forehead. He looked Renee over and gestured them inside.

As they entered the house, a woman with black rimmed eyes and messy, blonde hair approached them. She shrieked and hugged Renee but ignored Derek. She took Renee's hand.

"Come! I have something to show you!"

Renee rushed off and Derek scanned the room for a familiar face, but there were none to be found. He watched Renee and the woman share excitement over a human skull the woman revealed to Renee.

"Mr. K. had it in an old trunk. How bizarre, right?"

It was as though they spoke their own language and Derek was a foreigner. He noticed that down the hallway from the central room, a bedroom door was open just a crack. A young woman stood inside with her skirt flipped up. Then, a blonde, clean-cut man injected her.

"I don't know if I should be here," Derek said to Renee.

"Why not?"

Derek hesitated, in search of the right words, but his brain, foggy from his early rise, refused to offer censorship. He gestured to the girl in the bedroom; she rubbed her wound.

"Is she okay?"

"Listen," Renee began, "you say you don't see me around, so I ask you to come out with me. Then, you insult this party, this place of... liberation," she referenced the strange house. "You're becoming who you're around. It's like you're absorbing Angelene's pretentiousness. I remember you used to come out all night and dance. You wanted to be *in* the scene, immersed in the absurdity that gets people out of their heads enough to create something new."

Guilt set in and Derek attempted to better perceive the edgy surroundings. The Marseille muses were bizarre, but not in the same, abrasive way as what was going on around him. In the house, as the sun rose, people moved about wildly. Two young girls skipped down a hallway to his left, then tumbled onto the floor. They laughed and Derek smiled along with them, but his grin faded when the man from the front door joined them on the floor. The man persistently attempted to run his hands up their skirts.

"What? I'm good at this," the man said.

Derek started to approach the man when Renee stopped him.

"Are you crazy?" she asked in a hushed voice. "This is *his* place. He *owns* the record label."

Derek glared at their host. He turned toward Renee but kept his eye on the girls who appeared to be years younger than his sister. "I'll stay for a bit, but is there anything *regular* here like booze or weed?"

Renee gestured toward a shaggy-haired man in the corner of the kitchen.

"Reg," Renee said. "Ask him."

Derek couldn't help his surprised expression as he recognized the face from Marseille. He followed Renee to meet Reg.

At first, Reg furrowed his eyebrow, then Derek saw that he recognized him.

"What brings you here?" Derek asked, surprised to see Reg outside of Marseille.

"I just got signed, now I'm here," Reg answered.

"Just you?"

Reg nodded, "Yeah. Love Dan and Marcel, but they're too set in their ways. They would never 'sell out,'" Reg scoffed. "They act like that's what I'm doing, but the label will make me better. And get me paid."

Derek was distracted when, from the corner of his eye, he detected movement in the hallway bedroom where the young woman had been shot up. The room was lit by the sun, and inside the woman and a partner began to have sex. Reg's attention was also stolen by the spectacle, and their conversation stalled.

Derek snapped out of it and re-evaluated his surroundings. He was reminded of his need for a dramatic shift of perspective and asked Reg for a blunt, but Reg's focus was still held by the live pornographic film playing out before them.

Derek spoke into Renee's ear, "Is there anyone else I can talk to? Anyone else that I know? Where are all the friends we met in the country? At the artist's villa?"

She chuckled, "They're still here. See?"

Renee pointed to another man watching the bedroom spectacle and sure enough, there sat their summertime artist host with first row seats to the public intercourse. A wry grin was painted on his face. Derek realized that the woman in the bedroom was the blonde actress from their weekend in the country. She looked different, strung out and rail thin. She turned her face to the side and Derek could see her more clearly; she looked years older than before.

"I think it's time you lightened up," Renee said and dropped her head. "You never made me feel like this before."

Derek's heart dropped, "What do you mean?"

"Ashamed."

An appropriate reply was lost on Derek, so he remained silent. He contemplated whether he was changed by the past few month's events or if the world he lived in surpassed some line he'd drawn without meaning to.

Renee looked at him with hurt in her green eyes, then walked away from him, out of the kitchen to the opposite side of the main room. There, two men began to engage Renee in conversation. She laughed, and Derek watched her from across the room.

"Sorry, bit distracting in there," Reg said to Derek. Derek forgot Reg was in the same room. "Did you need anything or just come over to say hello?"

"You got a joint?"

Reg nodded. He pulled a generously packed joint from his pocket and placed it in Derek's palm. He named his price and Derek slipped him the cash.

"Got a light?" Derek asked.

The musician reached into his pocket and tossed a matchbook to Derek. Derek strummed the match's tip across the tread. He lit his joint and handed the matchbook back to Reg.

"Keep it, man," Reg said.

The more Derek smoked; the more Reg grew on him.

In the bedroom, the lovers built up to their climax. The volume of their moans escalated and drew a crowd. Her partner gripped her waist to speed up his pace. He went on to flip her onto her stomach and thrust from behind.

Derek started to roll and couldn't tell if her face read ecstasy or misery. They finally finished and the crowd cheered. The actress lay face down, stunned. Her partner shoved her aside and she tumbled off the bed. The crowd erupted with laughter. Derek looked around and everyone's face looked evil.

He turned to Reg.

Reg laughed halfheartedly to follow the social cue, but when he met eyes with Derek, his expression sobered. The crowd dispersed and resumed their conversations with one another.

A knock came at the door. The host sent his right-hand man to answer. The assistant opened the door and greeted three fresh-faced young women. Derek watched with disgust as the host ushered them in and inspected them. He gave each of them a once-over before admitting them inside. Derek's stomach turned when the host spanked Renee as she passed to greet the new guests.

Derek's surveillance of the greasy man in power was interrupted as the actress emerged from the bedroom wearing underwear and a long mac jacket. She avoided eye contact with the bystanders as she walked into the kitchen. She procured a wine glass from the cabinet and poured herself a glass from one of the many bottles scattered across the kitchen.

Newly emboldened by his high, Derek approached the actress.

"Are you okay?" He asked the beauty.

She looked at him with a confused expression. Then, she softened. She recognized him from the artist's villa. She chuckled.

"Okay?" She said in a Nordic accent, "I think you see I am quite good," she laughed. "Remind me of your name, I remember you from last summer. The photographer?"

"Yes," Derek said, surprised she remembered. "Derek," he reintroduced himself.

Derek's eye was drawn to a growing pool of blood that seeped through the actress' jacket from her elbow.

"Are you hurt?" Derek asked and pointed to the wound.

He remembered her fall and the look in her eyes as the crowd cheered. Derek pulled a handkerchief from his pocket. He ran water onto the fabric and extended the square to the actress. She pulled one arm from her jacket and draped the garment to cover her breasts as she pressed the piece of fabric onto her scrape.

"I am not hurt," she stated. "I don't feel much right now," she giggled. "Many people like to watch, and that is my choice to keep the door open. I saw you; you were watching too."

Derek felt ashamed of his own hypocrisy.

"Thank you for the rag," the actress said, and with that, she returned to the bedroom where she sprawled across the foot of the bed and chatted with the artist who had observed the entire spectacle from the front row.

Derek started toward the back door for some fresh air. The back exit of the host's luxury loft led to a fire escape where Derek landed. He held onto the rusty metal rail with one hand and brought the remaining inch of the joint to his lips where he took a long inhale. The thin paper crackled in the early morning air.

Birds chirped as the sun continued its ascent to the crest of the city's buildings. Though the pure morning light steadied Derek's bewildered mood, he found himself processing the progression of Renee's life from last summer up to that point. In doing so, he also digested his own chain of events.

The world and all of time was laid out before him, but he remained here where Renee was beyond his reach. Meanwhile, Angelene faded into the background. Everything around Derek was moving, but he stood still. Just then, two of the young girls who recently arrived, stepped outside.

After a hushed conversation between themselves, they approached Derek at the edge of the balcony. They watched the sun's rays begin to peek over the edge of the small building across the alley. Derek glanced over to see their faces. One had round cheeks with spry, blue eyes and wavy blonde hair, the other's wheat-colored hair was cut with heavy bangs which outlined her eyes.

"Some party, right?" the wheat-haired girl remarked. "Wish we could have gotten here earlier, but we were east last night."

"You girls come here a lot?"

"Yeah! Mr. K *always* has the grooviest parties," the blonde replied.

Derek cringed as he remembered the host's persistent advances toward the pretty young girls.

"It's good you're *both* here," Derek said, "together, you know, to look out for each other. Where's your other friend? Weren't there three of you?"

The girls looked at each other and burst out laughing. "Relax, she's just inside."

Derek felt his cheeks redden and he realized how old he must have sounded.

"It can be dangerous," he reasoned.

"With all those people in there," the wheat-haired girl began, "we'll be fine. Especially with Renee, she'd never let anything happen to us. Patty's probably with Renee right now."

"And, in case you didn't know, we both have parents," the blonde quipped. "We don't need another one."

"Sorry," Derek apologized, "I wasn't trying to be a bummer. It's just you're so young, both of you. Are you even sixteen?"

They cackled.

"I wouldn't want you to get in any situation where you're," Derek hesitated, "taken advantage of."

They rolled their eyes.

"We *choose* every situation we get into," the blonde continued. "We *want* to be here. No one forced us to come."

The wheat-haired girl started in, "We know who to stay away from. They've told us not to get in a room alone with Mr. K. Nothing to worry about, you see? We just go where the action is. We show up at hotels and we go to the parties where we know *they'll* be and we're not scared because we get to be a *part* of it, you know?" She paused. "Have you been a part of anything like that?"

Derek thought back to the villa.

"Once."

———

Derek went downstairs to find Renee. He needed to feel connected to the scene and she was the way into the moment. When he returned to the main room, the party had thinned. The remaining guests were either holed up in one of the host's many bedrooms or passed out.

The actress was asleep on the couch, still loosely wrapped in her jacket. Derek lay a blanket over her and continued to search for a familiar face. After wandering through the kitchen and walking down the hallway, checking open bedrooms as he walked by, Renee was nowhere to be found.

Finally, Derek ran into a conscious human, Reg. He was putting his coat on to leave.

"Heading out?" Derek asked.

Reg nodded, "Yeah, on my way to the studio. May catch a few hours of sleep, then see if we can finish the next bloody track. The song's been slowing us down, but I think we'll really come out of it with something."

"Well," Derek began, "it was good running into you."

He shook Reg's hand and noticed the musician's calloused fingers. Cold metal tapped against Derek's hand and Derek looked to see what touched him. Mia's charm bracelet was secured around Reg's wrist. Derek was thrilled to find the treasured keepsake.

"My sisters' bracelet!" Derek began. "She's been looking for this."

"I hoped she wouldn't want it back," Reg stated. "I quite like thinking of her. Though our time was short, she really touched me."

As Reg thought back to their night together, he remembered Mia's sweetness and her beauty. His memories were quickly pushed aside when he noticed the look on her brother's face.

"It's from our grandmother," Derek said. "I'll take it back, please."

Derek saw Reg's sadness as he unhooked the clasp. Until then, Derek didn't understand that the musician connected with Mia on more than a physical level. Derek took pity on Reg and began to fumble with the bracelet.

"Which charm do you want?" Derek offered.

Reg ran his fingers along the trinket. Finally, he held one between his fingers.

"The star."

———————

The bracelet jingled in Derek's pocket as he exited the front door. He was edgy and in desperate need of rest. The boutique was closer than his flat, and Derek made the decision to fall asleep on the storage room chaise lounge. So be it if the Uni girls discovered him there.

When he arrived, he turned the key to the backdoor and stepped inside. Rather than stepping into a dark room as he expected, Renee was there, folding the scarves she'd flung around the room just hours ago.

"Decided to stay a bit longer, I see?" she stated.

Derek nodded, "I stepped out back for a spell, sorry I missed you leaving. I looked for you. I left once I couldn't find you."

"Right," Renee continued, "and I'm the crazy one. I'm the one who stays out too late and attends too wild of parties," she smirked.

"I never said that."

"You didn't have to," Renee's gaze went from playful to stone cold. "I saw it. When I met you, I felt as though you were searching for something. That's why I invited you in, because we are too. I thought you were like us, living and learning as we go, but no," Renee shrugged, "seems you've got it *all* figured out for us."

Derek's foggy brain couldn't assemble the right words.

"I haven't got it figured out," he said. "Not at all. Since my parents—"

Renee sighed and placed her handful of scarves on the desk.

"I'm sorry love. It's been so long since I've lost someone; sometimes I forget how hard it is," Renee admitted. "Goodness, I barely knew my mum. She's probably around here somewhere. Lurking in a backstage dressing room. Or perhaps she's captured herself a country estate owner. Maybe that's why it hurt me so much to see your reaction to this lifestyle. Maybe I'm scared I'll end up like her, like my mum. Slipping up when I should be walking the straight and narrow."

Derek shook his head.

"Renee, the straight and narrow," he hesitated, "it's not for you. It doesn't deserve you. That path would dim you too much. You deserve to be in the action. In the spotlight. If I embarrassed you back there or made you feel bad, I'm sorry. Control…familiarity… both are things that I crave right now. That kind of party, I'm just not used to it where I'm from."

"Well," Renee said, "despite where you are from, you can choose to *be* anywhere."

Derek let the recurrent message absorb into his being.

"But" she finished, "you can't control where *I* go. Not even I can do that."

After a few more minutes, Renee walked to the backdoor.

"We'll talk soon. I'll ask William to remind me to check in on you more often."

'You need a reminder *to check in on me?'* he thought.

"Please do," Derek said and kissed Renee's cheek.

It was close to noon and Derek laid down on the daybed and indulged in the gift of sleep. The Uni girls arrived and giggled at him; his mouth open, fast asleep on top of the blankets.

The hum of the boutique's crowd and the occasional chime of the register were not enough to rouse Derek from his deep slumber. He slept restfully for a while, then fell into a dream.

He was driving fast on the interstate. He passed numerous exits without slowing. But Derek didn't revel in the thrill of endless destinations. Instead, he was overwhelmed by the options.

"Where are we going?" Lucia asked from the passenger seat.

Derek took a deep breath and drove off the interstate. They were airborne. They landed in the sea and Derek struggled to push open the car door.

'You can go anywhere,' reverberated throughout his subconscious, *'yet you choose nowhere.'*

"He's out cold," a bright voice said. "Should we leave him here for the night?"

Another voice laughed, "He's flinching! We should ask where they went tonight when he wakes up. I caught a glimpse of Renee walking down the street on my way here this morning. I think she's back for a while. My, how I'd love to see the parties she goes to."

"All I know is next time he gets after us for being a little slow," Ettie sassed, "I'm gonna bring this up. Dig this, the manager.

Sleeping at work. See his camera anywhere? We should get evidence!"

The Uni girls laughed in unison.

Derek cracked an eye open. Once the overwhelming sensation of disorientation subsided, he muttered the words, "Don't touch my camera."

The girls shrieked.

"Derek, I hope you didn't hear all that!" Bea exclaimed.

Derek sat upright and rubbed his eyes.

"Listen," he said in a groggy voice. "Renee..." Derek began, then stalled.

"We know," Bea sat next to him and placed her hand on his shoulder. "You love her. We do too."

Derek laughed. He looked out the small, cubed backroom window. Night had fallen. Derek searched for a clock.

'9:00.'

A groan escaped from his throat.

"Why did you stay here so late?" Derek asked.

"We got a new shipment. For Spring," Ettie retorted. "We turned the sign at five, like usual." She glared at him. "Sorry we stayed to make sure everything is checked in and put in its spot."

Derek rested his head in his hands.

"I'm sorry. You can go whenever you're ready, I've gotta figure out a faster way to get the order to Renee for approval. I forgot to ask her earlier. Then I'll go home."

Derek dreaded the waiting game of hunting down Renee's latest location to get her final approval on the monthly order. When she left for her first string of shoots, she made Derek promise that she would still have the final say on the seasonal clothing. He couldn't break his word.

"We can help track her down," Bea offered. "While you were out, we spoke with her agent, and he's given us her tentative schedule for the month."

Derek deflated, "Well, I guess I'll let you two take care of getting the order to her. Not much for me to do around here anymore, is there?"

Ettie and Bea exchanged a look.

"We won't let anything slip," Ettie assured.

Derek gathered his camera bag and the developed pouches of film which were stored in the bottom drawers of Renee's desk. Derek was surprised he didn't have more to collect.

The girls followed him out to the floor. They sat down on the register platform and waved goodbye. Derek stepped out into the night air and decided to leave *En Blum* behind.

Chapter VI

Mia watched the coffee pot fill, drip by drip. The aroma brought a sense of familiarity, and, for a moment, she forgot that she was back in 1998 and that Vaughn was still fast asleep in her bedroom. She tiptoed down the hallway and opened the door a crack. The hinge creaked and Vaughn rolled over to face the doorway.

"Morning," he said.

Mia's cheeks flushed.

"Morning."

Vaughn put his nose in the air and took a whiff of the coffee.

"You read my mind."

Vaughn beckoned Mia to the bed and pulled her down beside him. He wrapped his arms around her waist and kissed her shoulder. Mia did her best to practice self-restraint.

Today had to be productive. She couldn't spend a second day off the grid with Vaughn. Today, she would reveal her mission; to stay in the nineties and work to mend the era starting with the Tuesdaze and work her way out.

She would tell him her plans today, but not right away.

Forty-five minutes passed, and Mia and Vaughn finally made their way out of the bedroom.

Vaughn pulled a barstool out for Mia to sit at the kitchen island. After opening and closing most of the cupboards, he located the coffee mugs. Vaughn filled their cups and sat beside Mia.

"So," he began, "now that *that's* out of the way, what's next?"

Mia took a deep breath.

"I've dreaded this conversation," she said. "I'd ask you to share first, but if our plans don't line up, it will be harder for me to stick with mine."

Mia plucked her UpgrAid from the tabletop and showed Vaughn the block which was latched onto the device. Vaughn pulled the device from his pocket. The block was secured to his device as well.

Mia let out a sigh of relief.

He knew about mending. He was in on Rae's plan.

"I can't believe we're both on Rae's team," Mia stated.

Vaughn looked puzzled, "Wait, I couldn't get you to leave with me over the holidays. How did Rae get you to join her?"

"Things here are different than before I left. Even after Psilopram, the differences between my life now and six months ago hit me all at once. There *are* things to mend here."

"Did something happen with the Tuesdaze?" he asked.

"Lars is back."

Vaughn's mouth dropped open.

"*What?* Even after the holiday bash?"

Mia nodded.

"His return made me realize that, when I arrived, I only saw this era as a vacation. I think most Travelers feel that way at first, detached, there to have fun, free from the problems of OT. But now, I see things differently. And I want to make a difference. Even if it's small."

Vaughn shook his head.

"You're treading in deep water. We don't know what's below yet. I'm sure Rae filled you in on sequences, right? And the status of where they are with accessing mended projections of time?"

"N-no," Mia replied.

Vaughn chuckled, "Of course she didn't. Mia, you don't *know* if the effort to mend will pan out. Neither do I. Neither does Rae, nor any of her 'teammates.'"

"But you have the block. I thought that meant you were *in* on this. If not in OT, at least in some time sequence?"

"I only have the block because I was..." he paused, "Rae offered me one over the holidays. I just have it for times like these last couple of days, times I want to keep private. And Mia, the sequences, the planes of time you're hoping to alter haven't been tapped into yet. They're working on it, but this project is so off-the-radar that it's moving at a snail's pace. Do you really want to commit to impacting a time you don't even know exists?"

Mia shrugged, "What harm is there in trying to make things better?"

Vaughn tucked a curl behind Mia's ear.

"You're right. I can't decide your purpose for you. I'm just asking you to take a step back. We *have* enough monitors again. Since the new year, I've built up TRN's staff. Now, you and I can finally enjoy all this, all of time, together. You don't like to have to look over your shoulder and make sure Lars isn't following you, right? You don't like pop music's conquering of the airwaves. I say, leave," Vaughn swiveled his chair to face Mia. "Come with me."

"And let Lars tighten his grip on the Tuesdaze? Act like things in this era are fine as they are?"

Vaughn held up the eight-ball charm which dangled from the bracelet on his wrist. "When there's a clear answer, let me know," he said. "I'll stay for a couple of weeks. After that, I guess we'll see."

Mia was about to ask how Vaughn was granted so much free time and how he recruited so many TRN employees over the holidays, but he changed the subject.

"How's Derek holding up?"

"He's," Mia hesitated, "alright. After I found him in the sixties and broke the news, we went to Marseille. We visited Germain's family." Reg popped into Mia's mind, and she felt a streak of guilt for her lack of commitment to Vaughn. "To get away after losing Mom and Dad was just what we needed. When I left, Derek went back to London. I worry he will go back to chasing Renee and get his heart broken again, though I understand his infatuation with her. I saw her. She's magnetic."

"Just like someone else I know," Vaughn smirked. "But, unlike *their* time together, *this* doesn't have to end."

———————

Mia lay in bed. The room was perfectly lit by the cloud-muffled morning sun. She soaked in the feelings of Vaughn lying next to her again. She had nowhere to be and for the first time in a while, wished to be nowhere else.

She heard her UpgrAid buzz and Vaughn stirred.

He rubbed her arm, "What's it say?"

Mia read the tiny screen.

'*TRN: King's Records has a potential buyer. Mia and Derek Hayes to return to OT.*'

———————

Mia approached Macy's entryway buzzer. She wished to return to the simpler times when the two of them cohabitated in the apartment.

"Hello?"

"It's Mia."

A large plop of water dropped from the roof onto Mia's head as she awaited Macy's answer.

The entryway door clicked open. Mia took a deep breath and stepped inside. She hoped to gauge the group's plans and work around them for her trip back to OT.

Mia walked down the familiar hallway and knocked on Macy's door.

"Come in!" she heard Macy shout inside. "It's unlocked!"

Mia walked in and heard familiar voices coming from the living room. Though the aroma of smoke was stifling, Mia was reminded of her good times with Macy. She was elated to see the back of Tiffany and EJ's heads over Macy's couch. The group made her forget about Vaughn's proposition to Travel, about the loss of her family's legacy, about the fact that mending a moment in time was possibly a waste of energy. Tiffany and EJ turned to face Mia and grinned at the sight of her.

"The place has really come together, hasn't it?" Macy asked. "Ready to move back in from Rae's? Where has she been anyway? Come to think of it, where have *you* been?"

"We decided to spend a few days in the city," Mia bluffed.

Mia took stock of the apartment. Empty beer cans surrounded the kitchen sink. Ash trays overflowed on every table.

"It looks like you guys partied last night."

"We sure did," Macy replied.

"Sorry we didn't call. It was last-minute," Tiffany stumbled.

"And you were with Rae in the city anyway, right?" EJ said.

"Yeah. It's all good," Mia said, attempting to sound aloof.

Despite Mia's twinge of sadness caused by the group's separation, she wouldn't have changed the days spent with Vaughn. Mia suppressed the thought of him and refocused her energy on connecting with the Tuesdaze. She was happy to see Lars wasn't present.

EJ made room on the couch for Mia. She sat down and sighed. *'Here we go.'*

"I found out last night that they're selling the record store and venue," she stated.

"Oh man, I remember you talking about that place," EJ said. "The one your grandparents started, right? I'm so sorry."

"It was coming sooner or later," Mia admitted. "I'll have to go home as soon as I can get a decent priced ticket out of here. I wanted to give you plenty of heads up in case we have shows on the horizon."

"Lars told me he's got gigs for us almost every weekend once it's nice out," Macy said. "Guess we can start practicing without you. It's not like we got used to you being back anyway."

EJ shot Macy a look.

"Give her a break. It takes time to get back into it," EJ snapped. "Mia, you'll play with us until you have to go home again."

Heavy silence fell over the group and EJ stood. "Time for me to go home."

"Yeah, I better get going too," Tiffany said, and she walked out with EJ.

Mia and Macy sat quietly for what felt like longer than it was.

"It's nice out today. Want to sit on our balcony?"

"*Our* balcony?" Macy scoffed. "I didn't realize you still consider this place to be *ours*. Sure, you paid rent, but I guess I didn't think you'd choose living with an estranged friend over someone who has been here for you, someone who invited you into this band, someone who was," Macy paused, "so close to you."

Mia's heart sank. She could tell that Macy had been holding back the emotions for a long time, and her words came out marinated with months of repression.

"Listen, I know you've been through a lot, I'm not trying to make this about myself, but we've been here, waiting to help you through everything. Instead, you've completely cut yourself off," Macy said. "This fall, through the holiday season, we were together nearly every day, all of us. It's been painful to not be able to help you. You're not *here*. I don't know if you think you're better than us or if you don't care about us, but when I'm around you, it's like no one's home. Lars may have done some messed up things, but at least he's *here*."

"I guess I forgot I could turn to you," Mia confessed. "It all happened so fast. And I'm doing fine. I didn't want to drag any of you down."

"I know you've gone through so much; it just feels like in those tough times when you realize your priorities, you'd think of us."

Mia felt as though they were going in circles, but Macy's reiteration of the time Mia was gone made her realize how impactful her absence was. Rather than feeling cherished, Mia just felt further uncertainty surrounding her priorities.

"I'm sorry, Macy. It's all been confusing for me too and… I'll do better. I promise," Mia said. She wished she could conjure a fraction of the emotions she felt before multiple Psilopram doses, but the reactive part of herself was dormant. "It's too beautiful of a day to be arguing inside," Mia said, to diffuse the awkwardness. "Maybe we should go to EJ's. It would be good for us all to be together."

"You're right. Let's go to EJ's. I need to smooth things out with him. I was kind of a bitch to him last night," Macy admitted. "*You* came up."

Mia remained quiet.

Without another word, the two of them stood and left the apartment. Mia trailed Macy as Macy strutted ahead of her.

They made their way to the parking lot and slid into Macy's Cavalier. The sun shone brightly, but dark clouds lined the edge of the horizon. Their time to enjoy the weather was limited. The realization prompted Mia to close her eyes and enjoy the warm air as it blew in through the open window.

On the way, Mia watched Birchmont pass by. The familiar landmarks on the short drive to EJ's made her feel more at home. They passed Campustown and the Loop and Mia's brain filled with pleasant memories.

She wondered if she was overcomplicating her return to the nineties. Rather than engulfing herself in Rae's scheme, she could have spent the last few weeks jumping back into her previous scene, both feet first. She knew Macy's pissed-off front would be hard to penetrate, but Mia dedicated herself to the effort.

"Are classes going better for you?"

Macy rounded the corner then pulled into EJ and Jaq's gravel driveway.

"Not really. It's a snooze," Macy stated. "I'm barely going." She turned to face Mia, "Still passing though," she said with a wink.

Mia was encouraged by Macy's hint of openness. They walked around to EJ's side patio off the kitchen where the two of them had smoked cigarettes on Halloween after their night together. As Mia stepped up the creaky stairs to the small patio's platform, she felt optimistic.

Jaq was lounging on the patio in a fold-out chair.

"EJ, get more chairs!" he shouted. "Mia and Macy are here! You and Tiffany need to get out here. The air will help your hangover!"

After a few minutes, EJ stepped outside with two wooden chairs from the kitchen. He placed them down and patted the seats for his guests to use. His mood appeared to have brightened since Macy's apartment living room. Macy and Tiffany sat in the wooden chairs and Mia went to sit on a cushioned patio chair.

"Wait!" EJ said and ran inside to get a towel. He returned and handed the towel to Mia, "Sit on this. The chair is wet."

EJ took the remaining seat and got comfortable.

Jaq patted a cooler beside his chair.

"Help yourselves," he offered.

"Pass them out," EJ said, "here, we'll toss them down the line."

They passed the beverages until they each had a beer. Mia cracked the can, took a drink, and felt her body ease. They went on to chat about light matters; celebrities, classes, whether the Jaquez brothers should host a spring fling party; it felt like a continuation of Mia's life before January 1st. But, when she thought of what the next few weeks would bring, she knew better than to think she returned to the way it was.

They emptied the cooler, and no one volunteered to refill it. Mia's bladder was full, so she offered to restock after a trip to the bathroom. As Mia heaved the plastic container inside, Macy stood to follow.

"Here," Macy said and opened the door for Mia, "I have to go too."

Mia sat the cooler by the refrigerator. She stood upright and noticed that the buzz kicked in. Mia and Macy walked upstairs to the bathroom together. Macy sat on the toilet and Mia closed the door behind them. Mia decided to break the conversation open.

"I'm sorry it was so abrupt about having to leave again earlier," Mia began, "especially because I've been M.I.A before."

Macy chuckled at the bad joke.

"I'm sorry I was so harsh about our place. I understand not wanting to move back in with me. I see why you've stayed with Rae. You and I have history. And Lars *does* come over a lot. But like I said earlier, you've been completely unreachable, even when you're around. You've got a lot on your mind, don't you?"

Mia nodded, "That's an understatement."

"I just wish you'd talk about it," Macy changed the subject, "want me to flush?"

"No," Mia replied and switched places with Macy.

Macy hopped onto the bathroom sink and Mia sat on the toilet.

"I've been wanting to clear the air about Lars coming back into the picture for a long time, but you haven't given me the chance. That's why I came up here with you. Can I give you a quick rundown?"

"Sure," Mia said. She wiped and pulled up her pants.

"When he started getting us those gigs in the city, I don't know, he encouraged me to go all in. He built me up rather than constantly jabbing at me," Macy rolled her eyes, "it was a nice change after the holidays with my family. They're becoming harder to deal with, ya know. Especially with my sister's picture-perfect life."

Macy slid a pack of cigarettes from her pocket and extended the box to Mia.

"Want one?" she asked.

Mia shook her head and flushed the toilet.

"Suit yourself," Macy answered and flicked her lighter.

"Should we go back outside?" Mia asked, uncertain whether the Jaquez brothers would appreciate Macy's smoking in their house. "We can go around to the backyard and talk."

"Ugh, forget it," Macy said. "There's no use trying to explain it to you."

Macy opened the bathroom door and stomped downstairs to the kitchen. Mia followed her and busied herself with refilling the cooler. Macy reached to the top of the fridge. She stood on her tiptoes and barely wrapped her fingers around the handles to the liquor cabinet. She flung open the doors and grabbed a bottle of lime-green spirits.

Macy shrugged, "Let's kick it up a notch."

They returned outside to Tiffany and the Jaquez brother's laughter. The contagious joy sparked a jovial mood and diffused Mia and Macy's tension.

"What's so funny?" Mia asked.

"Oh nothing," Jaq answered. "You two were just in there for an awfully long time."

The group burst out in laughter and EJ elbowed Mia. Then, he turned to Macy.

"Pass that bottle."

Macy screwed off the top, took a long pull, then complied with EJ's request.

They passed the tart liquor between themselves and took on a carefree attitude offered by the warm day. They saw the dark clouds drawing nearer but savored the time before their arrival. Macy stretched her legs, her feet resting on the small patio's railing. Jaq cradled his hands behind his head. Even Tiffany slumped in her chair. Mia felt EJ looking at her and met his gaze. He flashed a dashing grin and Mia felt guilty as her thoughts drifted to Vaughn in their temporarily shared apartment. Vaughn was there, in the same town and era training new TRN hires remotely through the UpgrAid, and Mia wasn't with him.

A drop of rain fell on Mia's cheek. She ignored the first splat, but then another fell from the sky, followed by several more. Mia watched the precipitation speckle the patio boards.

Jaq groaned.

"I knew those clouds would get here sooner or later."

They gathered the chairs and libations to retreat indoors.

Just as Mia pulled the large, folded-up towel from her chair, she saw a car pull into the Jaquez' driveway. The vehicle parked behind Macy's car and blocked in the Cavalier and Tiffany's new Geo. Mia watched him open the door and step out into the building storm.

Lars.

Tiffany, Macy, and Jaq collected the empty containers, but Mia hurried inside to join EJ where he hung their towels to dry. Mia heard Lars and Macy converse outside and hoped Lars had just stopped by for a brief visit. He stepped inside; Lars was here to stay.

They kicked off their wet shoes, returned the remaining beers to the fridge, and went to gather around a bag of chips in the dining room. Macy brought the green liquor and sat it in the center of the table. She rustled in one of the kitchen drawers and pulled out a deck of cards.

"Cards, anyone?" she asked.

"I'm in," Lars responded.

Tiffany, painfully aware of the room's social dynamic, looked at her watch.

"Actually, I've gotta go. I have a quiz tomorrow." Tiffany looked out toward the driveway and scowled at Lars. "But I see I've been blocked in."

"C'mon Tiff," Macy pleaded, "just one game of cards."

Tiffany knew any hangout that involved Mia and Lars together would not end well.

"Sorry, it's a big quiz. This professor says the entire grade is based more on quizzes than on tests. Plus," Tiffany attempted to downplay her desperation to leave, "you know you can't just play *one* game."

Lars got the hint and stood.

"Maybe I'd better go," he started, then Macy cut in.

"No," she said. "I think we can all get along for one game of cards. Plus, Mia," Mia's skin prickled with Macy's acknowledgement, "we need to savor the time before you leave again. We never know how long you'll be gone."

"Leaving again?" Lars responded to the news.

"Yeah," Mia hesitated to explain, "I've got to go back to Maine. I don't know when though. I need to coordinate with my brother."

Macy rested her hand on Mia's leg and Mia furrowed her brow at the gesture.

"They're selling the record store," Macy filled Lars in on the development.

Anger bubbled within Mia. She didn't want Lars to know the vulnerable parts of her life.

Macy continued, "Have you and your brother thought of running it someday, Mia? It's not too late to switch to a business major."

Mia had considered the option but didn't need more decisions to make than the ones piling up.

"Right now, I just want to remember King's the same way it was when I was young."

"Maybe you shouldn't even go back," EJ suggested. "Keep the old image in your head."

"I don't know, revamping the place is definitely something to consider," Lars chimed in. "There's a venue below, right? Is that up for sale too? Maybe I could branch out to Maine, get some east coast connections to play there," Lars schemed.

Mia knew it wasn't a possibility, especially with her grandparent's fabled lineups of concerts in the nineties. She attempted to backtrack but was uncertain how to sever Lars' interest without blowing her story as a Traveler. Mia thought back to her training with TRN on how to formulate a no-strings-attached story to the natives of the era.

"It's just the record store they're selling," Mia said. "Not the venue, not yet at least."

Lars nodded, "That makes sense. A venue would be tough to let go of right now, but man, I know it sounds harsh, the reality is that record stores are becoming ancient history. You should be glad King's isn't falling on you. Maybe someone will buy it and you'll be able to pay off college."

Mia clenched her jaw.

Though Lars had no idea that records would make a comeback later in his life, she was livid at his assumption that he knew what was best for her. Despite her efforts to remain civil with Lars, she couldn't comply. Mia didn't respond and her lack of words said everything.

Macy dealt four cards to them but before everyone had five, Tiffany stood.

"I really do have to go," she said.

Tiffany walked to the kitchen patio door.

"It's not raining anymore. I'm not far, I think I'll walk from here."

No one stopped her.

"See you guys on Tuesday," Tiffany said and made her exit.

Macy took another long pull from the bottle and dealt the last card. They played the game in silence. The tension was uncomfortable beyond measure, but the one person who could have lightened the night with his absence, chose to linger.

Macy, who was starting to feel drunk and unable to help herself, drew closer to Mia. She played with Mia's hair; it had grown since her return and hung just above her waist. Macy smoothed the fuzz from the earlier raindrops.

Mia shrunk back. She noticed Lars' eyes darting from his cards to Macy's contact with Mia. Mia wanted Lars to look her in the eye so she could send him all her rage, but he never did.

Eventually, the game concluded, and Macy turned to face Mia.

"Ready to come home?" she asked with a dazed smile.

"I'm ready to *go* home," Mia answered. "I'm staying at Rae's tonight."

Macy shook her head.

"God, I throw myself out there and you just shut me down."

Mia raised her eyebrows, "Now you know how it feels." With that, she pushed her chair back from the table and headed toward the front door.

Months ago, she would have leaned into Macy's invitation back into her life, but now, Mia had more options. She hurried down the street. Once she lost sight of the Jaquez' house, she planned to signal through the Aid for Vaughn to pick her up. Mia heard a vehicle trailing her and snapped her head around.

"Want a ride to Rae's?" EJ shouted.

Just then, the rain intensified and down poured on Mia.

"Sure."

Mia got into his car and felt her pants drench the seat.

"Sorry," Mia said.

"It's okay."

EJ wove through Birchmont and Mia directed him to her apartment. She was relieved by the weather which lessened the chances of Vaughn stepping outside and running into EJ. Vaughn's residence in the same building as Mia would be hard to explain away.

They arrived and Mia worked up the nerve to run through the veil of rain to her building. She wrapped her fingers around the passenger side handle, but before she could push the car door open, EJ rested his hand on the middle of her back. Mia turned to face him.

He rendered her breathless with his rain dampened lips and dark hair. They connected on a level that wasn't just a whim and Mia realized she'd been avoiding something so deep in a situation so temporary. Rather than reset the boundary she put up for the charismatic, kind-hearted EJ, she let herself get lost in the moment.

EJ pressed his lips against Mia's.

The sound of the rain coupled with EJ's calming demeanor created an untouchable cocoon of reassurance for Mia that everything was right in the world. They pulled away at the same moment. They held each other's gaze, then Mia's vision was drawn to her balcony where she knew Vaughn waited inside.

EJ grinned, "Tell Rae I say hi."

"I will," Mia agreed.

"Remember, you're always welcome at our place. If Macy was not so talented, man, she'd be on thin ice. Jaq, Tiffany, and I have got your back."

"Thank you," Mia said and pushed open the car door. She ran through the rain to the entrance of the building, exhilarated. Her hands trembled and she struggled to get her key in the door.

She finally got inside and hurried to her apartment to check if Vaughn had been looking out the window and seen the whole thing. When Mia opened her entryway door, she was hit with the savory aroma of garlic and herbs. Her mouth watered.

Vaughn welcomed her inside with a kiss. He furrowed his brow and sniffed. Mia's heart rate spiked; could he taste EJ? He wasn't a smoker. Maybe she smelled like his cologne.

"Did you do some day drinking?" Vaughn chuckled.

Mia let out a sigh of relief.

"Yeah, we went to the Jaquez brothers' after you dropped me off near Macy's."

"How did things go? Were they upset you'll be gone again?"

Mia shrugged, "I don't know, they understand, but they're not happy. Especially Macy. She can sense I'm not myself. She kept saying she couldn't *reach* me. Have you noticed a change in my personality?"

"Of course, Mia. No one could go through what you've endured and come out as the same person. It's selfish for Macy to believe that's possible. Why is she making your tragedy about herself?"

"I don't know. I think that's a good point. Though, isn't it kind of weird that I haven't had a good cry about Mom and Dad? Or that I'm not heartbroken about losing King's?"

Vaughn pursed his lips.

"You might not remember the emotions, but you've gone through *plenty* of breakdowns. Your first couple of Acclimations were... rough. I wasn't there, but I asked about you. I wanted to make sure you were okay. Now, you're through it, why dredge up something that's going to hurt again, just to seem 'normal' to Macy? Who, if we're being honest, isn't the model citizen for dealing with her emotions."

"Right again. Imagine that," Mia smirked. She changed the subject before Vaughn asked more questions about her day with the Tuesdaze. "This place smells delicious. What's the occasion?"

"Well, a celebration is warranted. You know how I facilitated training through the UpgrAid today?"

Mia nodded.

"It was perfect! TRN will continue to have the standard, two-week training in-person, but once we go through the basics, and they're in the field, our communication can be virtual! We covered so much information today. Based on their projections, TRN said remote post-intensive training is going to free me up for a *three-month* break at the end of the summer! Plus, the team has grown so much, there are other monitoring leads to cover for me. Finally, the last year of hell has paid off!"

"I can't believe it," Mia said, stunned.

Vaughn read her expression.

"I'm not telling you this to pressure you. I just wanted you to know. And I needed someone to celebrate with."

Mia was unable to get the magic with EJ off her mind. Vaughn noticed she was distracted.

"Too many options," Vaughn said. "Right on brand for you, Mia Hayes."

Mia avoided eye contact, unable to conceal how correct he was.

She spilled, "The longer I'm here, the more problems I see with the past. If those problems were corrected, they wouldn't have piled on and influenced so much in OT, or whatever version of the sequence would play out. Every generation has been forced to see their Original Time sequence though, but what if we could change things somewhere? I'm not ready to give up on the idea of mending. I just don't know where to start. I'm getting nowhere with fixing Lars' hold on us."

Vaughn nodded, "I'm thrilled about the idea of mending, I just don't know how long it will take to see if the changes *fix* the future projection of the era or if new problems arise. It's a possibility you have to consider, Mia. Often, if it's not one thing, it's another."

"But this whole mission could take Travel to a new level. Rae's idea could make Time Travel more than TRN ever intended it to be. More than a vacation. We tend to get involved with the eras regardless. Why not try to create a better future?"

"It's hard to deny that mending is a great idea, it's just whether the logistics work."

"I know. Rae *did* seem hopeful though. Let's say I leave with you after returning home," Mia paused. "I love our time together, Vaughn, but what would we *do*? What's the point of bopping around to all these different times, going through several Acclimations if we're not making some sort of difference?"

"And I thought I was a workaholic," Vaughn smirked. "Look, I don't have an answer for you, and I'll only be here another week or so. Come back here if you want. Try mending but be careful. You have the block, but you'll still get flagged by TRN if you cause too much rift within a time. Work on a subtle level. Rae was right, starting with Lars might be good. If you can undercut his status by exposing his dark side to everyone, that's a lesson for all chauvinistic men at this time. You could cause a positive ripple. Just don't get lost in trying to fix everything. You can only control so much."

Mia nodded. A timer went off and Vaughn pulled a sheet pan of roasted potatoes from the oven. Mia salivated.

Vaughn prepared their plates and uncorked a bottle of Chardonnay.

"Tonight, we celebrate an extra link being added to the chains TRN has around my wrists."

As they ate, Mia thought of Rae.

"Do you know where Rae is assigned? Is she in another era or training new monitors in OT?"

"I haven't heard from her in a while. We don't talk much anymore."

"Why is that? I figured you two interacted a lot with monitoring and training."

Vaughn shrugged, "We *did.*"

Chapter VII

She hurried along the bustling street as the rain poured down. She finally reached another string of storefronts and sheltered herself beneath the awnings. Her boots splashed in the puddles as she ran.

Her dark, detailed eyeliner melted down her cheeks. She pressed her hand against her face and laughed at the black streaks on her fingers.

'No use trying to keep up appearances now.'

She disregarded the Carnaby crowd and stepped out from beneath the awning. She opened her mouth to catch raindrops, something she hadn't done since her childhood. She noticed a man seated on a bench by the bus top. He looked up at her from beneath his umbrella. She watched his eyes follow the streams of black running down her cheeks.

"Share my umbrella?" he asked. "I'm Grant, by the way."

"No thanks," she said. "It's way more fun out here. I'm Rae."

The man further engaged her in conversation, desperate to make a connection.

"Your things must be soaked," he gestured to her suitcase.

"They'll wash."

"Where are you off to? The airport?" Grant asked.

"To be honest, I'm not sure where I'll go yet."

Grant smirked.

"A drifter, huh? I used to be like that. San Francisco."

"Far out," Rae smiled. "I was there a few months ago. I wouldn't mind going back."

Then, their attention was stolen by a painted van that pulled into the bus stop. The driver looked for signs of authority as the vehicle parked illegally. Rae looked at Grant and, with no words, they exchanged an idea. A young man with sun-bleached hair slid open the backdoor of the van. Inside a smiling woman waved them in.

"You're either on the bus or off the bus."

A crowd gathered to watch the stylist swirl his model's hair into a work of art. Renee was seated just feet away from the salon chair. She was in awe at how the stylist's fingers worked with the model's hair as though it was fabric. Though Renee was astounded at his skill, she didn't know how the model had remained still as the stylist wrenched her hair into place.

Finally, he completed his masterpiece. He pulled off his model's cape with drama and revealed her airy pink dress beneath. The combination of her whimsical updo and the delicate dress reminded Renee of the breathless feeling she got every time spring arrived.

Renee caught sight of herself in a nearby mirror and found her reflection drab. Her chin-length cut dragged her down. "Mod," her agent, William, had called her cut, but it felt heavy like the winter. Renee hoped the stylist would choose her as his next canvas.

William was still flustered as he attempted to diversify Renee's image from—what he perceived to be—too suggestive.

"No publicity is *bad* publicity," Renee had told him after her centerfold appearance, but he wasn't convinced. He was the one who read the letters Renee received.

'Sex pot.'

'Dirty.'

'How could such elegance resort to such trash?'

He kept most of it from her, but he couldn't stop virtuous housewives and old bags from shouting at Renee in the street. So, he convinced her to hire his contact, Vic, as her security man. Vic shadowed her every outing. He kept the gropers and violent Christians away.

Just weeks ago, William also convinced Renee to lob off her long tresses.

"Chic, mod, geometric," the previous hairdresser said.

Renee knew chic, and the pageboy cut she received was not *chic*. She wore it better than most, but the time had come for a change. Renee wanted the man before her to create her new look.

With increasing frequency, Renee considered dropping William and riding her wave of connections. The new bubbling scene didn't require an agent to find jobs. Many called the new scene "underground," and they all relied on each other's word to set up their own makeshift sets and shoots. The underground was composed of a seedy bunch, but Renee's photographer client was their ringleader and she saw brilliance in his eccentricity.

Renee stood and pretended to stumble forward; she caught the hairdresser's attention. The motion reminded him of other knock-kneed icons whose signature cuts he crafted.

"Sorry," Renee said, "I lost my balance."

A whimsical look painted the hairdresser's face. He dissected Renee's face and body. Renee began to step back into the small crowd when the hairdresser extended an open hand toward her.

"Come," he guided her to sit in his black, leather-upholstered chair.

He pumped up her chair, so she was eye level with him. He used the mirror in front of him and familiarized himself with her dark locks. He tucked her hair in various places to explore the contours of her face. He fussed a bit more, then he revealed just the right amount of Renee's forehead, perfectly accenting her green eyes. Her pout became more irresistible. Renee saw him lock in; he found his lines.

"Should we get rid of this tired mass?"

Renee beamed and nodded.

She watched her hair fall to the floor. Every snip the hairdresser made, felt like it brought her one step closer to freedom. As he situated the fall of her hair from one side to the other, Renee heard the small crowd "ooh" with admiration.

Smaller tufts of hair began to float onto Renee's nose. He made his shape and was now tailoring the cut. She had mutual respect for his sense of design; Renee missed playing with lines and proportions at the boutique.

He got out a small makeup brush and fluttered the bristles back and forth from her forehead all the way down to her chin. She felt his final details along the nape of her neck. The brush then tickled along the back of her head. Just as he'd done with his previous style, the hairdresser pulled the cape off Renee.

She opened her eyes and was dazzled at the woman staring back at her in the mirror. She saw satisfaction on the hairdresser's face as he presented his work. Even William nodded with approval. Renee felt so light she wondered if she would float away.

———————

Derek saw her through the window from across the street. It was the first time he'd seen Renee in months, the first time he spotted her since he quit *En Blum* and resolved to live off his modest inheritance. Not much had changed; crowds of admirers still gathered around Renee. He was pulled in by the perfect structure of her face. He watched her stand and put on her sunglasses to leave the salon. Derek hurried along before she could spot him.

They never crossed paths, even as Derek's time with Germain and Tom increased. He wondered if Tom and Germain spent time with Renee when he wasn't there or if their next-of-kin relationship had also dwindled.

Derek was reworking his time in the sixties. He grew to appreciate discovering places on his own rather than following Renee or Angelene's lead. Derek realized, especially after spending time with Mia, that since arriving in the sixties, he was falling into the old pattern of building his identity around significant others. He was doing his best to break the habit.

Now that it was springtime, music could be found in nearly every park. Germain and Tom led Derek to the best places in the city.

The only downside to spending time with the two of them was the provoking of Derek's temper. As Germain and Tom grew braver by letting their love be seen, names Derek hadn't even heard were spewed at them. Because Derek was with them and well dressed, he was also subjected to baseless hate.

Unlike Derek, Germain and Tom brushed it off. Often, they had a better, wittier quip with which to strike their bully, leaving the bigots speechless and embarrassed. Derek loved many parts of the sixties, but there were several things that time had yet to change. He often wondered how strict TRN was about leaving the era untouched.

As he walked through the building shadows and pondered how to spend his evening, the chill from the lack of sun sent a shiver down his spine. Derek was more uncertain than ever of what the future would bring, but he attempted to make peace with the variability.

Derek adjusted his camera bag to the opposite shoulder. Over the winter, Derek immersed himself into photography. He mostly did it for himself; taking photos from the front row of concerts, capturing the first flowers to emerge from the ground, snapping images of women who made him think of Lucia and Renee. Most recently, he had been asked to capture album covers for local bands and was even working on turning his spare room into a dark room.

The side gig was perfect for Derek. It allowed him to be close to fame without having to engage and exhaust himself trying to be interesting. That was his subjects' job.

Derek turned the corner to go to Tom's. Tom would just be getting home from work. He'd complain about selling out his drawing skills to the ad company. Both Tom and Germain would be ready to hit the town for a drink. It was Thursday night, and Derek was ready to begin the weekend early with his two dependable mates, free from the judgment of Angelene and the feelings of inadequacy triggered by Renee.

'Rap, rap, rap!'

They were at the door again.

"This is the third time this week," Angelene whispered. "Go!"

Grant went to hide in Angelene's bedroom. He was sick of running. He wanted nothing more than to purge the night, to tell them he remembered nothing besides the knife. The bloody knife. But Angelene wouldn't let him tell the investigators his side of the story.

He listened from the bedroom, but the voices were muffled by the rain outside.

"Is your brother around?"

"He's out," Angelene bluffed. "Will you please tell me why you're looking for him? He's the sweetest, my brother, really. I can't imagine he'd be in any trouble."

"Just let us know if you see him," the voice said.

The door closed. Grant's heart raced. He knew, when he walked out and looked at the kitchen table, another scrap of paper with a phone number would be laying there to remind him of the forgotten night. He walked into the kitchen to face Angelene and took a deep breath on the way.

"I'm going to the station," Grant told his sister. "I can't bear the burden any longer."

"Grant, no. Don't tell them anything. We still don't even know what happened. And look at it outside. It's pouring. At least wait until the rain lets up."

"I'm going," Grant said.

He took an umbrella and left.

"It's just here," Tom gestured to their destination.

Their walkway led to a venue. The outside was made of stone, and the venue was built into the earth. The sidewalk led further downhill, and Derek's interest was piqued by the small structure to where the path led.

"What's down there then?"

Tom cringed, "I think it's someone's flat. Was probably a bomb shelter before, now someone's renting it out cheap."

'Who would live below a sunken music venue?' Derek wondered. Then he remembered how much time they spent above the Court at King's Records. Les often slept on the listening room's couch, unbothered by the noise below at the Court's bar after the show.

"Right this way," Tom led them inside the venue.

The inside was cavernous. The walls were made of large, crumbling stone blocks. The air smelled stale. Despite the dawning of springtime, the crowd felt heavy, like there was some source of dissatisfaction which they all were forced to live out in the current world. Derek understood. He felt the same about Original Time.

The hours passed and the drinks went down easy. Derek finally grew to appreciate the venue's grungy charm. The hour grew late, and a band filed onto a small stage at the front of the bar. Their appearance was like the bands of the time with their shaggy hair and volatile demeanor, but this group was greasier than Derek had seen. They started up and Derek was drawn in by their slightly off-kilter rhythm and dynamic melody.

By the beginning of the third song, the crowd got rough, and Derek's initial enthusiasm shifted to annoyance. People continued to flood into the bar. Derek was shoved and elbowed. Though he was exhilarated to be a part of the energy, he needed a break. Derek remembered that outside, the temperature was no longer frigid. He yearned for a breath of fresh air.

"I'm going to step outside," Derek yelled to his friends.

Germain shook his head.

"What?!"

Derek pointed to the stairs that led to the exit.

"I'll come back soon!"

The bar was jam packed, but eventually Derek made his way to the exit and climbed the creaky, wooden stairs. He made it out but was not alone. A half dozen other smokers lingered outside. Derek felt for the joint in his shirt pocket and was thankful it hadn't snapped.

Before he lit the joint, he waited for the smell that he was in good company. Within seconds, the pungent aroma of marijuana wafted into his nostrils from someone else's supply. He pulled a lighter, gifted by Marcel, from his pocket and lit the paper.

———————

Renee followed Lorraine inside. The room was thick with the smell of incense and weed. She was no stranger to the city's fringe, but this was shocking, even in her dulled state.

The apartment was set just below a music venue. The band had yet to begin, but Renee heard a churning crowd above. The walls were covered with tapestries and there were no windows. There were just two large rooms, a kitchenette, and a bathroom.

"Isn't this the perfect hideout?" Lorraine asked. "I see why she does her work here."

"How did you find her again?"

Lorraine's expression sobered. "She helped me get rid of a problem."

Renee kicked herself for bringing up Lorraine's backstreet abortion. "I'm so sorry, it's been months. I forgot."

"Welcome," a woman greeted Renee and Lorraine. She opened her arms. "Lorraine, my dear, so wonderful to see you in good health. You look beautiful."

Lorraine embraced the woman.

"Lena, your tonic did the trick."

"Few know that there are other methods than chemicals or crude instruments. I see you've brought a friend," Lena turned to Renee and stood eye-to-eye. "Beautiful emeralds," she said. "Have you come for the same reason as Lorraine?"

Renee shook her head, "No. We were told you have methods of healing. I've been so tired the last few months and..." Renee placed a hand over the tracks on her arm, "...I'm trying to kick some bad habits."

"I see," Lena eyed Renee's inner elbow. "How long has this been a problem?"

"Since winter. When I went to America, I've taken more and more. Last time, I barely made it down. I-I'm," Renee paused, "I'm coming down... now. I don't want to feel that way again, like I did before. I'm so scared I'll go back."

"She needs assistance with her coming down. Her agent doesn't know she's here. Neither does her bodyguard. I snuck her here tonight."

"If they knew I came back to the stuff, they'd lock me away. They'd make things worse," Renee panicked.

"I thought she could hole up here for a few days while she gets clean. Don't worry, Renee," Lorraine rubbed Renee's back, "I'll keep Will and Vic occupied."

Lena gestured Renee and Lorraine into the next room. "Come, I've got some ideas." They followed; Renee barely hobbled through the doorway.

Lena revealed a wall of glass jars. Each container held various herbs, many of which Renee had never seen. Lena rubbed her chin and scanned the shelves.

"I've got an herb from the far east," she said. "It is very rare, very costly, but it may help you to push through the drop more quickly."

Lena named her price.

"I don't know if I can afford that," Renee stated.

She blew all her centerfold money on the very thing which brought her to the apothecary.

"Well then, I'm sorry, I cannot help you."

"Can she at least stay here while she comes down?" Lorraine pleaded. She got close to Lena and whispered, "She made a mess last time. Plus, she has more eyes on her than ever before. The press knows where she resides. If they were to get photos, the humiliation would *kill* her."

Lena pursed her lips. "Alright. She can stay. But I'm just keeping her in the next room and covering the space with disposable linens." Lena spouted another price, significantly lower than the cost of using her precious herbs. Lorraine fumbled in Renee's purse and handed over all the cash she had.

"And you'll give her water and a bit of food when she can handle it?"

Lena nodded. "Three days. Come back to check on her. We will know the worst of it by then."

———————

Renee came to. She was soaked. A putrid smell flooded her nostrils.

She was in the dark.

She felt around for a light switch, for anything. She wondered if she was dead. Based on how she felt, this was certainly hell. Renee rolled over and, through a crack in the door, she saw a woman in the next room. Her face was lit by candles as she read a book. Renee squinted to read the book cover.

'Female Anatomy,' was the title.

Renee's heart raced. She had to escape. The woman's phone rang, and she seemed concerned. She looked in Renee's direction. Renee closed her eyes and pretended to be asleep.

The woman bought it and stretched the phone cord into the kitchen to speak in privacy. It sounded like she was sobbing. Renee made a run for it.

Derek looked at the clock. Fifteen minutes until midnight. The last time he'd been so exhausted from a band's endless energy was in Marseille.

"I've gotta go soon," Derek told Germain. "I'm fading fast."

"You can stay with me and Tom," Germain offered. "Our place is closer than your flat."

As they left the bar, Derek noticed the once vivacious crowd had died down. The band was still going strong, but Derek saw several members of the crowd turn away from the stage. They were in tears.

Derek wondered if he was paranoid, but then, a group of young people sobbed at the top of the stairs. Something was going on. They exited the venue and started toward Germain and Tom's apartment.

'Wham!'

Someone shoulder-checked Derek and fell to the ground with him. Derek pushed himself up and prepared to yell at the person who knocked him down. He stalled when he saw it was a dark-haired woman; he wondered how she had the strength to knock the wind out of him.

"Renee!" Germain shouted at the woman on the ground. "What are you doing here? Were you in the club?" He paused to examine her face and his eyes grew large.

Derek didn't even bother to brush himself off before tending to Renee.

"I was down there," Renee pointed to the bomb-shelter apartment.

"What on earth were you doing *there*?"

"I don't know, I remember Lorraine earlier. Perhaps she brought me there. She's jealous of me, you know. She's trying to get rid of me."

Renee shook so badly, the guys could barely understand her. Rain began to fall, and Renee shivered harder. Derek took her hand. Her palms were slick with sweat. He noticed dots of purple near her elbow crease and held his hand to his mouth.

'Heroin.'

Derek woke with the morning sun. Though Tom's place was beautiful, after the night he had, he longed to be in his own flat. He wondered if he should stop by the hospital to check on Renee or, more importantly, to ensure the press was giving her the privacy she needed.

Derek left Tom's apartment. His heart dropped as he saw the headline on the newspaper outside Tom's front door. He understood why so many tears were shed at the venue; the reverend who had a dream was killed. He picked up the paper and signaled a cab. Derek resolved to go back to his apartment and shower, then stop by the hospital and check on Renee.

As soon as he got inside his apartment, the phone rang. He rushed to the receiver.

"Hello?"

"I got here as fast as I could," Derek said to Angelene.

"Grant's been gone for two days now," she shook her head. "I don't know where he went. He was off to the station to confess about the night last fall. The night… he lost. Officers, investigators, they've stopped by to question him. He's had enough. I walked the route he would have taken to the bus station. I've lingered at the nick. He was so set on going through questioning and now he's just gone."

"Did he mention anyone new he's spent time with lately?"

"No. He mostly stays in. If he does go out, I'm there too."

Derek was struck with guilt for not being there for Grant, but Angelene had become so controlling of his life and the tension was hard to be around. She treated Grant as though she was saving him from being institutionalized, which drove Grant even crazier.

Derek, still drowsy from the eventful night before, spoke unfiltered.

"Ang, you've been suffocating him. I can see why he wants to get the night off his chest. He's had no resolution."

"You think you know what's best for him?" She seethed. "Fine. You go find him."

Angelene dismissed Derek and he started toward the hospital. He passed through a park where a guitarist strummed as though there was no darkness in the world. Derek wished he could retreat to the dreamworld in the musician's song.

Then, his UpgrAid buzzed. Derek searched for a place he could be alone. He stopped at *En Blum* which stood between Angelene's flat and the hospital. He turned the key to the back door and hoped the Uni girls didn't hear him come in.

Though the showroom sounded chaotic, the backroom was dark and quiet. He used the seclusion to read the message on his device.

Mia: 'We'll meet in OT in June. King's has a buyer.'

———

Renee fought to break free from her restraints. It was no use. She was too weak.

"Sweetie," a voice said, "sweetie, calm down. You're safe. You're okay."

Renee turned her head away from the nurse. She imagined the nurse attaching electrodes to her head, shocking her until her brain was mush. Renee didn't know what she did to land herself in this place where she had no rights. She couldn't get up to go to the bathroom. She couldn't make a phone call. They wouldn't give her the fix, the fix she was certain would make this all go away.

Renee struggled to escape until she exhausted herself and fell into another dark dream.

———————

"For years, I've rehearsed what I would say to you if we met. I imagined how good it would feel to let you have it. Now, I can't think of anything to say."

"You're not alone in your imaginations of us meeting. Anything you would have said, I have pictured you saying to me, cutting me down to my core. Unveiling my deepest insecurities."

Vivienne, Renee's mother, sat down on the edge of the hospital bed. The movement caused Renee's muscles to ache. She winced.

"So sorry, love," Vivienne said and stroked her daughter's face.

The sensation hurt Renee's skin, "Don't touch me."

"She may be a bit... sensitive," the nurse advised from the corner where she sat.

"Can you leave us alone?" Renee snapped.

The nurse complied, "I'll be right outside the door."

Renee's memories of Vivienne were limited to her life before six years old. She remembered receiving one last gift, an expensive bottle of perfume, which she shattered in her teenage years. Renee's grandmother Sylvia understood Renee's frustration but couldn't help her disappointment surrounding the destruction of the elegant perfume bottle as it splayed across *En Blum's* floor.

"I have been so unfair to you, Renee," Vivienne said. "I've hated myself for it for years, more than even you could hate me."

"I wouldn't be so sure about that," Renee responded.

"I see you now, and I know you. I know how you're feeling."

"I wouldn't say you *know* me," Renee stated. "How did you even find me?"

"I have seen your face on the storefronts when I'm in the city and I've seen you in my lovers' magazines. I know the life you are living and no matter how wild it is, we cannot resist it. I saw you were," Vivienne paused, "hospitalized. It was in the paper," she mumbled.

A tear rolled down Renee's cheek.

"So, now is when you choose to find me. God, I can't fathom having a baby right now," she began, "but I'd love her. I'd be there for her." Tears of anger welled in Renee's eyes. "Why did you leave me in the first place? I tried to be good. I did what I was told. My whole life, I've searched for the love only you could give me."

"I've always loved you Renee, even if you didn't know it," Vivienne wiped a tear from her own cheek. "You wouldn't have loved me. I know it. *Maman*, she wanted me to run the store, to keep the craftsmanship in the family, but I didn't want to be tethered down. She worked so hard, but I couldn't do it. My designs were never good enough, my technique was imperfect. It wasn't just my sewing, but it was the way I took care of you. I never fed you at the right time. I held you wrong. Seeing you out there, so beautiful, so full of grace and wonder, she brought you up so well, in a way I couldn't have. Once I saw what you became, I pulled further away from you, further away from anything."

Renee shook her head.

"You didn't even try."

Vivienne nodded and bit her lip.

"I wish I could say I regret it, but I was so resentful living the life of a mother. I lost myself. I had to come home when I wanted to stay out. So, eventually, I stayed out.

I inspired many artists. They bought me plane tickets to visit them and offered me the world, but I had to come home to a crying baby. I'm awful, Renee, and I know it. I can't believe I'm telling you any of this," Vivienne cradled her head in her hands. "This is why I've just stayed away; I knew all of this would hurt you and I've already done that enough."

Renee was silent. "Let's get you better. Then, when you get out of here, we'll make sure you're okay. We'll send you off with your friends."

"So, you're just going to hand me off again?"

"Renee, *bebe*, you're better off with *anyone* than you would be with me."

———

Derek approached the hospital. He slowed when he saw a cluster of reporters. "Renee Blum," buzzed through their conversations.

Derek rolled his eyes.

"Come *on*! Let her be!"

"You know her?" A group of reporters frenzied around Derek.

Derek shut down and did his best to move past them without making eye contact, but one reporter grabbed his sleeve. The reporter's eyes were wild.

"I'll give you forty quid for twenty minutes!"

"Get your hands off me you piece of shit! You people are destroying her!"

"Renee Blum, undergoing self-destruction. Straight from the boyfriend's mouth," the reporter smirked.

Derek sprinted toward the hospital.

"Whoa now, young man," a security guard stopped him at the door. "Who are you here to see? You didn't bring your *friends* with you, did you?" He scanned the crowd of reporters.

Derek searched his mind for the name of Renee's security guard with whom he'd only spoken once when trying to finalize one of *En Blum* orders. 'V...V...'

"Vic!" Derek shouted. "It's me, Derek. Renee's old… employee. I brought her here with Germain and Tom."

"Right," Vic nodded. "You can't see Renee right now."

"I've got to see her. I want to take care of her, Vic."

Vic sighed and led Derek inside to a private waiting room.

"This day has been a long time coming, kid. None of those reporters out there are paying you, right?"

"No," Derek replied. "They couldn't pay me enough to spill anything about Renee. Is she coming around?"

"Yes, but it's a long road. What she wants, it's still out there. And she can get it easily. Will's beside himself trying to recover her image. First the dirty magazine, now this. She might recover physically, but I don't know if she'll ever get into them posh designer's doors again."

"I don't know what there is to be done about the press," Derek hung his head, "but we'll watch out for her. We'll keep her from getting in too deep again."

———

Three days passed and Renee was released. Vic called Germain, Tom, and Derek to greet her in the hospital lobby. Renee looked as though she had aged ten years, but her friends disregarded the change and did their best to lift her spirits.

"No press is bad press," Tom stated. "Trust me, I work at an ad agency."

"Ready, kid?" Vic asked Renee before they stepped outside the hospital entrance.

"Not sure I have a choice," Renee said. "I can't stand to be in this place another minute. What's out there can't be nearly as bad as what's in here."

———

Throughout spring, while Derek waited for June to arrive, he tended to Renee's every need. When night fell and the reporters couldn't see her face, he brought her on walks around the park. He sat with her to do *En Blum's* monthly order. The spring air made it feel as though the past year was a bad dream and Derek was just meeting Renee again for the first time. The return of bliss into Derek's life made him want to throw his UpgrAid into the Thames and live out the rest of his days in Renee's orbit.

Though Renee was grateful for her friend's loyalty, she had an itch, a constant longing which dwelled within her. She passed a storefront and saw Lorraine's image plastered on a makeup advertisement in the window. Renee missed being on set. She missed her old crowd.

"Now that you're feeling better, there's something I need to talk with you about," Derek said one late day in May when he returned home from the boutique. "I've got to leave in a few weeks. My parent's record store is being sold, so Mia and I must return home. I figured you could stay with Tom and Germain while I'm gone, you know," Derek paused, "in case you need company."

"You think I need a babysitter, am I right?" Renee asked. "At some point, I must pick up with my life. I can't live as a shadow anymore."

"I wouldn't say you're a shadow. You've seen the papers."

"Tom said it best, *bad* press does not exist. Perhaps I should call him. Have him pick me up. Maybe his agency has an account who is in the market for a face like mine."

With that, Renee stood and gathered the one bag she'd had since her time in the hospital. She kissed Derek's cheek. The further she lifted him, the harder the drop always was.

"You know where to find me."

———

Vivienne laid her head on a cushion. Her self-hatred softened as her blood circulated.

Robert laid next to her. Though he had a few more lines on his face, he was still as beautiful as she remembered. Vivienne couldn't believe she found him. The man who made her a mother. The man she destroyed.

She met him outside the hospital when she went to visit Renee.

When he first saw Renee's ads, he wondered. Their faces were similar. She was the right age. The night of Renee's overdose, Vivienne confirmed his suspicions.

Vivienne still had the junk, and Robert couldn't resist. He was the father, and their daughter laid, alone, in the hospital. His two months clean came to a swift end.

Vivienne and Robbie spiraled off together, for the first time in twenty-three years. How they survived so long was a mystery to them both.

Vivienne first tried it after the war, back when it was clean. Robbie remembered meeting her in the jazz club. He brought her home after the show. She was magnetic.

"Shell shock. I can't imagine. The bombs here were unforgettable, but nothing compared to what you saw," she said. "I've got something. I tried it recently. One of our musicians said it's the bee's-knees and my, was he right. It may soothe your fits."

Robbie chuckled, "I know what *it* is. And I don't need *it*. I'm fine. They say we're closing in on them from all sides. Before long, there won't be anything to fear."

That night, Vivienne Blum made him forget anything else he knew in the world besides her eyes, her curves, and the feel of her skin. She wore his shirt into his kitchen the next morning. She dug through his cupboards and found a French press, tucked away.

Robbie walked into the kitchen and smirked.

"Of course, you found the press."

"It appears unused," Vivienne raised her eyebrows.

Robbie sighed, "A wedding gift. *She* selected it."

Vivienne looked around his apartment, "You're *married?*"

"Separated. Soon to be divorced. She's grown tired of my fits," Robbie shook his head, "wish I could get a damned handle on myself. Slowly though, I'm getting better. Her nagging didn't help the matter. Perhaps I just need the right person."

Vivienne had sympathy for Robbie. She got close to him and pressed her lips against his. Then, the earth shook. Bombs exploded just streets away.

Robbie's face reddened and he screamed. Vivienne pulled his stiffened body under the kitchen table. He crumpled and wrapped his hands around his shins.

"Is there a shelter nearby?!" she shouted.

Robbie didn't respond.

"*Robert!* Where can we find shelter?!"

"S-Stairwell! To the basement!"

Vivienne pulled him out of his flat and they rushed down the stairwell. The building was hit, and bits of ceiling rained down from above. Robert collapsed. Other tenants rushed down the stairs in waves. Vivienne extended her hand toward Robert, but he was unreachable, and she was carried away with the mass to the shelter downstairs. Once she was in the basement, she tried to move about and search for Robbie, but the bodies were smashed into the small refuge and left no room for movement.

The booms finally subsided. Silence prevailed. Then came the shouts of family members as they attempted to reunite. Everyone filed out of the shelter, but the stairwell became impassable with huge, blown-out gaps that extended down to the basement. Vivienne stepped outside and scanned the bombed-out structure.

She stood outside for hours. Nightfall came and she sobbed for her lost love whose shirt she still wore.

Throughout the following months, she asked everyone at the club if they knew Robert. It seemed their night together was the only night he visited the club. Her stomach was in knots for weeks, then she grew even more sick. She went to the doctor, and Vivienne was told about the gift from Robert, the gift of life.

———————

When the attack subsided, Robbie went back up to his flat. He planned to go down the fire escape to search for Vivienne if the exit was still intact. When he stepped inside his flat, he was relieved to see the place was barely touched. Vivienne's purse was still on his kitchen table. He picked up the satchel and a vial of white powder fell out. He picked up the container and his hands trembled. Robert was certain the contents would get him past his unbearable fear.

And he was right. For years, the substance made him forget the horrors of his best friends' guts spilling from their bodies. He no longer dreamt of brothers in arms being launched into the air like ragdolls. Robbie even forgot how badly he wanted to find Vivienne.

Now, they laid together and tried to remember what it was like to feel something, but they were too heavy to move from the darkness to go out and find the life they shared.

———————

Derek was released from Acclimation.

He left the TRN facility and, for the first time since leaving over a year ago, stepped foot into his hometown. He anticipated a rush of nostalgia. Or sadness. Or something.

Instead, he felt clear, light, nothingness. It was pleasant.

His Aunt Donna pulled up. Derek looked to see if her son, his cousin Theo, was in the backseat. To Derek's relief, he was absent.

"Mia's arriving in a few days," Donna stated as Derek slid into the front seat. "How are you doing?"

"Better than I've been for a long time."

Chapter VIII

Mia savored the last few moments of her time onstage with the Tuesdaze. Only weeks remained until she returned to Original Time. Who knew what would happen after that.

She locked in with EJ. Tiffany pushed the bass line to the front of the rhythm and propelled the song forward. Macy repeated the chorus' end and milked the encore for all it was worth. She was in a trance-like state as the crowd chanted along with her.

The Tuesdaze's wavering spine of melody kept time for the crowd's hymn-like repetition of Macy's final lyrics. Sweaty bits of Macy's hair stuck to her damp forehead. Her velvet voice was full of soul. Mia thought she had lost it. Macy prolonged the song and repeated the words until she herself was convinced of their meaning.

Backstage, Lars nodded with satisfaction. He felt a tap on his shoulder and turned to face the promoter who grinned ear to ear.

"Just wait," Lars said.

He watched Macy give the last bit of her energy to the crowd and finally she collapsed onto the stage. She lay there for what felt like minutes but was only seconds. Macy's recent addition of the physical dramatics to the end of the show was a crowd annihilator, but Lars fought to suppress the panic that she may not get up. His anticipation broke as she pushed herself onto her feet. Sweat lingered where she laid.

The rest of the Tuesdaze joined Macy for a final bow and the audience erupted. What had begun as a wobbly return on Mia's part had evolved into one of their best shows to date. Lars and the promoter met eyes.

The promoter nodded, "Yup. Just as good as you said they were." He rested a hand on Lars' shoulder. "The guitarist looks like a girl I knew when I was young. They're hot. Full of life. I'd heard you were good, kid, but wow you've got an eye. And they're not even drinking age yet!" He chuckled.

"Well, one is, the guy EJ," Lars responded.

The promoter sighed, "Shame it's not all ladies. I can just picture a little tart like the other three seated at the drums, mmm," he shivered.

Lars shrugged. He did his best impression of modesty. An air of humbleness was one of the many desirable characteristics he learned to portray since working the city. The fast-paced environment was better for him, it kept him busy. He'd struck the perfect balance between remaining in the action but not losing himself in it, not spiraling down into the night life and emerging as the monster he knew he could be.

Since the holidays, Lars chipped away at his own guilt, but it sometimes resurfaced, especially when he was around Mia, the person he'd damaged most besides himself. Lars had also grown increasingly concerned with Macy. Despite his own benefit from her medically induced lack of inhibitions, her tightrope walk kept him on edge.

Macy let the scene become a part of her identity before Lars re-entered the Tuesdaze's circle, but he couldn't help but feel a twinge of responsibility for her instability. He knew the rest of the band was skeptical of his late-night visits to her place and the spells of time they spent together, but they had it wrong. He wasn't there to take advantage of Macy; he was there to ensure her safety. If he couldn't convince her to kick the pills, he at least wanted to monitor her benders and be there to bring her to the hospital if needed.

Lars knew he should take greater action, perhaps suggest the Tuesdaze set up an intervention, but when he saw the way her medication allowed her to open up and pour her heart across the stage, he couldn't keep the fuel from her. It was his greatest conflict, but he bandaged the emotion with excuses.

'It's got to be her choice,' he told himself. 'I'm still on thin ice; if I try and tell her what to do, she'll cut me out. They're making a name for themselves, and soon they won't need me.'

So, Lars resorted to keeping the rest of the Tuesdaze off Macy's back. He knew from his inherited struggle with addiction that unsuccessful interventions could break up families, and, in this case, break up an up-and-coming band.

The promoter lifted his brow as the Tuesdaze walked offstage and he saw the look in Macy's eyes. Lars handed out their waters and removed Macy's cap before handing the bottle to her. By the time Lars studied the promoter's expression and looked back to the Tuesdaze, Macy had finished her water. She hung her lanky arm around Mia's neck.

Mia smiled, relieved and exhausted.

"We pulled it together," Mia stated. "Glad you decided to give me another shot."

With nothing to do but wait for June to arrive, Mia practiced non stop while the Tuesdaze were in class. She was better than ever. The distraction was welcome as major life decisions loomed on the horizon.

Macy, on the other hand, let her talent slip. She struggled to achieve consistency at their practices with her constant limbo of ramping up, then coming down. The group saw her growing reliance on the pills that had once been prescribed with the intent to regulate her mood. The substance began as a welcome moderator, but she struggled to figure out the correct dosage.

Macy's highs were atmospheric and contagious, but her lows were unbearable. Macy saw the band getting frustrated with her, so she began to doctor up her own concoctions with some success and some failure. Tiffany and Lars were the only ones able to temper her emotions, Tiffany with her sobering crackdowns and Lars with his personal understanding of addiction's roller coaster.

Daily life was a challenge for Macy. She teetered on the edge of failing college, but her natural charm kept the professors offering extensions and extra work to prove her intellect.

Mia had her suspicions of the exceptions given to Macy by the male teachers, but she was too busy stewing over her future to tangle herself in Macy's web.

Despite the Tuesdaze personal chaos, the stage offered focus to their noisy lives.

That night, when they stumbled to the dressing room, nothing outside the venue mattered. Lars joined them. He added to the post-performance hype by sharing the enthusiasm of both the owner and the promoter.

"I'll give it one more performance before you're their house-band!"

"Mia, do you *have* to go back next month? I mean, what is there to do?" Tiffany asked.

Mia often asked herself the same question. "I don't know, I guess I have to be there to sign King's over."

"Well, get used to signing your name! You drove the crowd crazy," EJ said.

"You think they'd want *my* autograph with that rocky start?" Mia asked and dwelled on her mis-timed opening solo.

"It wasn't so bad," EJ said.

The retreat of the stage quickly faded, and Mia's pending departure flooded into her mind. She plummeted from her high. As the band celebrated, she remained quiet.

"C'mon Mia, you'll always have a place here, even after the solo, even after the other night," EJ looked around for Macy who lounged in a blow-up chair in the corner of the room, "if anything, they'll want to replace me with a beautiful woman," he joked.

Lars overheard EJ and chuckled.

EJ shook his head. "It's true, isn't it?"

"Not entirely, but it helps that you're behind the drums and the three knockouts are up front," Lars stated.

The comment made Mia cringe.

Macy went to the dressing room's corner sink and splashed water on her face. After that, she staggered her way to a couch and laid down. She placed a towel over her eyes, a signal not to be disturbed. Lars spewed more accolades, then left the room.

Earlier that evening, Tiffany and Mia's instruments and equipment were placed in the dressing room by the stage crew, and, to their relief, EJ had been invited to use the house drum kit which left little packing up to do. Tiffany and Mia began to lug their various cords and cases to the back door where Jaq's van awaited.

Right after they finished loading the vehicle, thunder cracked in the distance. It was late spring, just before Memorial Day. The barometric pressure shifted, and the Tuesdaze grew concerned about their drive into the storm.

Jaq rolled down his front window.

"Let's go! I want to get out of the city before it downpours. The radio said the system is building," Jaq said.

"We just need to go get Macy," Tiffany yelled through the increasing rain.

Mia, Tiffany, and EJ descended the stairs to the dressing room. Macy hadn't moved a muscle.

"Mia, help me with her arms, Tiff, you get her legs," EJ instructed.

Macy roused, "I've got it," she slurred and batted them away.

"We've got to hurry, Macy," EJ said gently, "there's bad weather."

"Alright, I'm up," she replied and heaved herself from the couch.

Just as the headliners opened, the Tuesdaze hurried out to the van. On the way out, Mia caught a glimpse at the promoter with whom Lars had been chatting. Mia only saw him briefly before hitting the stage, but now, she held back a gasp when she saw his full face.

Reg from Marseille.

He was older, but Mia knew it was him. She contemplated how Reg's life as a musician had led him to the United States. Mia was pulled along by Tiffany but found herself wondering if he could still sing songs which made her heart hurt or if his days as a musician were over. She was filled with sadness that his life put him behind the curtain. She forced herself to move on and piled into the van.

They pulled out of the parking lot and splats of water fell onto Jaq's windshield. Mia's heart ached for the days when they stayed to watch the main show. Mia looked in the backseat and Macy was asleep between two guitar cases reminding Mia how much things had changed.

Jaq slowed down. He struggled to navigate the Saturday night traffic in the heavy rain. He turned the radio off and merged onto the interstate. Thunder boomed, causing Macy to jump awake. She shook her head.

"Sorry, I was out cold," Macy apologized and sat up. "That show took it out of me."

Mia heard Macy fumble in her purse for something to pep her up. Just as Mia was about to question the need for more substances, the downpour unleashed. The windshield wipers were on high. Mia had no idea how Jaq could see anything. Ahead of them, cars started to pull off. They approached an underpass and Jaq slowed to a crawl.

"Should we wait it out?" he asked.

The Tuesdaze nodded in agreement.

They sat there in silence. Mia heard Macy zip her purse closed. She wondered if she'd made a selection or decided against dosing with the delay in their trip.

Jaq turned on the radio. A song, frequently covered by the Tuesdaze, was on and Macy started to sing from the backseat. The rest of the group joined, and their spirits began to lift. The thunder cracked again, closer this time.

"Ooh," Macy said and squeezed Mia's shoulder.

Lightning flashed and Tiffany attempted to read the sky. She was frightened of storms. Tiffany's eyes were wide as she searched for signs of a funnel cloud.

"Relax, Tiff," Macy said. "Under an overpass is the best place you can be during a tornado. I heard it on Storm Chasers."

"I think that's a myth," Tiffany replied, her voice wavering.

Mia watched five minutes pass on the clock. The rain didn't let up at all. Mia's eyes grew heavy as she watched the minutes go by. The radio offered no reprieve with one bad song after another. Macy climbed over the seat to join Mia and Tiffany.

"What do you say we have some fun while we're stuck here?" Macy asked.

"Did you bring a game of Mad Libs?" Jaq referred to his favorite road game.

EJ chuckled, "We can't even play the license plate game with no new cars passing us."

"I've got something else in mind," Macy stated. "Come on."

Macy climbed around Mia and opened the van's sliding door. She took Mia's hand.

"Let's play."

"No," Mia resisted. "We'll be soaked!"

Macy hopped outside and gripped Mia's hand. The rain was coming down sideways. Macy's blonde hair was instantly drenched. Her clothing hung on her narrow frame.

Jaq joined in on the scheme and gently pushed Mia outside to join Macy.

EJ laughed and shrugged his shoulders. He swung open the passenger door and came outside to join Macy in her tug of war. They pried Mia outside the vehicle, and she shrieked. She expected the rain to chill her to the bone. Instead, the air was warm. A stream of rainwater flowed across the tops of Mia's feet, and she wiggled her toes.

"Tiff, we're waiting on you!" Macy shouted.

Then, as if someone turned off a faucet, the drops lightened to a sprinkle. A rumble of thunder rolled in the distance.

"Alright, the fun's over," Tiffany said.

Jaq extended his palms toward the sky.

"I guess we can get on the road again. Tiffany," he pointed at her, "you were spared this time, but next rain, look out," Jaq teased.

They got back on the road and, while flipping through the channels, EJ hit a country music station. The five of them belted the cheesy words. In the midst of the song, EJ leaned back to speak into Mia's ear.

"How come it's always raining when we're together?" he asked. "The night you returned, the day at our place, now, tonight."

A hair sprung forward onto EJ's forehead. Mia smoothed it back.

"You have my next sunny day," she answered and remembered how his lips felt against hers.

———

"How was the show? Aren't you glad we can talk on this thing now?"

Mia clipped the block onto her UpgrAid as she spoke with Vaughn through the device. She was still puzzled how it was possible to speak with him with the sound-diffusing block attached, but the impossibility of the technology was a testament to the brilliance of Josh's mind.

"The show was great," Mia said. "Lars thinks we're contenders for the venue's house band. If he's right, I'll be going to the city a lot this summer before I go back to Original Time. It… complicates things, though it is different than I remember from before. Hanging out with Macy is like being on a rollercoaster."

"Well, remember, you have options. Why not leave, if things are so tense?" Vaughn asked. "Come with me. You've committed to so many things, Mia. Drifting, possibly mending with Rae," he paused, "you've kept me on the line for a long time now. Your heart is in too many places at once. EJ, Marseille, The Tuesdaze; I love your connection with the people and events of the past, but at some point, you've got to stick with something. Or at least give me the chance to show you how good this life can be when you can go *anywhere*."

"And how am I to break away again? Once I shut this door, I don't know that I'll be able to open it again."

"You've got just weeks until you'll have to go back to King's. Take a look at the last few months. Has trying to change Lars worked? Have you made progress in improving *anything* social in the nineties?"

"I-I haven't had a chance. It takes time."

"I overheard Dr. Chandra talking about mending this week. People get too comfortable around me. It makes it hard to pretend I know nothing when the execs ask if I've heard of Travelers trying to fix the past. Anyway, Dr. Chandra seemed frustrated. I don't know if it's going to happen, Mia. I don't know if they're going to figure out how to access the mended planes."

Mia sighed, "Let's say I leave this all behind. What's in it for me? You say I haven't been committed. The only thing you've committed to is your job. You could have stayed in OT for that."

Vaughn was silent. Mia realized the harshness of her words.

"Sorry," she said. "Give me time to think."

They ended the call and almost immediately after, Mia received a call from Rae.

"I overheard Vaughn talking to a tech at TRN. He was coordinating a Shell for your return. What's going on?"

"They're selling King's Records, so I'll be back in June."

"Oh phew," Rae paused, "not phew that they're selling King's. I'm sorry to hear that. Phew that you're not picking up and leaving with Vaughn. Vaughn has put on a strong front with you. He's kind of a naughty boy around here. I mean, all those recruits didn't come out of thin air. And they're all attractive. And they all adore Vaughn."

Things started to make sense. Waking up from Acclimation after Marseille to the sound of laughter. The quick resolve of monitoring shortages. The only thing Mia didn't understand is why Vaughn wanted her to commit to him when he wasn't committed to anyone.

———————

Rather than calling Vaughn and confronting him that night, Mia decided to lean into the next few weeks of early summer '98. She awoke the next day, the first day of Memorial Day weekend, and Mia could see that her apartment pool was crowded. Mia took a leap of faith and called the rest of the Tuesdaze to come over.

Mia grabbed a boom box radio and her towel and went down to the pool. The day was divine. Even the breeze no longer held spring's zip of coolness. Macy and Tiffany arrived, and the three girls located four chairs and claimed them with their pool supplies.

Mia laid a large, color-blocked towel across her chair and got comfortable. She looked over to Macy and they smiled at each other, relieved to relax. Just as Mia began to doze off, she heard the gate to the pool rattle.

"What's the passcode?" EJ shouted.

"1998!"

"Security's tight around here," he chuckled.

Tiffany unloaded chips, suntan oil, and a stack of new magazines from her pool bag. A girl with red sunglasses smiled back at Mia from the May issue.

'*Ten ways to heat up your summer,*' was printed on the cover. Tiffany noticed Mia's interest.

"Looking for a hot summer, I see?" She teased, "It's good stuff," she handed the magazine to Mia.

EJ heard the conversation and held back a grin.

He thought back to the night they played in the rain and the sunny day which Mia had promised him. EJ still got shivers when he remembered their kiss and hoped the summer would lead to more after Mia returned from Maine.

The pool further busied until every chair was full. In the corner, by the gate, a group of upperclassmen set up camp. They plopped a massive water cooler on top of a table. Macy saw that the fluid streaming from the tap wasn't clear.

A scruffy man from the table began to circulate the pool and invited people to his cooler. Finally, he made his way to the Tuesdaze.

"We've got some jungle juice over there if you guys want some," he said. "Come on over, get some of the fruit too," he grinned, "it's vodka soaked."

The Tuesdaze took him up on his offer and, within an hour, they seemed to have transported back to before Mia left. Macy turned up Mia's radio and elevated the poolside energy. EJ grew more charismatic and flirtatious, and after learning about Vaughn's suspicious past, Mia leaned into EJ's light, vivacious personality.

"Okay, let's play never have I ever," he proposed.

The Tuesdaze agreed. Tiffany kicked off the game.

"Never have I ever," she paused, "had sex in public."

Macy knocked back her cup and Mia hesitated.

"Does it count if I was in a separate room from everyone, but the door was open?"

"Could anyone hear?" EJ asked.

Mia drank in response to his question.

"Ohhhh!" the Tuesdaze reacted in unison.

They continued with their game until clouds covered the sun. As the rest of the group continued talking, EJ leaned over to Mia.

"I thought you offered me a sunny day," he stated and pointed up at the sky.

Mia pursed her lips, "I'm sorry, must have cast a weak spell," she teased.

Though the sky became overcast, the temperature remained warm, and the cooler of spiked juice didn't seem to have a bottom.

Mia's thoughts drifted, and she wondered if Vaughn had tried to contact her. She pondered whether Rae knew for certain that Vaughn used his charisma to recruit or if she was just trying to get Mia to commit to mending. Mia wished for the time when she didn't have a device to connect her with the future. Her judgment skills waned with the emptying of her plastic cup, and she couldn't help but steal away for a glance at her UpgrAid.

"I'm going up to the apartment quick," Mia said. "Rae left some beer in the fridge. I'll bring it down."

EJ stood, "I'll come with and give you a hand."

Though the rest of the Tuesdaze shot Mia and EJ a skeptical look, their attention was stolen when one of the concocters of the juice cannonballed into the pool. EJ and Mia looked at one another and Mia forgot about her intention to look at the UpgrAid. They used the moment to sneak away.

Mia unlocked the door to her apartment building. She and EJ burst through the entrance and ran up the carpeted stairway with wet feet. As soon as Mia slid her key into the door, she felt the heat of the possibilities of her decision to be alone with EJ.

No Jaq, no Tiffany, no Macy, no Lars.

Mia turned the key and stepped onto her entryway mat. She dried off her feet and ran to the bathroom. After she emptied her neglected bladder, she patted her face with water and looked into the mirror.

She knew EJ waited in the living room. He was always there, waiting, and Mia knew, like Vaughn, he wouldn't wait much longer. She knew why EJ came up with her. It was now or never. Vaughn explored his options. Why shouldn't she?

Mia stepped out of the bathroom, but EJ wasn't in sight. She rounded the corner to their living room and saw him looking out at the pool from the balcony. He heard Mia and turned to face her.

"You've got a great view," he stated.

She replied, "Yes I do," and looked him up and down.

His breath caught, and Mia heard it. Unable to help herself, she walked toward him until their bodies kissed. Mia pressed her wet bikini top against his bare chest, warm from the earlier rays of sun. She ran her fingers through his dense hair then finally, they kissed, and it was better than she remembered.

They started to make out and he reached beneath Mia's swimsuit top. She placed her hand on his and sculpted her breast with his hand. Eventually, EJ moved both hands down her waist and into her swimsuit bottoms.

Then, a knock came at the door. They froze and looked to the unit's entrance, hoping the person on the other side would go away. The handle of the unlocked door twisted, and Mia kicked herself for not dead bolting her door as the entrance opened.

Macy. Her mouth dropped open. She saw everything.

"I thought it was taking a little long to 'just be grabbing beers,'" Macy said.

EJ and Mia remained silent. His fingertips still rested on Mia's waistline. Macy shot him a look and he pulled his hand away. He crossed his arms over his chest, but it was too late.

Macy gave them another searing once-over, then whipped around and began her descent down the stairs toward the exit. Mia looked at EJ.

"Sorry," she said, "I've gotta go after her," then chased Macy down to the pool.

"Macy!" Mia whimpered.

Macy didn't acknowledge her. She continued her angered strut into the gates of the pool. The drama caught Tiffany's attention. Macy turned to face Mia.

"God, you're such a slut! And you pass judgment on me," Macy shook her head.

"You're just mad at yourself because you passed up what we could have been," Mia retorted.

Their fight attracted attention. All eyes were on them.

Macy inched closer to Mia until they almost touched. Macy spoke into her ear.

"That night last fall meant as little to me as EJ does to you," Macy snarled.

Her eyes bore into Mia.

Mia remained silent, unable to formulate an adequate comeback. Macy placed her hands on Mia's shoulders and pushed Mia into the pool.

Mia's breath was taken away by the cold, early summer water. She popped back up to the surface and gasped. She wiped her eyes and looked around but wasn't ready to face what waited outside the water. Instead, Mia exhaled until she reached the bottom of the pool.

She opened her eyes. The chlorine burned, but she enjoyed the blue, blurry peace. Her shortcomings, her indecision, her impulsiveness, didn't follow her beneath the water's gentle surface. She wished she could stay there, but she knew that, if she wanted to continue with her life, she had to come up at some point.

Mia kicked off the bottom and rose back to the surface. The time beneath had served as a call to action, and she knew what her big move must be. Mia knew once she left, she had to join Vaughn. She complicated the era which was supposed to be a refuge. She failed to mend anything. Mia emerged to face her fate.

She felt her hair part with the water's weight as she breathed in the air. Macy stood above her on the pool's edge. She extended her hand toward Mia. Mia let out a sigh of relief. It seemed she and Macy were making a truce.

"Psych!" Macy shouted and pulled her hand back to flip Mia off.

"Macy, you don't have to be so mean!" EJ shouted. "Here, Mia, I've got you," EJ said and grabbed Mia's forearm. He dragged her out of the pool. Mia sat on the side and a light breeze caused her to shiver. EJ went to get a towel from his chair, but Macy intercepted him.

"I'm calling Lars. Take your shit," Macy said and threw a wet towel at EJ.

After Macy stomped off, Tiffany handed a new, dry towel to EJ. EJ went to wrap up Mia, but before he could get back to where she sat, Mia ran upstairs to her apartment. She started a hot shower. The water drowned out the sound of EJ knocking at the door.

"She goes all in on everything she does," Vaughn said to Rae through the UpgrAid, "but she *does* too much."

Rae shook her head.

"I don't think it's wrong to live that way, it just…complicates things," Vaughn continued.

"Complicates things for you or for her? I don't know why you're talking to me about this. This is supposed to be a call to evaluate how my trainees are turning out."

"I needed to get your take on this because you *know* Mia. You're more than a trainer to her, you're her friend. She's created these relationships and become a cornerstone of the group," Vaughn said. "Sometimes I wonder if she should have waited to Travel. I remember how I was at her age, blending into any group, looking for my people…" he trailed off.

"Hey, don't project your issues onto her," Rae warned, "this isn't about you. She wants to try and make the future better. And you're trying to stop her. To keep her to yourself. Because she's the only person who has made you *feel* something in months."

Vaughn didn't respond.

"If she leaves with you, it's not going to be 'happily ever after.' Make sure you're serious about this. Don't pretend that you have a clean past. You can't go flitting around, finding girls, and sleeping them into TRN. This is going to be taxing on Mia. She's gonna need a hard cut-off to get out of the nineties," Rae said. "Nothing is set in stone. Now, I've got to go. I'm trying to *do* something with Time Travel."

———————

Vaughn's UpgrAid buzzed. He smiled as he saw Mia's name pop onto the screen.

"Hey," he answered.

"I'm ready to go with you. After Derek and my trip to OT, that is," Mia said. "I just don't know how to get out of this."

"Mia," he began, "you weaved yourself into something. If you go, the Tuesdaze won't stop looking for you for a long time. I didn't realize how persistent they were until Rae told me about it when you were gone to deal with your parents' loss."

"I know she kept them at bay then, but now they might be ready for me to go."

Vaughn hesitated, but Rae had given him her blessing to spill everything if Mia asked.

"They fought to be there for you," Vaughn informed her. "And that's a rare thing. They were so upset when you got back because they couldn't give you the love they had to offer. Your absence changed their entire dynamic, I mean look at Macy, she got hooked on drugs. EJ sent you roses for Valentine's Day. Tiffany dropped off several mix tapes. They *won't* lose you again. When I asked you to come with me, I didn't say it would be easy," Vaughn said. "I don't want to feel guilty if you leave with me and regret it."

"So, what do I do?" Mia asked. "Just stay here forever? Some of the best nights of my life are followed by the worst," she paused as reality set in. "But that's just life, isn't it?"

"It depends on the life you want," Vaughn speculated. "This is why I've preached disconnection to you. Not because I want your life to be devoid of meaning, but because if you genuinely want to see more times, you can't get caught up in these things. It's not good for you and it's not good for the natives of the era."

"I know," Mia admitted.

"I don't want to be the one to tell you this, I wish it were your parents or Derek, but you've got to stick with something, Mia. You've got to move, or you've got to stay. If you stay in this plane much longer, I don't know if you'll be able to get out. And there's no guarantee that things will change for the better."

Mia remembered her moment at the bottom of the pool. She wanted to stay there, to avoid everything above the water.

"It's like I returned just for the ending," Mia replied. "I have to end it, don't I?"

"The sooner, the better. I can tell you from experience; cut-offs don't get easier with the passing of time."

Chapter IX

"Of course, this is the weekend shit had to go down. And flights are conveniently cheap for her to leave. The first time ever we're invited to play dock-opening weekend at the Lakehouse," Macy said, "and she's out. We should have never gotten used to practicing with her again."

"She hasn't *officially* backed out yet. We still don't know whether she's leaving Friday or Saturday," EJ stated.

"I still don't know why you told her about the gig."

"What are we supposed to do, kick her out? After everything she's been through?" EJ responded. "Look, we were both drunk. We can move past this. You two did."

Mia eavesdropped from outside the Jaquez' entrance. Though she was set to leave the morning after the patio show, and she hadn't spoken to Macy in days, her first instinct was to rush inside. To tell the band she wanted to play. However, Vaughn strongly discouraged Mia from caving into her desire to pursue the Tuesdaze any more than she already had.

"I want one last show with them," Mia told Vaughn when EJ broke the news of their last-minute invitation to play Birchmont's hottest event, the Lakehouse Summer Kick-Off.

"Playing will wrap you up tighter, Mia," Vaughn warned. "You *just* decided on seeing what else is out there. If you back out, that's it. For us, at least."

"You're right. It's just so hard to turn down something that was once everything I wanted."

Though Vaughn said a phone call to sever ties with the Tuesdaze would suffice, Mia went to EJ's anyway but stopped short from going inside. She overheard her name and couldn't resist knowing what the Tuesdaze thought of her strange comings and goings. Mia was also curious how irrevocably she ruffled feathers with her and EJ's make out after the pool.

"I know this isn't my decision to make," Mia heard Lars' voice, "but you guys *evolved* without her. Your newer stuff makes people want to dance. The sound is fresh. It's what young, cool people are listening to; not what their parents listen to on vinyl."

"But her solos and her guitar skill," Tiffany contradicted, "she's solid. And, God, it's *Mia*. She's our friend."

Silence. Mia worried they heard her outside. She remained still. Just when she was ready to knock on the kitchen door as though she just arrived, Lars continued.

"You've got to think of the Tuesdaze future, hell, you've gotta think about the future of *music*. Her rock-n-roll purism is outdated. Macy," the floorboards creaked as Lars paced, "you're the front woman, not Mia. What do *you* want to play? What gets *you* going? Everyone's going to feed off that."

From Mia's outdoor hiding spot, she felt the tension emanate from inside.

"It's time you guys get clear about what you want out of this. If you want to cover classics at parents' weekend and do house parties where you get paid in beer, be my guest. But if you want to play in the city, if you want to be on the radio and make popular music, you can't limit yourself. Mia's going to have to lean into that. You can't let her hold you back."

"We're getting ahead of ourselves," EJ said. "Let's just get through the Lakehouse show and see how it goes without her."

"Alright, but in the meantime, daydream a little. Summer's full of opportunity. Organizers are looking," Lars stated, "and you guys are *hot*. You're just what they're seeking."

Mia heard Lars' footsteps coming toward the door. She panicked and attempted to hide around the corner of the house, but she tripped, clumsy from her rush to the Jaquez' house. Lars popped his head outside and saw Mia.

"Well, hello."

"Hi, I just got here. I-I thought I should come over after EJ called about the show," she stammered, "before I leave."

"Come on in," Lars welcomed.

Mia saw through his kind façade. She stepped inside and pulled out a chair at the dining room table where the group was seated.

"Mia, before you got here, we were talking about where we want to take the Tuesdaze," Macy said. "I can't speak for everyone, but *this* is what I want to do. I don't want to go to class or end up working at a desk. I want to perform."

Tiffany and EJ remained quiet.

Mia could imagine all their lives branching away from performing, but not Macy's; her office had to be the stage.

"We know what we want, and we're not sure you can be a part of it."

Tiffany interjected, "We're *not sure*. We just don't want to force you to be something you don't want to be. I guess we've moved in another direction, into a style you're not fond of, and you have to be true to yourself."

Mia didn't put up a fight. She spared herself the awkwardness and walked toward the front door. Nothing she might say would change their minds. Nothing would make things how they were before 1998. And she was leaving anyway. Mia stepped outside and began to walk back to her apartment.

The weather was perfect, and Mia hoped the walk would clear her head. She made it two blocks when she heard a car pull up behind her. The Cav.

"Let me give you a lift," Macy said.

Emotions overcame Mia. Something about Macy's voice always cracked the plans Mia thought she had. Her objective mindset waned, and she accepted Macy's ride.

Mia opened the passenger door. Mia sensed that Macy was waiting for her to cave first. They drove in silence for a few more blocks, then Mia came clean.

"Macy, I heard you guys talking before I came inside, about getting on the same page with the future of the Tuesdaze," Mia struggled to utter the next words, "and I think you were right. I'm not the right guitarist anymore."

Macy shook her head. "I've sensed that from the moment you got back, the night you saw our involvement with Lars. Why can't you just let the past die? He was drinking then, he's changed. You always act like you're so open, but you're not if you can't let it go."

"Let it go? Just move on from his trying to *rape* me? You were so compassionate when we met. So supportive."

"Ha! I should say the same."

"I guess we've both changed," Mia said.

"Know what? Don't bother showing up for practice when you get back," Macy said, her expression didn't waiver. "*I'll* cover your part for the patio opening. To be honest, your solos were a bit much. Our crowd isn't into that. They just want to see a good show."

Mia nodded. Though she anticipated the pain of the moment, the finality stung.

"Rae told me she's staying in Birchmont for another year. I'll move in with her. I figured by the end of the summer, you could find a new place or someone to take over my half of rent," Mia severed the final cord.

"Should be enough time to find someone new as long as you don't leave me hanging for rent this summer," Macy said. "Hell, maybe I'll sublet the place. Kick the whole college thing and move to the city."

"I'll send a check for rent through August." Mia stated. She fished her and Macy's shared apartment key from her pocket. "Here," she said and handed it to Macy.

Macy took the key. "Sounds like you've got it all figured out. I don't know why you didn't give me this earlier; why you acted like things might go back to how they were."

Mia remained silent as they pulled up to her apartment. Macy put the car in park.

"Did you just offer to drive me here to kick me out?"

"I don't know, I guess I needed closure. I figured you did too. We had a pretty good run. I didn't expect things to go the way they did, but here we are."

Mia searched for the right words, but there was no way to explain the plethora of decisions she faced with all of time laid out before her. She opened the door and stepped outside.

Macy rolled down her window. Mia clung to a shred of hope; an imagined scenario where Macy said the Tuesdaze were wrong to cut her off and begged her to play one last show. Instead, Macy lit a cigarette.

"See you around," Macy said and drove away.

————

Derek and Mia walked up the familiar stairs, the same ones they ran up as kids. They half expected Les to be on the other side of the door, tidying and talking music with customers. But King's was silent. They trailed their Aunt Donna and her son, Theo, who had maintained King's since the Hayes' departure.

Mia's Acclimation was rapid after several Travels back and forth, but Derek's was much more time consuming. He got back a week before Mia to allow for the extra Acclimation time. Vaughn was there, waiting for them at the hub when they got back to Original

Time. Derek appreciated the supportive gesture, but had a feeling there was more going on between Vaughn and Mia than either of them admitted.

They finally reached King's entrance and swung the door open. She and Derek looked around. King's wasn't nearly as empty as they expected. Their favorite posters still hung on the walls. Though most of the record boxes were gone, the interior wall was still lined with crates of vinyl. Donna pulled Theo aside.

"Let's give Derek and Mia some space," Donna said to her son. She turned to face Mia and Derek. "Kids, we've still got some boxes in the listening room for you to sort through. If you want to keep anything, we can store it at our house," Donna hesitated, "or your parent's place."

Mia and Derek exchanged a look.

Derek began, "We spoke at the hub and, since the house is just sitting there, vacant, does anyone in the family want to rent Mom and Dad's?"

Donna sighed, "We've been hesitant to ask what you wanted to do with the place, given the shock of all of this, but have wondered if Theo could live there for a while."

"I understand if not," Theo said. "I know it was your home for a long time, it's just I'm starting at the community college here in town soon and—"

Donna interrupted.

"He's eighteen now, he doesn't want to live with us anymore," she laughed.

Mia joined in the laughter but was struck by the way Donna's eyes crinkled in the same pattern Ellie's did when she laughed. The sensation caught her off-guard and she took a deep breath which her brother noticed. Mia regrouped and got down to business.

"Francis can get a lease agreement together," Mia stated.

Derek and Mia meandered to the listening room. Inside was a large, rubber storage container with their names on it.

"That's for you to sift through," Donna said. "Les' personal record collection is in a storage unit, but we can talk about what you want to do with that later. Theo, shall we go to get the keys to the unit?" their aunt suggested.

Her privacy offering was appreciated by the siblings.

"We'll be back in a couple of hours. Call if you're done looking through things sooner and we'll pick you up," Donna waved goodbye and walked down the stairs.

"Will do," Derek said as he turned his Aid on phone mode.

The siblings pried the lid from the storage container. Inside were limited editions of each of their favorite albums. Mia ran her fingers across the plastic sleeves.

"Before I forget…" Derek said and reached into his pocket. He wrapped his fingers around his sister's charm bracelet and held it out for her to see.

"I thought it was gone forever!" Mia exclaimed and reached for the keepsake. "How did you find it?"

"You won't believe it, but I ran into Reg at a party," Derek stated.

"You went back to Marseille?"

Derek clarified, "No, he was at one of Renee's A-list parties."

"Ah ha," Mia teased, "I knew you weren't over her. Thank you, Derek," she said as she clasped the bracelet onto her wrist. She chose not to mention running into Reg at the Tuesdaze gig in the city.

"There's one charm missing, that was Reg's stipulation for giving it back, keeping the star charm," Derek explained. "You really made an impression on him."

"We accidentally get too involved, don't we? Both of us."

Derek nodded, "I suppose. Though, maybe when I return to the sixties, things will be better. I feel different after this trip. The Psilopram has really made me want to stay objective. Not get too wrapped up in everyone else's problems, you know?"

"Trust me, I know. It was a challenge feeling this way when I got back to the nineties. They were used to the more emotional, naïve version of me."

"If someone called you naïve when you first went to '97, you would have flipped," Derek laughed.

"I would have, but now I see myself for who I was in the past. Reckless, impulsive, emotion-driven," Mia shrugged. "It's funny, Macy used to think I was too attached, too deep. After I came back, she thought I was too cold."

"Think you'll go back to the nineties after this?"

"Not anytime soon," Mia said. "The Tuesdaze are done with me." Mia considered explaining her original scheme to mend, but Derek didn't have a block on his device and Mia didn't know how aware TRN was of Rae's secret operation. Plus, mending didn't seem to be worth bringing up with the delay in the scheme's execution.

Mia sighed and spilled her updated plans. "I'm going with Vaughn for a while. He was granted leave and he invited me to Travel with him."

"Wait, what? Where are you going?"

Derek was interrupted by the sound of the entryway door opening downstairs.

"Donna's back soon," Mia remarked.

"I'm actually ready to go," Derek replied. "I say we keep everything at the house for now. Decide what we want to hang onto once we've got our wits about us."

"What do you mean, 'once we've got our wits about us?'"

"Once the Psilopram wears off a little. I know myself, and I am not reacting in the way I normally would to that box of nostalgia. I know the contents *should* make me feel a certain way, but they don't," Derek stated. "Theo won't mind if we keep these things at Mom and Dad's for now. We're the ones letting him stay there."

"I'm not so sure I want to commit to that."

Though Theo and Mia had grown up together—with Theo just a year younger than Mia—their relationship was hot and cold. He was a narcissist, and he knew how to get Mia to take the backseat at King's and the Court, even though her taste was better and her marketing ideas more effective than his. He spoke over Mia when she gave recommendations to customers and disregarded her ideas to promote the Court. Les saw through Theo's fabricated knowledge of music and business, but Les was gone, and Theo was left to run the show.

Mia imagined their prized possessions stuffed into a closet while Theo had friends over for a party. She imagined beer seeping into the side of the storage bin and ruining the album covers. Mia questioned whether allowing Theo to rent was a good idea, but the Hayes had no choice but to rent or sell.

Footsteps reached the top of the stairs. Mia and Derek looked at one another, puzzled; the steps sounded far too heavy to be Donna's.

"Theo?" Derek called.

An unfamiliar man walked inside.

"Ah!" he shouted and held his hand to his chest, startled by the Hayes' presence. "Sorry, I didn't know you'd still be here. Donna told me you were stopping by. Pleasure to meet King Les' grandchildren. I apologize for interrupting y'all's time here. I can come back later," he said in a friendly voice and ran his hands through his light, curly hair.

"It's all good. We're done looking through things," Derek said. "Who are you?"

"Joe Mason," the man introduced himself. "You just signed this place over to me."

His hand was warm, and his presence was comforting.

"Mia Hayes."

"Derek Hayes."

"Quite a place your family built here," Joe stated. "I mean to keep the building up. I'm so sorry for the loss. If you two wanted to stay here, you know, in this time I'd—"

"We don't," Mia assured. "What will it become? I noticed the boxes and posters were still up. Are those for us to take?" Mia paused. "We're not quite sure what to do with anything. We can't take many belongings to other eras."

"I'd buy the posters off you if you don't want 'em," Joe said. "I did get myself a few records. Bought 'em and the money's in your accounts. They're records Donna said neither of you would want. There are still other albums in a storage unit. Didn't want to roll up the posters if you weren't gonna hang onto them. I think they'd look great in the bar if you don't want to keep them for yourselves," Joe pulled out his wallet. "Again, I'll buy 'em from ya. Donna explained you two's situation. The past has got to be cheaper, but I'm sure a little extra cash wouldn't hurt."

"Did you say you're turning King's into a bar?"

"Yeah," he nodded, and an uncontained grin took over his face. "The first vinyl bar in the city. You two probably don't remember me, but I've been coming to shows at the Court since I moved here ten years ago. I love this place and I want it to stay the same, only I want to sell cocktails instead of records," Joe explained. "I hate to say it, but the business of sellin' music has too many peaks and dips. Everyone likes a good cocktail bar. Figured it'd be a good built-in stop before the shows. Especially with how cold the winters get up here, nice to stay put for the night."

Mia and Derek paused and absorbed Joe's plans. They exchanged a look of approval. No discussion was needed to address the answer that had fallen into their laps.

"Would you want to take on the Court too?" Derek offered.

"I imagine Donna and Theo are barely keeping it alive," Mia thought back to the stress of keeping the venue running, even with her parent's and grandparent's combined efforts. She knew it must be a source of stress for Donna's family. "We can ask Donna how it's going when she gets back. We're working with a great lawyer, perhaps she can get something going in the next few days."

"Woo-eee," Joe stated, "that's a lot to consider. I don't know about runnin' that whole show, but I got a friend that might be interested."

Derek's Aid buzzed. "Donna's outside. We'll talk soon. Does Donna have your number?"

"Yes sir, she does," Joe confirmed. "I'll lock up the place. You want help with that box?"

Without waiting for an answer, he heaved the packed container from the floor. Derek took the other side, and they followed Mia down the stairs. Though the late summer air was humid, Mia opened the entryway, and the fresh air was a relief after the stifling air upstairs.

"I see you met Mr. Mason," Donna said as she stepped out of her SUV to meet them.

"Great niece and nephew you've got there," Joe said, short of breath.

"Donna, we wanted to talk to you about some things," Mia began. She took a deep breath. "We want to discuss selling the venue. Joe said he might know someone who wants it, and we know how much work it must be. We worked the venue all through high school and watched Mom and Dad and Grandma and Grandpa; it's draining."

Before Donna could answer, Theo joined the conversation.

"It's not so bad," Theo stated, "we've been running it fine since you two have been off in yester-year," he said and nudged Mia.

"We'll consider," Donna said.

Mia had a sense there was more to the story but went with the narrative at play. She exchanged information with Joe and bid him farewell. Derek and Mia climbed in the backseat and sat in silence as Donna began to drive them back to their parents' empty house.

"I wouldn't mind running the venue," Theo said, breaking the quiet. "I don't know why you wouldn't want to keep it in the family. If you two aren't going to keep things up, someone might as well step up."

"Theo!" Donna scolded.

"What? It's true and you know it," he said from the passenger side. "I'm sick of everyone acting like Time Travel isn't fuckin' weird. That drug they give Travelers turns 'em into zombies. TRN is full of con artists. They're in the government's back pocket. Even Jon and Ellie thought so, that's why they didn't go back more often."

"*Enough*," Donna growled.

Derek watched Theo's reflection in the rear-view mirror. Theo's nostrils flared and his lips tightened.

"You know *they* killed them, right? It was an inside job; it was TRN making sure you two didn't have a reason to come back and stay."

Mia and Derek were at a loss for words.

"Stop it right now, Theo!" Donna shouted. "No one wants to hear your conspiracy theory bullshit. You're lucky they're letting you stay in their house, you ungrateful little ass!"

Donna rested her hand on Mia's leg and looked back at her niece. She stroked her arm, then looked back at Theo. Her glare was fiery.

"Get out," Donna commanded. "Out!"

"What the fuck?" Theo whined.

"You can walk home, and not to *their* home," Donna said and pointed outside the vehicle.

Bewildered, Theo gave them all one last cutting look, then opened the door and stepped outside. Donna drove off without looking back.

Though Theo's outburst was potent enough to make the Hayes consider TRN's motives, as they returned to their childhood home, their cousin's cruelty led them to crave their oasis from Original Time: another era.

"This isn't our home anymore," Derek stated. "Being here," Derek gazed around their parent's boxed up living room, "seeing how Mom and Dad lived, how much they saved for 'once things slow down,' it gives me this sense of urgency to *live*. But I don't know what that looks like for me."

"So, hop around. I can see if Vaughn minds if you tag along with us."

Derek furrowed his brow, "No. I'm not tagging along with my little sister and her lover."

"I think I know what living looks like for you, and it's with her. Go get her, Derek."

In the morning, they consulted Francis Platt.

"Sell it all."

"Are you ever nervous about getting caught by TRN for trying to mend? Especially for a future you might not get to live in," Mia asked Rae through the UpgrAid.

"Anyone who has made a difference in the world could have asked themselves the same question," Rae responded. "Not comparing myself to the great leaders of the past, but what's in it for anyone to try and better the world when they could die tomorrow?"

Mia nodded, "True."

She imagined stopping her parents' death, being there on Christmas Eve to deter them from crossing the street. Mia wondered what it would be like to spend that night in their hotel, bringing in the holiday in plush robes with a chilled bottle of champagne.

Though Mia wasn't entirely sold on any one religion, the thought of 'playing God' paused her desire to mend as did Rae's team's lack of progress in accessing the future of the new and improved planes.

"I've got to level with you, Mia," Rae said, "right now, the only way we can see our efforts through is to live out the sequence we're trying to change. Some of the scientists are calling this place we have yet to access 'IF.' The acronym stands for Ideal Future. We can theorize the destination; we just can't get there yet."

"That's got to be frustrating. Knowing TRN's tech team, it's right there, isn't it?"

Rae sighed, "I hope so. But waiting around would be a lot to ask of you. I understand why you want to see what's out there and drift with Vaughn, just," Rae hesitated, "don't get your heart set on being with him forever. He's... had a history around here."

"You alluded to that before. What happened, exactly?"

Rae sighed, "Never mind. I need to let you develop your own opinion about him. I know he's really into you or he wouldn't be taking you on this journey. I'll keep you updated through the Aid. Maybe we can meet along the way. Do you know where you two are going first?"

"Not a clue."

The glares came from every direction.

Rather than look them in the eye or try to explain himself, Vaughn kept his eyes down toward his feet as he walked to meet Mia, the girl who made him feel something. His IF awaited with her, not them, and he refused to derail the perfect trajectory of his plan. They could judge him. They could hate him. But, he knew, they were just disappointed they weren't the ones to end up with him.

They acted like they would "never hurt someone like that." Like they would never "trick someone into something so all-consuming." But the future of TRN had not been placed on their shoulders by Adrian Glass himself.

Vaughn broke their hearts, but Psilopram would eventually soften their sadness. Or they would meet someone in another era who made them forget about their fling with TRN's monitoring recruiter, Vaughn. In the meantime, Vaughn reveled in saving TRN from implosion.

Next, he would weave together Adrian's plan of eliminating any reason for Travelers to return to OT and Rae's prototype of improving the eras. But it was a waiting game, so he took some time off. He hoped the technology to mend would be there when he returned.

Vaughn passed Dr. Lowell's office. The door was open. He looked at his watch.

'Ten minutes until Mia gets here.'

Vaughn knocked on the wall beside Dr. Lowell's door.

"Look who's in."

"Vaughn," Dr. Lowell stood with outstretched arms. "Always great to see you. It feels as though our paths haven't crossed in years."

"Technically, they haven't," Vaughn smirked. "What have you been up to? Now that the crisis has been averted."

Dr. Lowell chuckled, "Dodged that bullet, didn't we, thanks to your recruiting skills," he lowered his voice. "Adrian's plan to reduce Traveler volume was making me sick. I almost left TRN."

Vaughn stepped further into Dr. Lowell's office and closed the door halfway. He gestured out to the hallway.

"The organization may have been saved, but they hate me."

"They'd hate you more if their family or friends were stuck in the past due to a shortage of monitors. They'd hate you more if Time Travel crumbled."

Vaughn shrugged, "I guess it doesn't matter now. They're hooked on Psilopram. And Original Time is no longer enough for them. And," Vaughn beamed, "Mia has agreed to accompany me on my leave."

"Oh Mia, one of the sweetest Travelers. She's not gotten mixed up with Rae's whole scheme, has she?"

Vaughn's eyes grew wide. He shut the door behind him.

"You *know* about mending?"

"I've heard whispers. Must be something if you're reacting this way."

'Shit,' Vaughn kicked himself for not playing dumb.

"I thought about bringing it up to you. As another safeguard to keep Travelers in the past in case we lose monitors again. Might give them purpose, you know? If enough of them can get together and create an ideal future, they might not come back at all."

"Ah ha. So, this is a solid mission, is it? I knew something was up. Dr. Chandra's been on edge lately. I slipped into her office a few weeks ago. Saw a paper sticking out of a pile detailing her plan to access future planes of past times. Times which her not-so-secret team hope to mend."

Vaughn remained silent.

"Relax, Vaughn. I've heard inklings of this whole scheme for months now and I haven't uttered a word to Glass. It's still so hypothetical. Honestly, I like the idea of mending. I just don't know where they're going to get the volunteers to try it. Or how they'll even access these 'Ideal Futures,'" Dr. Lowell chuckled. "Sounds like a big IF to me."

"Guess we'll see," Vaughn stated. "I best be going. Mia's going to meet me in the upstairs lounge soon."

"Hope to run into you again after your leave," Dr. Lowell stated. "Safe Travels and, again, thank you for taking the hit to save all our asses."

"Let's just hope, where I'm going with Mia, things don't catch up with me."

———————

Mia felt free. Untethered from Original Time; and from the death which permeated the life she once knew.

As she walked up to TRN, she was reminded of the first time she arrived, nearly a year ago. She still adored the building. Ann Marie, the woman with the red lips, greeted Mia, only this time Mia wasn't redirected to the South Wing with the other Travelers. She was meeting Vaughn in the North Wing.

Ann Marie led Mia to a North Wing lounge where Vaughn waited. Mia wondered if she was paranoid or if the staff was on edge. They looked at her as though she wasn't invited.

'I did get off the hook early from monitoring. I'd be mad too.'

Unlike the onlookers, Ann Marie remained as poised and kind as ever. They climbed a spiral staircase, and Vaughn came into view. He was seated on a white chaise lounge. He stood when he saw Mia and unleashed his knee-weakening grin.

Mia rushed over and stood on her tiptoes to kiss him. The smell of him was intoxicating. He wore an expensive aroma.

"I'll leave you two alone," Ann Marie smirked. "Have a good trip."

Throughout Mia's entire visit to Original Time, she had remained detached and objective. Now, her senses turned on, as they always did when Vaughn was around. They both scanned the lounge to make sure they were alone.

Mia moved in on Vaughn. She wrapped her legs around him as he lifted her feet off the ground. He was the perfect kisser. Mia's open skirt against his belt buckle offered a welcome shock.

"Is there somewhere more private we can go?"

Vaughn nodded.

Just then, Mia heard footsteps coming up the staircase. Vaughn's gaze snapped to a door in the corner of the lounge. He carried Mia across the room and turned the handle. They stole away into the dark storage room. The tension heightened with the possibility of getting caught.

Vaughn descended to the floor and Mia straddled him. Voices grew close to the door. Mia and Vaughn exchanged a look.

"Fuck," Vaughn whispered. The voices drew nearer.

Mia noticed an old, beat-up couch in the corner of the storage room. She helped Vaughn up from the floor and led him behind the furniture. Just in time. Someone swung the door open and flipped on the light.

"See?! See what happened?"

Mia placed the voice. Dr. Chandra.

"I don't know why I can't figure it out!"

Mia peeked around the sofa. Dr. Chandra was pointing at a warped Shell which leaned against a wall in the corner of the room.

"He barely made it. Still suffering from head injuries," her voice cracked.

"Anchal, they signed up for this," the other voice stated. "And so did you. He made it to the plane, right?"

"Yes, but in critical condition. This is all too similar to the days when we first sent the early Travelers back in time. I don't know if I can stomach it again."

Mia heard Dr. Chandra's sobs. She hung her head. Vaughn stroked her shoulder.

"Anchal, Anchal, remember, this is to offer an out from where we're at now. This isn't for nothing. If Travel remained a vacation, an oasis for the playboys, an outlet of detachment, what would it all be for?"

"I know," Dr. Chandra replied. "It's just like an endless puzzle. An equation with no solution."

"The idea itself is the solution. We *invest* people in the betterment of the world. We make OT better by reducing the people here. Rae alone has recruited twice as many menders as Vaughn has monitors; and you know how much of a rockstar Vaughn was. Mending gives the Travelers something to *do*. If anyone can access the mended times, if anyone can make this a reality, it's Anchal Chandra."

Anchal took a deep breath. She didn't know whether Adrian Glass was encouraging her for the mission itself or for his own clout, but the funding was helpful, and it was nice to be on the verge of something so positive.

"Psilopram tonight? It could help with a breakthrough. We're too close to give up now."

Dr. Chandra nodded. They turned off the light and closed the door behind them. The mood between Vaughn and Mia had fizzled.

"Are you still in?"

Chapter X

Derek finished his morning coffee with the windows open.

A cool breeze ruffled the curtains. The night before, a cold front had moved through and fed a colossal storm, stronger than many Derek had experienced in Original Time. Storms typically lulled him to sleep, but the thunder was so loud that Derek now debated if he should finish his coffee or try to go back to sleep. He was still exhausted from Acclimation and the previous night's storm sapped any energy that remained.

A knock came at his door. Through the peephole, he saw Angelene and let her inside.

"Morning."

Angelene looked as though she hadn't slept either. Her typically clear eyes were red and puffy.

"Hell of a storm last night, wasn't it?" Derek began. "Come in."

Angelene sat at his kitchen table.

"Here, I'll get you some coffee. Everything alright?" Derek asked.

"I don't need any coffee, thank you. I'm anxious enough as it is."

Derek sat down with her.

"Still no Grant?"

Angelene shook her head.

"I'm sick about it. He's been gone for weeks; no note, no phone call, and no one's seen him. I was hoping you'd say he was on your flight back to America."

"No such luck. Have you checked in with Germain or Tom?" Derek asked. "They're all over town. They'd be the ones to check with."

"I have checked in with them and they have not seen him either. Germain is growing more concerned as well since, you know, he was there that night last fall. If Grant brings himself down, Germain could have the cops at his own door next. You were all at the same party, hell, they could show up here."

"Angelene, what's going to happen will happen regardless of your stewing," Derek said, still objective from his recent dose of Psilopram. "Frankly, you kept Grant locked away for so long. Whether he's turned himself in or run away, at least he's free now."

"What was I supposed to do? Let him wander the streets at night only to come home with blood on his hands? Let him get behind on rent rather than just having him move in with me? In case you haven't looked around, things are *tumultuous*. This world will gobble Grant up. We nearly let him slip away once, and I can't let that happen again."

"I understand wanting to be there for him," Derek remembered Cooper, his lost brother, and softened. "Unfortunately, I've fallen on the side of doing too little to help, and I don't recommend it. But, if he's found, take it easy on him."

"You'll tell me if you hear anything?"

Derek nodded, "Of course."

Derek felt Angelene's gaze on the bags beneath his eyes. "Are you doing alright?"

"Fine," Derek stated, "It's been a long week."

"Whatever could be making you so tired when you're on the dole? Last I knew, you weren't at *En Blum* anymore. Still more of the same?"

"What do you mean?"

Angelene smirked.

"Well, you keep running back to Renee, quitting the boutique was a big move. I wondered if the severance lasted," Angelene pried.

Derek sighed; he wasn't in the mood for her jealous interrogation.

"Not that it's your business," Derek began, "but I've only seen her in passing since quitting."

"And in the papers no doubt," Angelene said. "Poor girl. To see them tear her apart like that… no one deserves that kind of ruthless criticism."

"She's dealt with a lot, that's for sure. One *needs* a little medication to tolerate that level of stardom."

"Perhaps. Though, it appears she's not done making waves. Have you seen the lingerie in the windows of *En Blum*?"

Derek chuckled as he remembered Carole, serving as a live mannequin, in the windows of *En Blum* last summer.

"Did you come here in search of Grant or to get dirt on Renee?" Derek teased.

Angelene's jaw tightened.

"Your loyalty to her astounds me."

"I was joking."

"I showed you my favorite club when you were alone over the holidays. I stood at your door, right after your parent's passing. I took care of your best friend, my brother—whom we both adore—and none of it meant anything to you. A kiss. That's all we've shared."

"I'm sorry. I had no idea you really wanted something," Derek responded.

"Just let me know if you see Grant," Angelene said and let herself out the front door.

Derek meandered back to the couch. His joints ached and he attempted to fall asleep. Though his body was still recovering from Acclimation, his mind was active. For once, he was less emotionally committed than his partner. Derek thought back to Angelene's invitation to dinner early in the year after Jon and Ellie's death. She wasn't open about her intentions to comfort Derek, but, looking back, it was clear; he disregarded her.

Rather than rush outside to catch up with Angelene and try to win her back, Derek remained in his flat and thought of Renee and Grant. He was concerned about them both. The image of Renee, frightened, on the sidewalk outside the strange basement venue, flashed through his mind.

He needed company.

Derek got dressed. On any other day, he would have shown up at Germain's flat, unannounced, something he still found funny was not considered rude in the era. Instead, Derek dialed Germain's number; he didn't want to put his body through the walk if his friend was out.

"Hello?"

"Hey man, what are you up to?"

"I should ask you the same," Germain stated. "I rang several times yesterday when you were expected to return. Was your flight delayed?"

"I-I was sick."

"Oh, must have caught something on the plane."

"Must have. But I'm better today."

"Good. You've *got* to come over. We have some things to talk about," Germain stated.

"I'll be right there."

————————

"You'll never believe what happened while you were ill," Germain began.

Derek couldn't help but grin along with Germain. He expected the urgent invitation to come over was about Grant or Renee, but it appeared the news was positive.

"I didn't think I'd see the day...I thought he'd fuck it up before they got to this point, but my father has asked Corrine to marry him!"

Derek embraced Germain. "That's amazing, man!"

"I had to tell you in person," Germain said. "That kind of news just can't be shared over the telephone. It's happening fast. That's why I was so bummed you didn't answer your phone yesterday. You and Mia are invited to celebrate in Marseille! If she can get away from her studies, that is. You two gave such joy to my father and Corrine. They couldn't wait to see the two of you again."

"Of course, I will join! Though I can't speak for Mia, she's got her own commitments."

Derek wondered where his sister had gone by now. A year ago, if she told Derek she was drifting through time with Vaughn, Derek would have insisted that she reconsider. However, after their cutoff from Original Time, Derek knew they both had to do what was best for themselves. He would notify Mia of the wedding later that evening.

"Who else is joining?" Derek asked.

"Tom of course, and possibly Angelene," Germain paused, "though I haven't told her yet. I'd also love for Renee to join, but I have struggled to reach her. William is keeping her on a short leash. And, of course, Grant. If we can find him, that is."

———————

"Derek, great to see you again. It's been so long since the two of you have made magic together."

Renee rolled her eyes at William.

"Give it a rest, William," Renee chuckled, "this photographer doesn't require much schmoozing. Derek, you're still in practice, right?"

"Right."

"Renee, I reviewed his portfolio before hiring him today. You should have seen some of his photos. His book was on your desk at *En Blum* all week. Have you seen Mr. Hayes' latest photos?"

"I haven't stopped by my boutique since the night of the lingerie launch. Too much press. Anyways, I trust that Derek hasn't lost his touch."

It was the first time he shot Renee in months. William had invited him to photograph Renee just days before the shoot when the original photographer vanished from the face of the earth.

"You're reliable," William had said. "Plus, Renee's better with you."

Derek took a few test shots. Unlike the first time he photographed Renee in the amber backroom of *En Blum,* she didn't demand time to prepare before she was behind the camera. Her short hair didn't need as much rigid placement. Posing was now second nature. She stood before him and wore only a flesh-colored bra and panties; Derek found her irresistible.

"I think we're ready."

Two men carried Renee's wardrobe onto the set. She was to wear a designer dress which was comprised of a patchwork of mirrors. Light glared from the tiny, reflective shapes. Derek's jaw dropped. The silver reflections set Renee's skin aglow, and her eyes lit up. Derek couldn't believe he got to be behind the lens and, all the sudden, he wasn't certain of his ability to capture the beauty.

"Renee, my dear, this kind of dress *is* the future," William beamed.

A hired stylist studied Renee. He rested his chin in his hand. "Hmmm. Do you think we should do away with the undergarments? Might add a bit more shock."

"I think Renee has been shocking enough, thank you."

"I think he's right, William. People will study the photo more to see what I'm wearing beneath the panels. To see if they can catch a glimpse without having to buy the dirty magazine," Renee laughed.

The eccentric dress designer emerged from the backroom.

"Ah, Renee Blum. It fits you just perfectly," the designer gloated.

"We were discussing undergarments."

"What about them?" The designer raised his eyebrows.

The two clothing stylists removed the dress from Renee. She got naked, and, before Derek could conjure the memory of the last time they were together, the stylists placed the dress back on her narrow frame. The designer nodded. He fussed with the panels to cover her nipples.

"See? No exposure," he stated.

William was satisfied.

They began the shoot. It was hard to believe that, in front of Derek's camera, was the same girl who was nearly broken just weeks before. She was meant to be draped in couture. She *was* the art, whether the tabloids believed it or not.

The shoot wrapped quickly, and the designer burst across the set to Renee. He clapped his hands.

"*Radiante!*"

"It was an honor to show off your work," Renee stated.

"Well, remember me for your next event. Perhaps you would walk for me as well."

"Anytime."

The two stylists returned and lifted the dress from Renee's body. The panels clanked as they carried the garment away. William rushed to cover Renee with a silk robe. Renee slipped into the fabric without haste and took her time knotting the sash. William then made his way toward Derek. He pulled a checkbook from his jacket and began to scribble.

"Wonderful, Derek. You'll get the other half when we go into print," William said and tore the check from the pad.

Derek accepted the slip of paper. "It was wonderful to be on set again. Especially with her."

"You poor bastard," William said. He patted Derek's shoulder and sauntered away.

Renee procured her wallet and street clothes from a table in the corner of the set. She stepped into a curtained-off room to change. Derek packed his equipment.

Renee emerged in a lavender mini-dress and, after thanking the crew, started toward the exit. Derek caught up to her and they stepped outside together. The day was perfect, and Derek was reminded of the previous summer.

"Another iconic shoot. Imagine that," Derek said. "What are you up to after this?"

Renee slowed her stride and Derek followed suit. She turned to face him.

"Going to Mr. K's house. Care to join? Perhaps you'll have a little more fun this time."

Derek's heart sank.

"S-sure. I was out of line last time. I'll work on letting go."

Renee shook her head. "Sweet Derek. You took care of me, and I am grateful. But you don't have to *keep* taking care of me. William loves that you watch over me. That way, he doesn't have to."

"I'm not trying to be overbearing, I just care about you. I saw you when you were..." Derek trailed off.

"It's as though that's all you see now. Someone you must take care of. Someone you must keep out of trouble," Renee rested her hand on Derek's face. "Derek, you're my compass. You point me in directions which are familiar to me. You give me a sense of where I'm at in the world. But, right now, with all this madness around, to imagine any sort of control in this time would be crazy! All we can do is get lost in it. There is no roadmap to navigate any of this. We must find our own route."

"I'm not trying to water you down, Renee. I'm not trying to make you normal. Someone as extraordinary as you could never be normal. I just want to be *with* you. Whatever that means."

A tear streaked down Renee's cheek.

"Earlier today, I spoke with the designer of that dress. He told me he's lived in other eras, that he's met Christ. Do you know what it's like to meet Christ, Derek? To take a walk through heaven?"

Derek shook his head no.

"I think I nearly went to heaven that night. Though, first, I had to ascend from hell. That's where I met my mother. She was there, Derek. She was there that night. In real life. I'm sure of it."

"Did the nurses have a record of her visit? Did she leave an address or any information?"

Renee nodded.

"I could hardly believe it, but she left an address. I walked by the place one day and it's an old, run-down building on the hill. There's no chance she's living there. Not after the life of luxury she deserted me for."

"You never know, Renee. I'll come with you."

"Where I'm going, you don't want to follow. You think you do, but it's just a dose of heaven followed by a lifetime of trying to get another fix. That's what my life is, now. Not the shiny dress or the limelight, it's all about finding my way back into the shell." Derek didn't know how to respond, so he kissed her cheek and breathed in the smell of her rose perfume. "In another lifetime."

———————

'Any chance you'd want to Travel back for a Marseille wedding?'

Derek knew his sister joining was a longshot. The emotion of lovesickness was fresh within him. Derek could only imagine the way Mia felt about Vaughn after agreeing to join him for an extended period of time.

'Yes. When?' Mia replied.

Derek: 'Two weeks. Shall I tell them Vaughn will be joining?'

Mia: 'No. I'll explain when I arrive. Can Rae join? She's with me now.'

———————

Theo watched with begrudging wonder the ways in which the world around him changed. The sporadic return of many Travelers led to a drastic shift in society. People like him were always skeptical of good things, but despite their best efforts to be unhappy, they were sucked into the world's recent positivity.

Countries which, before Travel, suffered great oppression and famine, seemed to be thriving thanks to the replenished resources.

Theo expected that the media was portraying some big lie. That things weren't getting better, but he grew more and more hopeful. Though he rarely spoke to his parents since falling out with his cousins Mia and Derek, he called his mom to get her take on the situation and, of course, to share his perception.

"I can't believe they expect us to buy into this," Theo said to Donna.

Donna replied, "It's like it all changed at once. It's wonderful, but I'm waiting for the other shoe to drop." *'Have we entered the Utopian phase?'* ticked across the news crawler as Donna spoke with her son.

"All these people are coming back with their 'woke' ideas," Theo continued, "but they're the ones who *left*. We can't let them take over *our* time. We're the ones who stayed, for Christ's sake. We supported this new infrastructure while they were off, gallivanting in the past."

Donna shrugged, "I guess we'll see what happens."

———————

Rae's device buzzed. It was Dr. Chandra. Rae turned on her block to answer the call.

"Did you do it?"

"Yes, my dear, we did!" Dr. Chandra exclaimed. "We sent someone to the future track of the time *you* mended!"

"How is it?" Rae asked.

She feared the answer. Though Rae hoped they were making progress, she dreaded the other problems that may have arisen. Her mother used to say, "If it's not one thing, it's another."

"It's better than we imagined," Dr. Chandra said.

"How soon can we open the mended eras to Travelers?"

"We're not sure yet," Dr. Chandra answered. "I've still got some convincing to do. Some people in Original Time worry that everyone will leave for another era and play out the improved tracks of the past. I don't know how it will play out."

"Either way, the other planes have been accessed?!"

"Yes. And we're considering only sending Travelers back to the improved tracks rather than the original endings. We just sent a Traveler back to the ideal future of his desired era and he arrived safely. We've found that everyone has an ideal future lying deep within them. Some in Original Time have lived out their lives in the way others expected them to and it's made them bitter. Angry. Jaded. Acclimators have noted some of the first things Travelers say out of the Shell; we've learned why they *really* came to their chosen era. We've notified Glass that Travelers are not responding well to TRN's guidelines of detachment."

"*Glass* knows about this?"

"He sure does. And he is onboard with mending. He's dropping the 'no fame' rule."

Rae cheered.

"Wait," she paused, "does he know about the block?"

Dr. Chandra laughed, "No way. He's such a control freak, the block would shut down his openness to the whole idea of mending."

"What's next?" Rae asked.

"We will see how the research progresses, but as of now, we're thinking we will get Travelers in the most honest state possible during their consultation. We will edit the section on *why* they want to Travel to obtain *what* they want to do. Then, we will run them through all suitable tracks of time they could access. We will show them the possibilities. And, in the end, they will choose where to go."

"What if it doesn't turn out the way they are shown?"

Dr. Chandra sighed, "We can only do so much to ensure they live in the track most beneficial for them. We can give them the right circumstances, drop them into a track that has been mended, but, from there, they must make their own luck."

"Have you considered the resistant ones in Original Time? What if they ruin the progress being made? Or worse, create a terrible track for those native to OT? What about the people whose life's purpose is to cause chaos? Destruction?"

"That is something we are trying to work out. As you know, the consultation process has *got* to be updated. Though, for evil people, we've been upping the dose of Psilopram, and it seems to be leveling them off. It is only for those who are enlightened, for those who want a new outcome, that we're offering this new venture of mended futures," Dr. Chandra explained, "those who want something more than a vacation."

Rae's mind raced, "Once they choose an outcome, is that it? Or can they go back to their starting point?"

"Another aspect we're still working on. They *should* be able to come back if we can recreate the element for Travel in another time sequence," Dr. Chandra stated. "Theoretically, it's all there. We just need to make it a physical reality. They say you can make your own luck, but for many, the time in which they were born gives them no advantages, no realistic opportunities to pursue their calling. Mending changes all of that."

"Some will consider this advance to be too enabling," Rae said.

"They will, however, at its core, isn't *being able* good?"

Rae agreed, "It is." She thought of her team of over one hundred menders and couldn't wait to share the news. "May I tell my menders that everything they've worked toward is on the horizon?"

"Wait just a bit longer," Dr. Chandra replied, "though I would suggest gauging how happy your menders are in their chosen eras. If they Traveled there purely to mend, they may stay if they feel that the issue they're mending is worthwhile. But I'd caution them against returning to OT right now.

So many in Original Time, who've yet to Travel, are angry. They think we're doing all this to play God. They're resistant to the brilliant future it could bring. There is something about *living* the past that has changed Travelers who come back to Original Time. Travel virgins are not open to the new perspective.

They don't see that all this provides us with hope that we won't ruin everything we have. That we won't have to inhabit other planets due to lack of resources," Dr. Chandra stopped to compose herself. "We can work with what we have to make it better, to occupy the Earth with a different approach."

"Doctor," Rae began, "I am thrilled about this. Please keep me updated as to when I can break the news."

"I will. In the meantime, you should take a leave before announcing this progress to your team."

Rae complied. She contacted her network of menders and monitors and gauged their contentment with their eras. As she awaited their replies, Rae decided to use her time off to go to past concerts she always dreamed of attending.

She looked up the date of a Central Park spectacle. Rae also checked to see if anyone she knew was in attendance. She saw Mia and Vaughn's names pop up. She was surprised to see that they were still drifting together.

Rae walked to the nearest TRN hub. Throughout her entire life up to the point of her first Travel, Rae felt uncertainty around the future of Original Time. She was once told that 'the future is a source of anxiety and, the past, depression.'

She attempted to process that the future was the past, and she hoped the next dose of Psilopram would absolve her overly logistic thought process and bring her back into the moment.

It took only a few hours for TRN to provide Rae with a Shell. Rae took her dose of Psilopram and was en route to the past.

Chapter XI

"Lean in, baby," Vaughn grinned, "you're gonna love this."

Mia reached to pull off the purple silk scarf Vaughn had wrapped around her head across her eyes before they entered the venue.

"Not yet," Vaughn instructed.

Pure thrill welled up in Mia's chest and she laughed. She was certain she appeared silly to the onlookers, but the lights dimmed and their perception of her no longer mattered.

It was their first outing since their Acclimation period, which only lasted twelve hours. Mia agreed to go with the flow and indulge Vaughn in a "surprise for her."

Over the last year, Mia made far more decisions than she preferred, and she was ready to go with whatever Vaughn had up his sleeve. After a healthy dose of Psilopram, she was reset and ready to experience all that time had to offer.

Mia heard the wail of a guitar. The band's sound was undeniable. Vaughn pulled off the scarf and Mia was immersed in a sea of hair, bright makeup, and violet lights.

The performance was almost more than she could handle. Vaughn leaned forward and spoke into her ear.

"First stop on the best music of the nineteen-hundreds tour," he said.

Mia's mouth dropped open. Her eyes welled with tears.

"I've been waiting for someone to come with me," Vaughn said, "it's not as fun alone."

Mia craned her head back and kissed Vaughn. When she pulled away, she absorbed that she was standing in the front row of the show of a lifetime.

"This is the first of many."

"Compliments of TRN," Vaughn said as they walked into the luxury hotel after the show.

They stumbled up to their room and Vaughn lay down on the bed. He fell asleep after a few minutes. Mia laid there. Her ears rang and she was uncertain how Vaughn could rest after the show they just witnessed.

She walked to the window and took in the city. Few proper murals had yet to be painted. Instead, erratic graffiti decorated the brick sides of buildings. Once Mia processed the night she'd just experienced, she joined Vaughn on the bed. She grinned as he roused and fumbled with the eight-ball charm bracelet she'd gifted him long ago when she thought 1997 was her permanent home.

The weeks that followed were a dream.

Mia and Vaughn were surrounded by vast crowds of like-minded music lovers. Mia was certain she saw every type of person, only to be proven wrong at the next show. The concerts were better than her wildest dreams and being a part of the artists' collective fans made her feel at home as they drifted through several eras.

There was a gentle group of people with which they melded for a span of an entire region of the United States. The band gave their followers an exclusive experience, something not offered by their records. It was as if the musicians opened a new world for their audience. Through repeated melodies and exaggerated solos, they offered their viewers a gift before they laid it on vinyl for the rest of the world to consume.

At a punk show in the mid-seventies, Mia was jarred by the physicality of the crowd; bottles were broken, safety pins were embedded in skin, musicians leapt onto the sea of fans; they trusted they'd be caught. Most shows brought Mia to tears when she saw how much the crowd was *with* the icons on stage.

The more shows Mia saw, the closer to the music she longed to get. She was tantalized by her desire to be back on stage. Rather than being in the spotlight, Mia ventured backstage with Vaughn. It seemed he had unlimited funds and spared no expense in experiencing his leave to the fullest.

Mia was at a loss for words. Idols stood before her eyes. As she spouted accolades to one front man she'd dreamt of meeting her entire life, she noticed a group of beautiful women who lingered in the backstage corners. While Mia and Vaughn's backstage passes were paid for, she wasn't so sure the groupies were let in with the same currency. Mia recognized a head of curls on one of the muses and beamed.

"Lucia!" she shouted.

Lucia turned and looked for the person who said her name.

Mia repeated, "Lucia! It's me, Mia! We met in Marseille!"

Lucia hurried over to Vaughn and Mia. She was every bit as enchanting as Mia remembered, though a bit more ragged.

"Mia," Lucia said and placed her hands on Mia's face, "you haven't aged a day!"

Mia thought back to when they met in the late sixties. It was now the early eighties, and the time took its toll on many young beauties. Mia shrugged, "Good genes, I guess. You're still so beautiful as well."

Abra turned to see who Lucia was talking to. She shrieked when she saw it was Mia. Abra's arms offered the warm embrace Mia didn't know she needed. After their initial excitement to see each other, Abra gestured to Vaughn.

"Who is this?" she asked and chuckled.

Vaughn extended his hand.

"How do you all know one another?" Vaughn asked.

"Marseille," Lucia answered. "What magical days those were."

"Doesn't look too bad here," Mia said.

Though, as she scanned the room, her perception shifted. A knife stuck out from a fly infested rotisserie chicken. A dusting of white powder dulled the shine of a gold serving platter. The muses' once-colorful dresses were dull and spotted with holes. Mia realized that the muses were living their lives day to day, city to city, doing what they could to survive yet maintain their sense of bliss and self-preservation.

"Let's go out and claim our spot up front!"

They stood together throughout the concert. Mia thought *she* was enthralled with music, but the muses were on another level. They were *in* the songs.

When the time came to depart for the night, Mia was sad to leave them.

"We will be brought together again," Lucia said, "even if not in this plane."

With that, they parted ways and Mia was left to wonder where all this was going.

Vaughn noticed she was quiet.

"What's up?" he asked.

"I just missed them more than I realized. Everything in life must be held in such a delicate balance between leaning in and letting go," Mia stated, "I sometimes wonder how I'll get through an entire lifetime. It all feels too big, especially with all of time to experience."

Vaughn nodded, "I understand."

———

Mia and the muses got ready.

Earlier that evening, she promised to meet Vaughn at the park and was grateful for his consideration of her need for more time with the enchanting group of females. The day before, when they ran into Abra, Lucia, Chiara, and Phoebe in Midtown, all of them in the city for a concert, Mia couldn't believe her eyes. Something, God, the Universe, the Divine, was at work and continued to bring them together.

Mia wondered if some sort of mending had taken place and she'd fallen into the playout of a time in which she was destined to join their scene for good. She hoped so. Though she loved Vaughn and wanted to give him her all, she couldn't help but imagine her life with the muses as a vagabond. Then she realized she *was* a vagabond, but in a committed relationship.

Mia heard a honk outside the muses' temporary home in the Village. They put on their final touches, then scurried outside. One by one, they hopped in the convertible, careful not to poke holes in the leather with their stilettos.

Their driver reminded Mia of Reg. He navigated the flurry of vehicles which, it seemed, were all headed to the same destination. The driver's hair was long, and he wore a leather jacket. He popped a tape into the cassette player. Mia expected the lively harmonies and poetry they were about to experience at the park. Instead, the man played a song which they all sang at the top of their lungs, a lively punk song, new for the time.

He had the top down and Mia's hair blew in the wind. Among the beauties she felt like a rockstar herself. As she sang the lyrics with no inhibitions, the driver shot her an impressed look.

"Maybe *you* should take the stage tonight," he said.

"I'd love to," Mia replied, "but that ship has sailed. I've woken up from that dream."

"What woke you?"

"At some point, you just have to go with something," Mia recited Vaughn's words, "or so I've been told."

"Anyone who questions your dreams can just fuck right off," he said.

They drove much longer than anticipated; then Mia saw the crowd file into the park. Rather than stop at the concert, they drove past the crowd.

"Wait," Mia began, "where are we going?"

"A smaller place," Lucia replied, "a punk show."

Mia placed her hand on the driver's shoulder.

"Will you drop me off at the park?" she asked.

He made a confused expression.

"Really? You'd rather go *there*? Peace and love's expired, baby."

"I'm meeting someone there."

"Vaughn?" Abra asked.

"Yes. We came a long way to see this show. He brought me here."

"Alright, alright, drop her off," Abra teased, "but, Mia, I always pictured you with a musician, or becoming one yourself." Abra moved in close to Mia. "If you need us, you know how to find us."

Abra flashed her Aid and winked.

Before Mia could respond, a car behind them honked and she was rushed from the vehicle. The muses waved goodbye. She walked by herself to the North side of the park where she intended to meet Vaughn. Her thoughts whirred.

'Are they menders?'

Mia walked in a daze and eventually realized she was near the park's North side. She laughed as she saw another set of familiar faces: Germain and Tom. Mia was astounded at the night's synchronicity. She didn't know if some cosmic alignment was at play, but she chose not to question her good fortune.

The sight of Mia lit up Tom and Germain's eyes. Tom was dressed in drag and Germain unlocked arms with Tom to open his arms to hug Mia. She ran to him and was surrounded with love and, no matter how mind-blowing the music was about to be, at that moment, she didn't see how the night could improve.

"Mia, love, you haven't aged a day!" Germain cried. "It's been far too long since you've visited all of us. Since the wedding! Marseille misses you!"

"What wedding?"

"Oh, so you've lived such an exciting life as a musician that you've forgotten the wedding of the century? *Papa* and Corrine?"

Mia attempted to go with the flow.

"How could I forget?"

She wondered if by drifting so extensively, she and Vaughn had crossed into some other time trajectory. Mia itched to connect with Rae. To see if mending was live.

"Did you two come to New York just for the concert?" Mia asked.

"No," Germain answered, "just visiting for a spell. We *had* to see Stonewall. I thought nothing would change after the violence that night," he squeezed Tom's hand, "but it has. Hopefully the progress continues."

The fact that it was the early eighties baffled Mia. The era was notorious for misogyny and elitism, but she had yet to see it. Something about all the eras they'd visited felt different than Mia had anticipated.

After final embraces with Germain and Tom, Mia continued her search for Vaughn. She looked up to the sky, but the North star was blotted out by the city lights. She wandered wherever her feet took her, and, finally, Mia saw Vaughn across the way.

His hands were in his pockets, and he glanced around the kinetic crowd in search of Mia. She waved, but he didn't see her. Mia ran up to him and began to tell him about her night.

"You'll never believe this, Vaughn," she began.

"You won't believe this either," he said. "Sorry, you first."

"On my car ride here with the muses, just as they pulled away, Abra pulled out her Aid. They're menders or Travelers or *something!*"

Vaughn nodded. He looked lost in thought, "It's all coming together—"

Mia interrupted, "*And*, I saw Tom and Germain!"

"Mia," Vaughn paused and took a deep breath. "We made it! This is the track we're supposed to be on. Rae's done it," he said with a look of astonishment. "We're here."

"Are you serious?"

"I've drifted for a while now, Mia," Vaughn assured, "this era hasn't always been so good. I don't know how vast the menders' reach has gotten," he paused, "but things have changed. The ugly parts have been reconciled. Look," Vaughn took a deep breath, "while you were with the muses, I walked around the city. I don't know if it's just the magic of this concert tonight, but the city is borderline Utopian."

Mia shook her head in disbelief.

"It all happened so fast."

Vaughn shrugged, "We have been drifting together for a while," he stated. "Remember, in Original Time, Autumn has nearly begun. Soon, they'll call me back from my leave."

A gentle, sparkling guitar sounded across the city's green patch. The crowd began to migrate forward.

"Want to go up?" Vaughn asked.

Mia answered, "In a bit. It's nice here."

The trees had not yet turned, and the world had yet to dry out, but Mia was hit with the familiar, end-of-summer feeling. She looked at Vaughn and wondered if she could spend the rest of her life in a crowd, or if she'd get bored. After a while, they would run out of concerts. Then what?

Her thoughts quelled after a few songs. It felt as though her brain waves lengthened and everything was smooth. Non abrasive. Mia watched them onstage, and she longed to weave in harmony with another person.

When the concert was over, they walked home in silence. Once again, no words were adequate for the flawless evening. Though they had yet to exchange the words, Mia loved Vaughn. He felt like a natural companion and always took her into consideration. But the future was growing more and more uncertain.

"Drifting," Vaughn said as a bright streetlight illuminated the back of his head, "I find it so similar to how I imagine reincarnation. Every different time we visit, we can be something new."

They reached their temporary lodging and stood outside to savor the night air with its gentle coolness and sound of crickets.

"I think the constant newness will get us through," Vaughn stated, as if he sensed Mia's uncertainty surrounding a future with him. "Most couples only have one time to occupy, but we have endless tracks to choose from."

Mia sighed, "At the concert tonight, I found myself wondering if I should have given the stage a longer shot."

"Now that TRN is warming up to fame, I suppose things could have worked with the Tuesdaze," Vaughn said. "With Lars, though, who knows what you would have had to deal with, and no one was there to help if you'd gotten into trouble."

"I could have used the Aid," Mia responded. "But you're right, help was sparse after you left."

"I'm glad you chose this; we've seen so many amazing things together. I've wanted to do this with someone for so long; to see the best concerts of the modern era."

"Never in my life did I imagine this as a possibility. I'm still in awe of it all," Mia said.

Her UpgrAid buzzed.

"Inside?" Vaughn asked and gestured to the device.

Mia pulled out her hotel key and led the way to their room. Vaughn hung back as she walked up the plush stairway. Their TRN hotel displayed every positive aspect of eighties interior design: fluffy, white carpets, soft up-lighting, and long furniture which sprawled across entire walls.

"Rae wants to stop by," Mia said. "She is visiting for a short time. All my favorite people in one place, I never imagined. All, except Derek. Do you mind if I meet her? I can find out if they have accessed the other planes of the past."

"Sure, go ahead."

Mia wondered if she was too absent for Vaughn on this visit to the Big Apple. She debated whether she should feel bad for abandoning Vaughn so frequently: first, for the muses and now,

Rae. But she resolved to meet her anyway. Mia gave Vaughn a kiss and pulled on a sweatshirt. She hurried down the stairs and rushed to the street where Rae waited.

"Rae!" Mia ran into Rae's arms. "It feels like we haven't seen each other in a lifetime."

"I was just in town for the concert," Rae explained, "and I wanted to stop by and see how *you* are doing."

Mia didn't know where to begin.

"This entire summer, we've drifted through the eras. We've gone to every concert I've ever dreamed of seeing. It's been incredible, and my Acclimation period has been cut down to just a half-day," she boasted. "So, we haven't been slowed down by the Traveling process. I don't know if it's the continued Psilopram dosing or if it's all in my head, but it seems things have *really* changed. You must be making progress on your mission."

"We have been, but it's not set in stone yet," Rae winked. "Your summer sounds like it has been lovely," Rae responded. She looked exhausted.

"Was your Acclimation a little rough?" Mia asked and rested her hand on Rae's shoulder.

Rae shook her head.

"I've just been incredibly busy, that's all. We've taken big strides and it's been both exhausting and wonderful," Rae stated. "I'm on leave. Tonight's the first night I've taken the time to revel in the progress. The city feels different than it did when I visited in the past. Maybe it was the energy of the concert, but the bad parts I remember about this era seemed to have vanished and the good parts seem even better."

"Vaughn said the same thing," Mia shared.

Rae suppressed a grin, "I may have taken… certain liberties. Because of the rough year you've had. I wanted you to get a taste of the power of mending. Dr. Chandra recently worked out some kinks so I," Rae paused, "I had your Shell tech send you and Vaughn to a mended plane for this concert."

"You *didn't!*" Mia laughed, thankful they made it in one piece.

"I just put you on a mended plane for this trip to NYC. The rest of your trip with Vaughn probably felt perfect because, well," Rae shrugged, "you went to the best concerts in history."

Mia thought back to the electric ladies, rock 'n' roll deities, all the soul-driven artists they had the honor of seeing live.

'How could anything get better?'

"Vaughn has looked for his happily ever after for a long time. I was bitter at first, after our run-in, but now I understand that when he didn't get what he wanted from you over the holidays last year, he ended up diving further into TRN, using the job as his identity," Rae said.

"He was lost for a while, wasn't he? Right after he left the nineties. Not that it was my doing. He seemed to have other commitments."

"You have no idea," Rae responded.

"You never seemed to get caught up in TRN's desperation. You complied, but their shortcomings never took priority over your purpose."

"It's very easy to fall into seeing yourself as your job, not just in TRN, but in Original Time, throughout time. People compromise their daydreams to do their job. I think you... the music, both bring Vaughn back to who *he* is."

"Now, to figure out who *I* am..." Mia sighed. "Seeing how the city is now, I feel bad for dropping out of your mission," Mia hung her head. "It worked. I wonder if I could have changed the nineties."

"Remember, this is just one of the few mended planes. You'd be happy you left if you saw the Tuesdaze now. Macy's with another band, still crushing it, but at a high cost. Of course, Lars is milking his new band for everything they're worth."

"How are EJ and Tiffany?"

"They're alright, not as fun as when you were around," Rae said. "If we wanted to get really selfish, we could go back. Mend Lars out of their group."

"I don't know if it's worth it. Then again, even though I'm having one of the best summers of my life, I'm afraid I'm losing sight of what *is* worth it. I fear that once Vaughn and I run out of interesting eras to visit, we won't have anything to *do*."

"I understand what you're saying, and I'm here to remind you that you must put forth the energy to create the future *you* want. Remember, at any point, you can be whatever you want in whatever time you want, but time isn't slowing down.

You can change your setting, and Psilopram can smooth the landscape of your mind, but remember, it's all leading somewhere. Remember where you want to go and don't lose that in the experiences along the way."

Mia absorbed her words. "Thank you, Rae."

Rae rested her hand on Mia's face.

"One more thing, remember you can be a *part* of all this now. TRN has relaxed their no fame rule due to the alternate takes of time. Your dreams don't end in OT anymore. Keep playing."

With that, Rae wrapped her arms around Mia, then released her and walked into the night with much more to say.

———

Rae: 'Remember, you've tried this before. She's young, but she won't be forever. You're both having fun, but she's losing purpose.'

Though Rae's words cut Vaughn, he knew she was right. He'd drifted with several other girls before. All of whom became monitoring recruits.

'Mia's different. My motives have improved. You know that. We were desperate then.' Vaughn paused his message to Rae before sending. He deleted the part about desperation. Vaughn had been with Rae, too, and he knew she wouldn't respond well to the sentence. He didn't blame her.

Vaughn loved Mia for many reasons; however, his greatest draw to her was her talent. He was unsure if he would be able to fulfill her dreams. He feared their relationship was built solely on seeing the best of the best together. He heard Mia knock at the door of their loft and he sent the message to Rae. Vaughn unlocked the door and let Mia inside.

He took a deep breath as he closed the door behind her. Vaughn felt the ring in his pocket, a black diamond smoothed into a sphere, he still wore the eight-ball trinket on his wrist.

'The omen of chance.'

She sat on the bed, and upon seeing her face, Vaughn decided to pop a question he'd asked before, only this time, he was convinced it was the real deal.

Mia arrived with red, puffy eyes and moist cheeks. Rae invited her into the spacious loft and Mia curled up on the couch.

"I don't know why, I just couldn't do it," Mia stated. "I love him, but I still don't know where or how I want to spend my life. It wouldn't be fair to say yes."

"I guarantee he's not certain what he wants either," Rae said.

Mia looked at her, puzzled.

"I'm sorry," Rae began, "that wasn't directed at you." She knew it was the wrong moment to share the details of Vaughn's history. "I've known him for a while and he may think he wants to settle down, but I've seen him get restless. His contentment is always fleeting, which made him such a good recruiter. He makes people, both his lovers and friends, believe things. He validates his actions by convincing himself it's all for the 'greater good,' but he hurts people. I do believe he loved you," Rae hesitated, "*loves* you, but I'm not sure he's allowing you to live your Ideal Future."

"I guess I'm the same way. My contentment has been short-lived too." Mia's tears returned.

Rae rubbed Mia's shoulder, "Hey, you went with your instincts. If something was off, it was off. No question about it."

"I tried to explain, but he freaked out when I said no, so I left. It wasn't a never, it was a not now. When I saw the band playing earlier tonight, I wanted to be up there. I'm so scared I'll always wonder, Rae. I don't know if I should have left the nineties. What if it turned into something? What if Lars somehow got taken out of the picture? This summer has been heavenly. It's been everything I've always wanted. What's wrong with me? It's like I can't accept things just being good."

Rae handed Mia a tissue.

"Things can be perfect, but if you're not fulfilled, if there's a part of your being that's ignored and suppressed, I don't know," Rae shrugged, "maybe things here aren't *really* perfect for you."

Rae debated if she should tell Mia about the prospect of viewing the most fulfilling sequence for every person. But she didn't get permission from Dr. Chandra to spill the details. Rae feared that if she told Mia everything too soon, she'd lose her most prestigious ally in TRN, Adrian Glass; the genius behind making Travel a substantial turning point in history rather than a vacation destination.

Rae had already divulged enough information by telling Mia that this was a mended plane. She decided against elaborating on the individual sequences and let Mia make her own way. *'I've already destroyed her and Vaughn's engagement.'*

Instead, she redirected Mia. She thought of the muses. Those women were the sunshine of humanity, and Rae knew they'd bring joy to Mia.

"Care to go see Abra and the girls?"

Mia agreed. She had no direction now and decided to jump back into a flow which had healed her in the past. Rae led her to the muses.

"You came to find us!" Abra exclaimed when she opened the door and saw Mia and Rae.

Her initial excitement dropped when she realized what Mia's solo arrival meant.

"Things didn't work out with the boy?" Abra asked.

Mia shook her head.

"Come in, we'll get you mended up. It's kind of our specialty," she winked.

"The whole time in Marseille, you were in transit? Mending?"

Abra nodded, "You caught us taking some down time. By the way, has the future of the Marseille sequence been accessed, Rae?"

"She came here off duty," Lucia teased. "We don't have to talk about mending all the time. Though, I would like to know if we terminated the end of the sixties dream."

"Let's just say a few bad apples have been taken care of," Rae shrugged.

"Taken care of?" Mia repeated.

"It's complicated," Rae shut down the question.

"What's next for the two of you?" Abra asked.

Rae turned to Mia, "Shall we go visit your brother?"

Mia contemplated the idea.

"We? Don't you want to enjoy the rest of your leave?"

Though the time off was much-needed, Rae knew she couldn't allow herself to live on another era's time for long without purpose. She wanted to avoid ending up in Mia's situation.

When Vaughn and Rae were together, Vaughn brought Rae to some of the most beautiful places she had ever seen and in the prime time to see them, but she knew something was missing. Rae hoped Mia would take the action to fill the void of what was missing for herself, and she suspected a visit with Derek would realign Mia.

"Know what?" Mia said, "I'd love to go back for the wedding. Let's go see Marcel and Corrine get married."

Germain pulled up to the shabby building with Derek in his passenger seat. Though Germain didn't tell Derek, he had shoved a handgun into his book before they left.

"This is the place, huh?"

Derek read the slip of paper which was given to him by the Uni girls that morning. Earlier, when they phoned Derek and told him Renee had been out for weeks, he rushed to the boutique. On the way, he stopped by the apartment near the cavern bar.

"I haven't seen her since she escaped that night," Lena, the healer said. "Though, Lorraine stopped by after the fact. She told me Renee ended up in the hospital."

After speaking to Lena, Derek rushed to *En Blum*. The Uni girls tore Renee's desk apart and searched for clues as to where she could be. They found a folded shred of paper with an address scribbled inside. Derek read the address and remembered Renee's mention of her mother's address in the bombed-out area of London.

Derek phoned Germain from the boutique, and, within minutes, Germain drove him to the address on the scrap.

Germain parked the car. He and Derek exchanged a look.

"Here we go."

They went up to the front door and knocked. Minutes passed. Derek knocked again.

"Hello? Anyone home?"

A man answered. He had a gapped smile.

"You here for Miss Renee?"

"Yeah," Derek answered.

"She saw you pulling up. Didn't want to answer, but mum told her to. Her mother saw you," the man pointed at Germain. "Said she remembers you as a little boy. She wants to see you grown up. Renee! Come out here or your mother's gonna get after you for bad manners."

"Derek, Germain," Renee stepped out from around the corner.

"Renee," Germain said with more concern in his voice than intended.

Derek stayed quiet. He suppressed the urge to whisk Renee back to his apartment. To care for her and bring her back into vibrant health. He looked around.

His shoes stuck to the carpet. The place smelled like rotten food and mildew. But there Renee stood, in the middle of the decaying flat.

"We came to share good news with you," Germain started. "My father and Corrine are finally getting married! They request your presence at the ceremony."

A woman overheard and joined their circle.

"After all these years," she said. "Wish I was in better condition."

"As I live and breathe," Germain shook his head. He recognized the woman, "Vivienne Blum."

"*Bebe* Germain," she beamed.

Though Vivienne's teeth were discolored, her smile was still contagious. For a moment, Derek forgot about their surroundings. He looked back and forth between Renee and Vivienne as they embraced Germain.

"And who is your friend? Renee told me about your lover. Is this him?"

"No, this is Derek. We've… known each other for a while now. He tended to the store while I was away."

"Pleasure to meet you, Vivienne," Derek said.

"Likewise," Vivienne's hand trembled as she shook Derek's hand.

"Will you come to celebrate?" Germain asked.

Renee sighed.

"I don't know, it's so far."

"Says the globe-trotting supermodel," Germain teased.

Then another man joined them. He was rail thin, but the resemblance between himself and Renee was undeniable.

"Renee's father," Derek said, in awe.

"Robert Griffin."

They shook hands. Derek noticed goosebumps on Robert's arms. The family's faces were ashen, and he wondered how long they'd been coming down.

"Germain, your father was somewhat of a ringleader at the club where I met," Robert put his arm around Vivienne, "Renee's mother."

"I didn't know you met there," Germain stated. "My father, Marcel, he's the one getting married. For the three of you to join would mean the world to my father and Corrine. Their reunion has been years in the making. Like your own."

Renee looked around the dumpy setting, as though she noticed the poor living conditions for the first time.

"What have I gotten *into*," Renee said with a sob. "And *you*," she pointed at her mother, "you led me here!"

Vivienne attempted to console her daughter, but Renee ran into the other room. A vacant expression painted Vivienne's face. She stood still and wrung her hands.

"Sweetie," Robert said and followed Renee into the next room.

Germain and Derek stood in silence.

'Should we leave?'

Then, Vivienne spoke.

"We gave into the stuff together. It made it easier. All of it."

Derek nodded. "I understand." He remembered Cooper.

"I've avoided mirrors for weeks. I don't want to see myself. I don't want to see the face Renee remembers walking out on her, though the face has changed. It's gotten older. Harder. I don't know that I could show it to your father, Germain. I'm ashamed to show it to my own flesh and blood."

Germain's face morphed in a way Derek had never seen.

"Know what, Vivienne? You act like you're stuck, but you have a decision to make. You can stay here and hate yourself even more when you see her rotting beside you, or you can come with us. Now. But you don't get to come back here. It's now or never."

———

Mia awoke to Rae and the muses.

"You had a rough Acclimation," Rae said. "Everything must have caught up with you."

The light shone in Mia's bedroom. Mia realized she was back in Corrine's building on the lowest floor, the muses' pad. She was in the city that introduced her to life without a plan.

"When is the wedding?" Mia asked.

"Not for a few more days. Derek and Germain are on their way now. Rest up though, love. Here," Abra fumbled with the knobs on the television, "would you like to watch some TV?"

"Sure," Mia replied.

She found it fascinating to watch news of the time as it unfolded.

"We're going out for a walk. There's so much to do here in the summer. When you're fully recovered, we will show you everything."

Mia waved goodbye.

She watched the screen and regretted staying in. Plane crashes, fiery palm trees, and collapsing apartments lit up the news. Mia was about to turn the television off when the story cut to a festival in California. Mia recognized the man with the dark beard, on stage, and longed to be in his presence again. The view flipped to the faces of the crowd. Mia wasn't sure if she was imagining the hippie's features, but she was almost certain the man in the front row was Grant, Derek's friend who took the siblings to dinner after Jon and Ellie's death.

Her eyes grew heavy as she watched the concert, and she wondered if she made a mistake; she turned down the chance to live in the crowd for an eternity.

Chapter XII

The train slowed at the platform and the doors opened with a hiss. After several passengers poured out, Mia finally saw a familiar face.

"Derek!" She waved

Germain and Tom trailed her brother. They saw Mia and beamed. Mia didn't recognize the older couple that stepped out next, but, without asking, she knew the beauty who emerged after them.

Renee Blum.

She looked different than she did at Tom's flat when Mia went to tell Derek about their parents. Now, the sixties it-girl had dark rings around her eyes. Her hair was short. The crop revealed the beautiful sculpture of her face, but it appeared she took a sabbatical from polishing her look.

Last to step out was Angelene. Mia made a mental note to ask how long Grant had been in California after seeing him on the televised concert.

The crowd thinned and Mia rushed to her brother. After a long embrace, she welcomed the rest of the crew. The unknown couple stepped forward to introduce themselves last.

"I'm Vivienne, and this is Robert. We are Renee's parents."

As Vivienne spoke, Mia noticed her stunning green eyes; they were the same hue as the emeralds that studded Renee's face. Though the couple was attractive, they looked as though they just got out of Acclimation themselves.

"How was the trip?" Mia asked.

Derek's expression warned to drop the question.

"A bit rough, but we're getting better, aren't we?" Robert replied and put his arm around Vivienne.

Tom chimed in, "Shall I flag down two cabs?"

"*Papa's* place isn't far, we can walk," Germain answered. The Blums exchanged an exhausted look. "Perhaps just one cab for Renee and her parents. The rest of us can meet them there."

Tom signaled a cab. He gave the driver Corrine's building address. He hoped Corrine had enough empty units to house their guests. The presence of Renee's parents was unexpected.

Tom, Germain, the Hayes, and Angelene started toward Corrine's building on foot. Light glistened off the water and illuminated Angelene's golden curls. The air gave no sensation at all, no oppressive heat, and no chilling cold. The sea was calm, and the city bustled. Around them was the perfect setting for a wedding.

"Angelene, how long has Grant been in California?" Mia asked. "I believe I saw him on the television a few days ago. I've only met him once, but I imagine he's so happy there."

"You saw him on the television?!"

"Yes, I swore I saw him when they covered the Newport festival."

Angelene shook her head in disbelief and Mia regretted her question.

"Ang," Derek began, "there's nothing you can do about it here. Just be glad he's safe. He seemed to be enjoying himself, right Mia?"

"Absolutely. It would be impossible to have a bad time there."

The group arrived at Corrine and Marcel's building. Corrine and Marcel rushed outside, and they were all given a warm welcome. While the engaged couple caught up with Germain, Tom, and Angelene, the Hayes siblings stole away to the balcony.

"Why was Angelene so on edge when I brought up Grant? Did something happen?"

"He vanished a few months ago. No one has heard from him since. Are you sure it was him on the television?"

"I-I guess it could have been someone who looked like him. It's hard to say."

"I hope you're right. I hope he's in a place where he's surrounded by peace and love."

"Me too. And while we're alone, I have to tell you, Rae, my TRN stylist, is downstairs with the muses. They've been working together on this *crazy* mission. They're using Time Travel as a vehicle to mend the past."

"Wait, I thought it was against the rules to influence past eras. How are they not getting pulled back to OT and sentenced?" Derek asked, astounded. "And they've done this in multiple time periods?"

"Yeah. They flew under the radar. TRN was severely understaffed when they started the mission."

Derek shook his head and absorbed the information.

"Get this," Mia looked around to gauge their privacy, "mending *works*. And Rae's team has just gained access to the improved futures of several eras. Glass is on it. This is huge, Derek. We could go back and save Mom and Dad. We can go anywhere we want and live the outcome we desire."

"This is blowing my mind, there are multiple outcomes of every era?"

"Yes. And we can go to any trajectory we want."

"Easier said than done."

"What do you mean? I thought you'd be excited."

"Think about what you just said. 'Any trajectory we want.' That means, we have to know what we want."

A commotion came from inside and stole their attention.

"Oh, *belote* partner, come on in!" Marcel shouted to Mia.

Mia laughed and shook her head.

She faced Derek, "More later."

———————

The sun painted rose-colored streaks across the water. Golden hour arrived. Then, the indigo side of the sky began to take hold.

"I think it's time we do this thing," Corrine said.

Rae put the finishing touches on the bride's hairstyle and grinned.

"See you in there."

Corrine waited outside. She took a moment for herself before she stepped into the ceremony. She waited a long time for this. She wondered why their marriage took so long, why so many things got in the way, but as soon as she noticed those thoughts, she cast them into her mind's abyss. She understood that it was that kind of thinking that held them apart for so long. Corrine stepped into the aisle.

As Corrine entered, she heard gasps from the assembly of their closest friends. Corrine was a vision in her wedding dress; the bodice was made of blue velvet and a train of light blue silk rippled behind her. Robert and Vivienne held hands, and Renee and Derek stood next to them.

Mia dabbed her cheeks. She wondered if she passed up her own love of a lifetime. Rae rested her hand on Mia's shoulder. Marcel and Corrine had their first kiss as a married couple in the presence of those meant to be there, unbound by the limits of time.

———————

Marcel used his status as a member of the reigning house band and reserved the venue for the night's entirety. The next-of-kin, muses, and Hayes siblings mingled as Marcel and Corrine reveled in the moment. Eventually, Corrine was stolen by the muses. Marcel wandered to Robert.

"How's it going? Seeing her again," Marcel gestured to Vivienne. "You've been gone so long."

Robert shook his head.

"I'm not sure what's real and what's not at this point."

Marcel gazed at his bride, "Me either. But let's not question it, what do you say?"

"I say that's a good plan."

Marcel patted Robert's back.

Renee joined her two paternal figures.

"Renee, so sweet of you to fit us into your busy schedule," Marcel teased.

"You spent so much of your younger years fitting us into your busy days," Renee said and rested her head on Marcel's chest, "it's the least I could do."

Marcel pulled away and gave her a wink, and Renee saw the untouchable bliss on his face. A guitar sounded onstage and stole the crowd's attention. Daniel beckoned.

"Come on up, Marcel!"

"I'm the groom, I'm not playing today!"

"C'mon, Marcel," Angelene encouraged, "I haven't seen you play in years!"

Marcel pretended he wasn't interested in playing but, with little effort, he was convinced and herded to the stage. He opened a closet backstage and procured a guitar for himself. When Marcel came around to the front, he shot Daniel a knowing look and began to strum.

"Of course, they play this," Corrine swooned, "we first danced to this song."

Daniel and Marcel sang in harmony. Marcel hit the rhythm and Daniel played the melody, then they both broke out into solos.

After the fast, Spanish number, the wedding crowd needed a break from dancing. Marcel strummed a glittering tune, and then, to everyone's surprise, Corrine joined him onstage and began to sing. She enchanted the crowd with her voice. At the end, she perched on Marcel's lap and landed a kiss on his lips. The tender moment concluded their live performance. Daniel coaxed Mia onstage, and they took over the tunes. Marcel found a table and whipped out a deck of cards.

They continued their game until the venue was dry and the ashtrays were full. Then they made the short walk back to Marcel and Corrine's building. The newlyweds crashed at Corrine's flat, and the guests split between the muses' dwelling and Marcel's old bachelor pad.

Derek and Mia went to the muses' along with Rae, and Angelene. Everyone besides Mia fell asleep. Mia tossed and turned, then finally rose and walked out to the balcony.

She thought of the evening's perfect series of events. Marcel and Corrine were married, Renee found her father and established a relationship with her long-absent mother, and Rae's mission was coming to fruition. It seemed Derek might even get the girl.

Though her heart burst with joy for those she loved, she was uncertain how she fit into it all. Mia saw why, after Vaughn's attempts at Travel—his extraordinary experiences throughout history and multiple relationships—he wanted to settle down with her. He craved a conclusion, as did she. Mia remembered Derek's words, "We have to know what we want."

———

The next day, a clear, bright summer sun woke Mia. She and Lucia stepped into the living room at the same time. They returned to the balcony. Mia's eyes were tired, but her spirit was a bit brighter, and she hoped that the new day's mood endured. The two of them grew impatient with waiting for the rest of the group to awaken, so they went to the beach. They sat in silence as the waves lapped the ground by their toes. The city was much different than it was on their last visit.

Back then, Mia intended to return to the nineties and live whatever version of happily-ever-after the time offered. She thought Vaughn left her behind. Now, she had done the same to him.

"You're not *here*, are you?" Lucia asked and pulled Mia from her thoughts.

Mia shook her head.

"It's the only place you've got to be," Lucia said and took Mia's hand in hers. "Discontentment creates our greatest problems but is sometimes our greatest motivator. Despite the importance of growing and moving forward, restlessness must be tempered, or it can lead to a troublesome life."

Lucia ran her finger along Mia's charm bracelet. She rested her finger in the blank space where the eight-ball and the star once were.

"If you're dwelling on the past, you're not living. Where there's nothing new, there's no life," Lucia said. "Come in," Lucia started toward the water.

Lucia peeled off her clothing. Mia laughed and looked around to see if anyone was looking. There were two more groups gathered at the beach. She noticed they were partially nude as well.

"Take it off, Mia!" Lucia encouraged, "So much of you is covered! We didn't work so hard to have you hold back!"

With a deep breath, Mia untied her borrowed bikini top. She shrieked as a wave crashed and cool water droplets splashed her chest. The water energized her. Mia followed Lucia and they raced along the waterline.

Eventually, they grew tired, and Mia heaved for breath. They clomped across the sand to the spot where they placed their belongings. Lucia's curls blew and she relaxed her head back into a rolled-up t-shirt.

"Ah," she said with the warmth from the summer sun.

"How did you get this way?" Mia asked.

"What way am I?"

Mia searched for the right words.

"Present, careless, thoughtful."

"You are those things too, you just have too much chatter in here," Lucia patted Mia's head. "Truth? I may have had some assistance. Most of the time, it's an advantage. Just as Vaughn was one of the first to Travel, I was a Psilopram test subject. Me and Abra both were. One of us had a high dose, the other, a low dose. It's obvious who had what," she chuckled. "But now, to me, every object is more alive. It's as though everything is breathing and that's the state in which I live. The only question we have is," Lucia paused, "what are the long-term effects?"

Lucia's smile faded.

"My memory is not so great, but I can recall the important things. That is why I meditate and slow down. To remember."

Mia rested a hand on her beautiful friend's forearm and squeezed.

"We should be heading back, hopefully the rest are up by now. We can come back later."

Mia's heart dropped when she saw Renee, Vivienne, and Robert's suitcases outside.

"Are you leaving already?" Mia asked.

Renee nodded, "William beckons," she rolled her eyes.

"He makes no sense to me. He 'worries' about you, yet he doesn't allow you time to slow down," Derek stated.

Renee got close to him and spoke into his ear.

"If I slow down, I'll go back to the dark."

Derek nodded.

Renee continued, "I can't give as much of myself as you want, Derek. You deserve someone who gives you all of life. All of their self."

Renee kissed him on the cheek then blew a kiss to the rest of the group. The driver popped the trunk and Robert heaved their suitcases inside. Marcel and Corrine exchanged whispers. Corrine nodded and stepped forward.

"Vivienne, Robert, I know Renee must go, but you should stay in Marcel's old flat for a while. Please. We will pay for your tickets back to London should you choose to return," Corrine said. "A new place does all of us good sometimes. You can come to Marcel's shows. We can walk along the beach. It will be like old times, Vivi."

Before they could answer, a car drove up and parked in front of Corrine's building. The Blum's driver popped his head out the window and yelled at the car.

"You're blocking me in!"

A passenger opened the door of the other vehicle. Out stepped a man with shoulder length hair. His face was somber as he searched the group for Mia's face.

"Vaughn?"

He spotted Mia and ran to her.

"Mia!"

Vaughn pulled her into his arms.

"I wanted to come to the wedding so badly, but I didn't want to ruin anything. Though," he looked at Renee in her getaway car, "it seems I'm interrupting a goodbye."

"How did you know about the wedding?" Mia asked.

Vaughn looked around and became aware of the spectacle he was creating.

"Derek phoned me. Renee, Germain, Tom, great to see you again."

"You called him, Derek?" Mia glared at her brother.

Derek shrugged and attempted to respect Vaughn's cover.

"Look, don't be mad," Vaughn said. "I called Derek to see how he was doing. Then, the wedding came up. You've let me take the lead, now I want to follow you."

"I can't make this decision right now, Vaughn."

"Of course not. I just had to find you. I had to be with you. For as long as you want me around. We've done," Vaughn paused and remembered their summer of music, "almost *everything* together. Everything except that which fulfills *you*. I want you to give your dreams a shot."

"Mia, if you want to play, I will share the stage," Marcel said.

"Thank you, Marcel," Mia held back grateful tears.

She looked to Rae who stood on the other side of Derek and Lucia.

Rae nodded. "Play it out," she mouthed.

"Okay," Mia said to Vaughn. She gestured toward Renee's family. "Can we bid them farewell now?"

"I have an idea," Renee started, "*Ma, Papa,* stay here for a while," she drew close to her parents and spoke quietly. "Make sure you've kicked it. Then, come back if you're ever ready," she turned to face the rest of the group. "Vaughn, Mia, why don't you come back with me to London? I know some of the biggest names in music. Hell, I'm going to the mothership of the British Invasion! Come with me. Or, perhaps, we can connect you with some people I know in California."

"You could find Grant," Angelene stated.

Mia looked to Derek.

"You won't know until you try," her brother assured. "Give it a shot."

"Alright," Mia agreed and grinned. "Derek, what will you do?"

Lucia locked arms with Derek. He blushed.

"I'll stay here for a while. Then, who knows. I'll phone you and see where you've made it to. I could take pictures of you on stage," he schemed.

Corrine beamed and extended her hand to Vivienne.

"I think everyone knows where they belong."

Rae smiled upon the group.

Mending was successful. Their Ideal Futures finally fit together. Rae's work was done.

Then, she felt a buzz in her pocket. Rae suppressed a groan. She scanned her circle of friends and colleagues; their attention was on the happy ending at hand. Rae slipped away from them and found a private corridor of Corrine's building.

'Time to bring them all back.'

Chapter XIII

Mia opened her eyes.

She looked at her phone.

'How do I have my phone in Marseille?'

She read the text.

'Vaughn: Come to the North Wing lounge.'

Mia studied her surroundings. She was in an unfamiliar place. The Time Regulatory Network's emblem was etched into the frosted glass door. She looked down at herself.

Rather than donning an Acclimation gown, she was fully dressed. Mia grabbed her phone from the nightstand. She walked to the door and stepped into the hallway. She felt for the UpgrAid in her pocket. It wasn't there.

Mia walked past the salon and saw Rae inside; she was working on a bridal updo.

Rae made eye contact with Mia and winked.

Mia shot Rae a suspicious look and continued through the South Wing.

She reached the North Wing lounge. The place where she met Vaughn before their summer of music. He stood there, again, with his dimpled grin.

"Welcome to the other side of the rules."

"What do you mean?" Mia asked.

"Remember? I told you. The no fame rule was tossed aside. So is the no-killing rule; I guess omitting that one was necessary for mending. They had to get some evil people out of the past."

"Why are we back here?"

Mia looked around. It appeared she returned to the day of her Travel consultation. She looked outside. The weather even resembled the day she decided to take the journey back.

"Was it a dream?"

"Not exactly. I know what you've seen. I saw it too. Some of it by your side, some of it on my own."

Mia's phone signaled a notification.

"My mom, she just messaged me. Where is my UpgrAid? Did any of that happen? Did we—"

"Go to all the best concerts together? Yes. Did I come to Marseille? Also, yes. But only to test run the future of that time. To make sure life panned out the way you wanted."

"I thought we were going to London with Renee." Mia raised her voice as emotion flooded in. "I want to get back there! Is it all lost?"

"It's complicated to explain, but Rae and I cleaned some things up and got you in the prime place and time to revel in the spotlight," Vaughn grinned. "If we go back, everything will be self-propelled, you'll still have to make it as a musician, but what better place to get on the scene than the late sixties?"

"So, all of that did happen? Or didn't it?" Mia received another message from Ellie. "And they're *alive?*"

"Mia, we're back at the beginning. But," Vaughn took a deep breath, "this is the last chance. We're bringing Travelers, the ones we can find at least, back to their point A. It's only fair to give everyone a shot at their Ideal Future or 'IF' as we're calling it; their perceived dreams didn't exactly work out. This time, once Time Travelers go back," Vaughn shrugged, "that's it. We're shutting it down. No more back and forth."

Mia's mouth dropped open.

"Don't worry. The things that have happened in those other tracks, the tracks you can return to, are not undone. You played with the Tuesdaze. I monitored you in the nineties, per your parent's request. We fell for each other, but you wanted to stay, and I couldn't. I was sucked into TRN for a while, then I found you again. King's was sold. We went to the concerts. Then I met you in Marseille. Now, here we are, back in Original Time. Before you Traveled. And you have a decision to make."

Mia shook her head, flabbergasted. She was struck with an unwelcome sense of urgency. She craved a conversation with someone wise, someone who *knew* her.

"Can I see my parents?"

"Yes. You can go home after this, but you must make a decision in the next few days. And, before you leave today, you must take this formula. You've had many rounds of Acclimation, and this is a new supplement to assist with recovery."

Mia shook her head. "Let me get this straight. I have to choose whether I want to live out this crazy sequence I've lived? Full of ups and downs, or if I want to return to OT? To see my parents live?"

Vaughn hung his head. He paced back and forth and ran his fingers through his hair.

"I knew I shouldn't have been the one to talk to you about this, damnit. I'm too wrapped up in it."

"You're right," Mia said. "Is there someone else who can walk me through the *details* of what's going on?"

Dr. Lowell rounded the corner. Mia raised her brow.

"Have you been *listening*?"

"Mia. It's more complicated than we anticipated, but this is the reality we face."

"Dr. Lowell, where are my parents? Where is Derek? Is he still in Marseille?"

"He has yet to decide. You two should discuss whether you want your paths to intersect or divide. We've played with several outcomes, but the one we showed you has the most variety of eras and keeps you connected with Derek."

"What about our parents?"

"They've made it clear what they want. They want to go back. To save Cooper. Once the planes were opened, once we came up with the concept of Ideal Futures, we brought our Travelers back here in shifts. We invited the public, your parents, back to TRN. Once Rae gathered her menders and Dr. Chandra's principles got off the ground, we accessed this whole new," Dr. Lowell grinned, "this whole new system of *being*."

"Why can't I be with my parents *and* fulfill my Ideal Future?"

"It's just not how it works. There is some version of you in another plane. A version that stays in this city. A version that goes to college and plays in a band at the Court. Your parent's IF involves their children staying close by. The three of you. There, they rescue Cooper from his darkness. One of the children takes over King's Records. You see where I'm going with this? Clearly, that's not the plane you want to access, so we offered you something else. You lived it enough to determine whether you want to continue down that track or try something else."

"Mom and Dad were supportive of me, no matter what I wanted to do."

"You're right," Dr. Lowell admitted, "but their turning point was Cooper. We owed them a trip back to save their son. Especially after what Glass tried to pull."

Mia's nostrils flared as she understood the truth about what happened to her parents.

"Their death wasn't an 'accident,' was it?" She seethed. "It was Glass. Trying to cut Traveler's ties to the future. God, I didn't want my cousin to be right."

Dr. Lowell nodded, "Glass, well, he went off the deep end. Dr. Chandra's pursuit of Ideal Futures versus *murdering* those close to Travelers was Glass' lifeboat. He manipulated Dr. Chandra and got in on her scheme. He tried to make the advance look like his own doing, but too many people knew the truth. Glass took it too far when there were other ways to fix our predicament."

Vaughn spoke. Mia had nearly forgotten he was in the same room.

"We bent the rules. We used Time Travel to resurrect those sacrificed for what Glass called 'the greater good.' Resources, injustice, corruption," Vaughn smirked, "they have no place in our elevated society's Ideal Future."

Mia's mind raced.

"I need to talk to my brother."

———————

Derek woke up in a cold sweat.

"Breathe, Derek," Rae said, "you're back. You're in Original Time. Do you understand me?"

Derek nodded.

"Did something happen again?" he asked.

"No, we're in Original Time. In your hometown's TRN hub."

"Why?" Derek's heart raced. One minute he was looking into Lucia's eyes, sipping a glass of red wine, now, he was on the edge of an exam table in a sterile room. "Where is everyone? Is Mia okay? I wanted to stay in Marseille. With Lucia."

Rae sighed. "We'll go back. That is, if you choose that plane. For good."

"What other option is there?"

"There are many, but we think we nailed *that* future down as the one which produces the best outcome for you. But we can start from scratch if you'd prefer. We're giving every Time Traveler the well-deserved choice. You can go back to 1967 if you'd like. Or to the nineties, or anywhere really.

But, I must say, you put yourself in a rare situation where your chosen destination and Ideal Future naturally merged. Without our help. You ended up with your muse.

You will become a photographer, after putting in the work of course. But the catch is, that's it. The option to return to your Original Time is coming to an end.

See, now that we've mended so many eras, Travelers are choosing to remain in those tracks of time, which is benefitting Original Time. When we first launched this idea of mending, TRN was not on board. Now, they understand the benefits of righting the wrongs of the past. Not for those remaining in Original Time, but for those who choose to reside in other eras.

Through Psilopram we're learning what our Travelers want out of their destinations; then our network of menders and monitors set them up for long-term happiness in the era of their choice. You get Lucia. Mia gets stardom."

"What about our parents?"

———

Vaughn tapped on Mia's door.

"Come in."

"We don't have to talk about it now," Vaughn said. "You've got just minutes left to savor this time if you choose to leave. Follow your instincts and don't let me sway you—"

"Stop. All the options are freezing me in my tracks."

"Does it help knowing that your parents will have you, the you they planned on having forever, in another plane?"

"I'm not sure. I won't have *them*. Though, I've come to accept not having them, haven't I?"

"I suppose so. I'm still on the fence whether Psilopram's effects are helpful in the grieving process or if the drug is turning us into robots."

"Same. I *should* feel guilty that I can't be the person my parents want me to be. The person who stays here. Who runs King's or plays the Court night after night. Who wants to live in an era where online presence is everything and showing up in person is so rare. Where our resources, along with trust in any system, have been depleted. It's too bad we can't mend *this*."

"You're wrong. We can. Just not this version. See, Mia, I've failed you in building your perception of Time Travel. I've jumped around too much, and I know that now. The Ideal Future where we are going has its own outcome," Vaughn stated. "But all of us who go back in time must continue to act fiercely as menders. If all goes well, if we fight to keep our world just and beautiful, our outcome will be different than what we see around us. So will your parents' outcome."

Vaughn smoothed Mia's hair from her face.

"Now that I've taken a step back, now that TRN's desperation is quelled, I see what I *was*. What I'm trying not to be: an observer. I never got my hands dirty. Not even with you. I was fine leaving *you*," Vaughn looked at Mia in a way that caused her cheeks to redden, "for this job."

Mia softened, "Don't beat yourself up. A lot of Travelers would be in trouble if you hadn't rallied the troops; though I don't love how you went about recruiting the monitoring army."

"Psilopram really has done you well, hasn't it? Forgiving me and all. I want to contribute to an era. Like you and Rae have done. I've been a ghost in the times I've visited."

"You've been a helpful ghost," Mia thought back to the way Vaughn put Lars in his place.

"I realize I'm not a photographer like Derek, or a seasoned mender, or a rockstar," Vaughn winked at Mia, "but I want to put myself out there. To pursue something that keeps me up at night."

'Bzzzt.'

"Time to go. For the last time. You ready?"

"As I'll ever be."

"You gave the Hayes some high-dose Psilopram right?"

"Of course," Rae answered. She thought back to Derek and Mia's toast to the beginning of their happy ending in Marseille. Rae patted herself on the back for slipping Psilopram into their champagne before they were strapped into their Shells and transported to their Ideal Future. "They won't remember that they ever hesitated to live their Ideal Futures. And Jon and Ellie will think the ICU was a dream."

Dr. Lowell smiled. "All those people that Glass meant to eliminate were saved. We found another option when TRN didn't. Or should I say, you *pushed* for another option."

Dr. Lowell nodded and avoided eye contact with Rae.

"Things got very... out of hand. Glass is paying for it now," he paused, "a *lot* of us are paying for it. The investigation is underway," he shook his head. "I didn't mean for things to get so out of control. We were desperate to keep Travelers from coming back and collapsing Time Travel's purpose."

"Which was?"

Dr. Lowell's expression sobered.

"You know what the purpose was. To build up Original Time's resources. To offer another era to those who were dissatisfied with the era into which they were born. A few people just lost themselves in it, compromised their ethics."

"On that note, I'm not so sure what Vaughn is doing is ethical. He's weaving himself into Mia's Ideal Future," Rae said. "He's really blurring the line."

"She loves him though, right? And he may not stay at her side forever. You know how he...gets distracted. Plus, if she becomes famous, she may not want him around."

"True. She's let him go before. So, we're all set on the Hayes? And you've emphasized this is their final plane?"

"Yes. From there everything is up to them."

"Well, Rae, despite what everyone said, including myself," Dr. Lowell shrugged, "it was worth your team's efforts to make amends to the past. I just wish we would have thought of that option first."

"We're not done here," Rae stated. "Several more eras need to be carried out in a better way. And, the more eras we mend, the more we can place Travelers in their most Ideal Future. When Francis returned to TRN as the Chief of Operations, she proposed that we reopen Time Travel every five years to natives of Original Time. We can keep resources abundant and allow humanity to live in a time which best suits them. Though mending took a *while*," Rae smiled, "having TRN onboard really pushed this thing forward. Dr. Lowell, thank you."

"Don't thank us yet. We've yet to see the outcome."

————————

Derek followed Lucia's footsteps.

She turned back to face him, and he snapped the photo. She walked close to him. His eyes darted across the full length of her body.

"Ready to see the night outside the glass?" She tapped his zoom lens.

Derek nodded. He shuffled across the sand and wrapped his camera in a towel. He stuffed the bundle into a bag and rolled up the bottom of his pants.

'See outside the glass.'

Derek thought of the planes that way. Each period offered a different view; and the bad images were being edited. Like the records in his family's store, which now sat in a different track of time, the sound of their world was being remastered by people like Lucia. Derek. Mia. Rae. Vaughn.

Even Jon and Ellie impacted their IF.

Though Derek and Mia's parents chose to live out a path separate from their OT children, their lives were mended with the salvation of Cooper. Jon and Ellie took the mended version of their kids to see their beloved, aging bands. Years passed and Jon and Ellie watched the trailblazers of their time pass on. Those impacted by the legends' tenacity to keep the eyes of the world open, carried on with their mission: to hold a mirror up to society.

"Derek," Lucia splashed through the water, "join me!"

Derek beamed.

'You can go anywhere.'

About the Author

Hallie Baur, historical fiction novelist and poet, views the world through a nostalgic lens and uses her fascination with the past to transplant readers into the settings of her stories.

Baur lives in the Midwest with her husband and Maine Coon cat. When she's not writing she can be found dancing, making her way to the front row of a concert, and seeing the world.